RAWHIDE JAKE:
LONE STAR FAME

THE LIFE AND TIMES OF DETECTIVE
JONAS V. BRIGHTON, BOOK II

RAWHIDE JAKE: LONE STAR FAME

JD ARNOLD

WHEELER PUBLISHING
A part of Gale, a Cengage Company

GALE
A Cengage Company

LIBRARY OF CONGRESS CIP DATA ON FILE.
CATALOGUING IN PUBLICATION FOR THIS BOOK
IS AVAILABLE FROM THE LIBRARY OF CONGRESS.

ISBN-13: 978-1-4328-9588-4 (softcover alk. paper)

Published in 2023 by arrangement with JD Arnold.

Printed in the United States of America
1 2 3 4 5   27 26 25 24 23

Dedicated to all my children

CHAPTER ONE:
ON THE FLYING XC
1883

Jake trotted Jasper through the arches of the gates of the Calhoun ranch headquarters. He slowed the big black and white paint with the golden mane and tail to a walk. They crossed the ground of the lots that were damp from the rain the day before. He headed toward a couple of hands who were sitting on the top rail of the corral next to the barn. The afternoon was quiet in the lots, with only the sound of a metal windmill on a wooden tower behind the barn singing in the breeze and a buck fly buzzing around Jake's face. He pulled off his Stetson and swatted at the fly, but it got even more excited and tried to burrow into Jake's thick black hair. He saw the ranch hands were watching him, so, he gave up on the fly and put his hat back on. The fly apparently gave up, too, because it quit pestering him. When he got up to the cowboys, he inquired, "Howdy. Boss around?"

"Yer lookin' to hire on?" one of the cowboys asked.

"Yep. Kin yer point me in the right direction?"

"What's yer name?"

"Jake Brighton."

"Rawhide Jake Brighton?"

Jake nodded his head *yes* and kept a
steady eye on the speaker, who was wearing
a pistol in a holster, and not so much on
the other cowboy, who wasn't armed. "Yer
the feller that killed Charlie Dalton down in
Seymour. If there ever was a rattlesnake
needed killin', it was Charlie Dalton. Ain't
that right, Slim? Wal, my name's Johnny
Raymer," he said as he jumped down from
the fence and held out his hand for a shake.

Jake dismounted, and as they shook hands,
Raymer said, "I be one of the top hands
and line rider. This here is Slim Butler. He's
the top wrangler."

Slim jumped down and shook hands with
Jake, while stroking Jasper's neck with his
other hand. "Nice to meet yer," he said.

"C'mon," Johnny said. "I'll take yer over
to meet the boss. His name is Walt Guthrie.
He's in the office. Prob'ly arguin' with the
bookkeeper." He chuckled and grinned at
Jake.

Johnny Raymer looked to be in his late

twenties, about eight years or so younger than Jake. He stood about the same height as Jake and was stocky like Jake. But his hair and mustache were a sandy-brown color, and he had a cheery, lean, and tanned face with bright and twinkly brown eyes.

Jake walked Jasper behind him as he and Johnny headed across the lot past a long and low adobe building with a full-length covered porch jammed with wood chairs and spittoons. Johnny said that was the bunkhouse.

They came up to the ranch office, and Jake tied off Jasper's reins to the hitch rail. He followed Johnny in and saw the book-keeper sitting in a wooden swivel chair with its back to the roll-top desk. A lean stock-man sat in a straight-back chair with his legs stretched out in front of him, crossed at the tops of his boots. Jake knew right off that he was the boss because there was an air of authority about him. He wore an expensive looking Texas style felt sombrero. It was pushed back on his head and revealed his baldness with fringes of salt and pepper hair on the sides. His face was lean and leathery with prominent crow's feet wrinkles at the corners of his eyes, deep creases in his cheeks, and a prominent wrinkled chin under a drooping handlebar mustache.

"Boss, this here is Rawhide Jake Brighton. Yer might a heared a him. He killed Charlie Dalton down in Seymour. Rawhide, this here is Walt Guthrie. Yer might a heared a him. He's cow boss a the Flyin' XC ranch, one a the biggest ranches in the whole state a Texas." Johnny was all smiles.

Jake stepped forward, held out his hand, and said, "Pleased to meet yer, Mister Guthrie."

Walt stood, rising an inch or two over six feet, smiled slightly, and said, "Likewise. This is Ed Saunders. He's the ranch bookkeeper." They shook hands and exchanged greetings.

"Rawhide's lookin' to sign on," Johnny said.

"Wal, y'all heared 'bout the cowboy strike gonna start up pretty soon in the panhandle," Walt said. "Gonna be some rustlin' I'm afeared. Reckon we can use 'nuther cowboy good with a gun. Johnny's a crack shot. Yer a crack shot with a rifle?"

Jake nodded his *yes* and was about to speak when he was interrupted by the bookkeeper. "Now, Walt. You know that ain't in the budget. We're full up on employees," Saunders said, a tad edgy.

"Oh, it ain't gonna bust the budget. 'Sides, I didn't know there was gonna be a strike when we made the budget. Xavier told me the association is sendin' Wes Wilson up there to watch over the sit-chashun. Guess that tells yer somethin'."

"Well, I'll have to check with Xavier before we sign him on."

"Yer just sign him on. I'll talk to Xavier. Welcome to the Flyin' XC," he said to Jake. "Johnny, yer can ride herd on Jake here for a spell 'til he's broke in. Maybe ride out together and look for rustlers. Git his horse settled and him bunked in. Comin' up on supper time. Crew'll be in soon."

"Will do, boss."

"First, let me have a confab with Rawhide here."

"Sure. I'll take yer horse over to the barn," Johnny said to Jake, who nodded his head.

Walt sidled up to Jake and started walking slowly in the opposite direction. He talked quietly in a subdued tone. "Wal, we're, me and Xavier, glad to see yer here. I ain't got the men to spare to be ridin' all over the range lookin' for rustlers. That's Johnny's job, but I think they got him outnumbered. So, yer comin' on undercover to work as anuther line rider is good. Just wanted to let yer know, me and Xavier are behind yer, and we're the onliest ones who know who yer are. So, good luck, Detective." He gave

Jake a friendly slap on the back.

That evening, after supper, it was cool and dry. Jake had met all the cowboys and wranglers and even sat in on a few hands of one of the two poker games going on. But it got stuffy, and he decided to get some fresh air on the porch. When he walked out, there were already a couple of cowboys sitting and talking at one end of the porch. Jake stepped over to the other end, sat in one of the chairs, and lit a cigar. His thoughts drifted back to ol' Wes Wilson, his mentor and partner, who was working up in the panhandle. Now that Jake was fully trained, they would be riding separately. His thoughts were interrupted when a scraggly looking cowboy named Scruffy came out and sat in a chair next to him. Jake sized him up on the sly and figured him for the weaselly type. He was on the small side for height and build. He was dirty. There were dried sweat rings on his shirt and the crown of his hat, and he smelled. His left eye held a perpetual squint, even in dim light. His beard was short, and from the looks of it probably scissor cut by one of the other hands. He was in bad need of a haircut. He seemed to be always twitching, but he wasn't.

"So . . ." he began as he sat and pulled

the fixings from his shirt pocket under his vest. "I heared yer is the famous Rawhide Jake Brighton." He glanced at Jake with his good eye as he rolled a smoke.

"Ain't famous," Jake said tough-like, having previously decided to play the rough, hard-hitting type individual.

"Wal, folks hereabouts heared a yer," he said as he lifted his thigh and struck the match on his pant leg, then lit his cigarette. Jake said nothing.

"I was in Seymour the night yer killed Charlie Dalton."

Jake maintained a placid expression and posture, but inside he tensed. All the cowboys had dropped their gun belts on their bunks, and so Jake did likewise, which left him unarmed and feeling vulnerable. He snuck a few glances around to discover any kind of weapon, rock, bottle, spittoon, anything. He saw one spittoon that was out of reach. He said nothing.

" 'Course I was over next door at the Aces Wild when Charlie started shootin'. But I ran over in time to see yer shoot that snake Charlie Dalton. Then that other big feller shot Whitey Morgan, and Charlie lying on the floor in a pool of blood, and yer standin' there with a smokin' pistol. 'Course when I saw the marshal running up, I hightailed it back to the Aces Wild. Him and me don't git along."

"What were yer doin' in Seymour?"

"I had business," he said in a tone that implied Jake shouldn't ask anymore about it. "Why'd yer kill him anyway? Not that it makes no never mind to me. Everbody knew Charlie Dalton would git kilt sooner or later. He thought he was a gunman. But he weren't. Yer must be though, wearing that cross-draw and all."

"Ain't no gunman neither. I witnessed him shoot an unarmed man in the back, and I drover-whipped hell outta him for it. Few days later he broke outta jail and came to the Brazos lookin' for me to kill me. Instead, I kilt him. That's all." Jake puffed his cigar until the tip was bright orange, then took a deep drag, and blew the smoke between him and Scruffy like he thought a tough hombre might do.

"Wal, I heared he already had his pistol pulled, and yer shot him while he was takin' aim at yer." Jake shrugged and said nothing. "That sounds like a gunman to me," Scruffy continued. He stared at Jake, who stared back at him with the ever-present natural look of challenge in his eyes. He reached across his vest to pull his pocket watch, and Scruffy skidded his chair back and jumped

14

up. "Hold on. Hold on now," he stammered while holding his arms at full length in front of him, palms facing out, as he quickly backed up. "Didn't mean no offense." Jake pulled the watch all the way out and dangled it in the air. "Aw, gosh dawg it. Thought yer was pullin' iron on me." He made a low kick at the vacant space in front of him and turned sharply to stomp back through the bunkhouse door. Jake chuckled. Little did Scruffy know that not only was Jake not a gunman he was, in fact, an undercover stock detective working for the Stock-Raisers Association of North-West Texas, headed up by James Loving, and assigned to the range around the Flying XC at the request of the owner, Xavier Calhoun.

Two days later, Jake and Johnny were riding the western edge of the Flying XC range, counting cattle, and searching for any sign of rustlers. They came to a high rise and climbed just far enough for their heads to show over the crest. Pulling out their spyglasses, they spent several minutes searching the terrain. "Right over there in that big meadow in the gulch with the long red bank, see it?" Johnny queried.

"Yup."

"We had a hunnert heifers and were fixin'

to bring in anuther couple hunnert and turn out the bulls. Plenty a water in the creek all year, and the grass's good. Wal, those hunnert heifers is gone. Rustled right before a storm that washed out all sign. Ain't got no ideer where they took 'em. That ain't gonna happen soon as the whole range is fenced in."

"Calhoun's fencin' in his range?"

"Yep. Surveyors workin' out to the east right now."

"Mmm. That's interestin'. Rustlers are probably makin' up a herd farther to the west. Whose range is that west of Flyin' XC?" Jake asked contemplatively as he looked through his glass.

"Ain't nobody's. Open range."

"Uh-huh. What say we take a little ride out thataway? Past the farthest yer been out west and see what we can see. Play out a couple a days' ridin'."

"Fine by me. Long as it don't rain. I hate ridin' in the rain and snow. Done enuff a it."

Jake glanced up at the western horizon and at the sun that had just begun to slant to the west. There was not a cloud in the sky. "Looks like a good chance it ain't gonna rain. Yer brought yer slicker, didn't yer?"

"Yeah," Johnny growled.

Jake touched his spurs to Jasper's side, and off they loped down through the meadow where the heifers had been, and on out the other side over the low end of the gulch.

On the next day of searching, the air was dead calm and warm. The sun was bright in a cloudless sky. Flies buzzed about their heads, and the horses swished their tails rapidly side to side to clear their flanks of the pests. They were walking the horses toward the mouth of an arroyo they intended to check and then turn back for the barn, when they suddenly turned their heads to look at each other. "Did yer hear that?" Johnny asked.

"Yep. They's cattle bawlin'. Cummin' from that low canyon yonder, don't yer think?"

"Yep. Let's git on over there."

They both vaulted into their saddles and trotted the horses toward the arroyo. As they drew close, Jake held up his hand. "Why don't yer go up that side and I'll go up this one. Try and stick to the edges of the mesquite and scrub to stay outta sight." They split, and each worked their way up the canyon. Soon, they came to an area where the floor widened out into a large

17

meadow of good-looking grass with a little stream running through it. And sure enough, there were cattle grazing all over the meadow. Jake found a good spot higher up under a mesquite tree in a thicket of scrub, hopped out of the saddle, and pulled his spyglass to search the whole area. He looked over at Johnny and noticed he did the same. He glassed all around the edges of the meadow and found what he was looking for. There was a deserted campsite on the southern shoulder of the arroyo. He kept searching, but it was the only one he found, and there was no sign of any cowboys either in the meadow or on the edges. He caught Johnny's attention and motioned for them to go forward. As they moved through the cattle, they checked brands and then came together at the campsite.

"All Flyin' XC. What a yer think?" Johnny asked as they sat their saddles and kept looking over the meadow.

"How many head do yer figure?"

"At least the hunnert missing head I told yer 'bout, and I say anuther fifty."

"Wal, we got some choices. We can hide out here and wait for the rustlers to come back and catch 'em or kill 'em and then drive the herd back to the Flyin' XC. But who knows how long it could be before they bring in any more cows? How many more head yer figure this little valley could hold through the summer?"

"Oh, I'd say at least anuther couple a hunnert, maybe three hunnert."

"So, they want to keep buildin' this herd. They'll be back prob'ly purty soon, but we don't know how soon, and it could rain between now and then?" Jake smiled as he gave Johnny a quizzical look who, in response, waved his hand over his head.

"Or we can just drive this herd back. Then come back out here to see if we can pick up their trail when they come in with more cows. Cuz they won't want to keep 'em here anymore now that we know about their hidin' place."

"I think that's what we should do. It's a fer sure. I don't like maybes."

"Yeah. Yer probably right. Plus, any kinda gunfight might stampede the herd. And I don't know 'bout yer, but I'm gittin' low on provisions. We got half a day of light left. Let's round 'em up. Once we're made up, yer take the point. Jasper and I'll take drag."

They loped off and in half an hour had the little herd made up. Jake tied his blue bandana around his mouth and nose as high up as he could without blindfolding himself and pulled his hat down low over his eyes.

Then he and Jasper took up the drag. Jake hollered out, "Head 'em up! Move 'em out!" And he popped the bullwhip several times over the heads of the last cows. Johnny whooped up the lead cows. The cattle started moving, and they headed out of the arroyo turning east. While they were working, the thought crossed Jake's mind that if they had more provisions, they could have stayed at least three or four days to see if any rustlers came in. At his contract rate of five dollars a rustler it would have been worth it. Well, at least he would have a bill to give to Loving for $150 for the recovered cattle in front of him. Including the $65 he previously billed for the Jonesboro recovery, he would be owed $215 plus his regular monthly wages for a total of $290. Not a bad month. He smiled to himself.

The herd was kicking up heavy dust. Jake's eyes watered, and he sneezed seemed like every two minutes. Jasper wasn't liking it as well. But they stayed rawhide tough and, in a day and a half, pushed the herd to the meadow in the gulch where they first went missing. Once they got the critters settled, they came together, slid out of their saddles, led their horses to the little stream, and let them take a long drink. Jake swatted his Stetson against his thigh to shake off the dust, put it back on, and pulled off his pale-blue bandana that looked more beige from the dust than blue. He shook it out, dipped it in the water, and wiped his head and face, smearing the dirt at first and then, after repeating the process several times, had a clean face. "Guess yer ate 'bout a acre a dust. Told yer I'd spell yer," Johnny said.

"Aw, we were all right, me and Jasper. Next time yer can ride drag." Jake knelt and dipped his cupped hand into the stream, sucked in the water, and swished it around his mouth, then spit it out. "Whew," he said as he submerged his canteen and let it fill. "Reckon we kin make it back to the ranch inside a two days. Travel faster than when we came out. Get re-supplied and come back out here. See if we can catch them rustlers."

"We ain't gonna take a day or two to rest up?"

"Yer can if yer want. Me and Jasper's goin' right back out. He's a tough old bronc. They's rustlers loose on the range, and we aim to catch 'em or kill 'em. It'll be their choice."

"Yer talkin' like yer some kinda Texas Ranger or sumthin'."

"Ain't no Texas Ranger. But Walt sent us out to see what we could do. So, I say, let's go out there and see what we can do to cut these rustlers outta the herd. Toss 'em and jail 'em or send 'em to see they's maker. What a yer say?" He grinned big at Johnny, who caught the enthusiasm and said, "Wal, guess that's why I was hired on as line rider. Better git to it." And he grinned back at Jake.

On the second day they trotted into head-quarters just before supper time. They took care of the horses, washed off in the stock trough, and drug into the bunkhouse to sit with the rest of the hands on the long bench at the table. Johnny couldn't stop boasting about their accomplishment. Jake watched the reactions and noticed that Scruffy seemed to be more quiet than usual. Every-one else seemed to react normally. They ate their fill and retired to the porch for a smoke. The sun was still up but sinking fast. Walt walked up and motioned for them to come over and talk to him out in the lot. They did and while they strolled with him toward the office, Johnny reported their ac-tivities.

"That's good boys. Yer done good," Walt said. "Yer say they's 150 head there. All heifers? All right. We'll pick 'em up and bring 'em in on the roundup. Plus, I gotta turn the bulls out in the south and east ranges. Only got four hundred. Hope it'll be enough. Want to try for twenty thousand calves next year. Better talk to Xavier. See 'bout pickin' up some more bulls." He was looking out over the lot talking to himself more than them, then turned to them and said, "Wal, yer boys take a couple a days to rest up. Might have to send yer out to pick up some more bulls."

"We're plannin' to head out in the mornin' and catch them rustlers," Jake said as he stared eye to eye at Walt. He could feel the challenge in his eyes, and he saw immediately that Walt was starting to get his back up. Jake said softly but firmly, "Walt, both Johnny and me are of the mind that part a the reason we were hired on is to catch rustlers. I'm guessin' there's a bunch a them workin' down to the southwest. Maybe we could ride on down thataway to the L Bar and see if they got any extra bulls to sell. And along the way —" Jake shrugged and smiled friendly-like.

Walt held his stare, and Johnny looked from one to the other of them, kind of expecting to see Walt brace Jake and, if need be, knock him to the ground with one punch like he'd seen him do more than once. Instead, he saw a line of white show under Walt's mustache and his crow's feet crinkle up. "That sounds like a pretty good ideer, if yer think yer and yer horses don't need the rest," Walt said.

"All right, we'll be gone before dawn." Jake's smile widened. "Maybe we can bring back some bulls and rustlers. Okay to take a packhorse outta the remuda?"

"Yeah, sure. We could use a lot more bulls. Make sure they are all working bulls. Don't want no young ones but not too old neither. Make sure they's thick. We'll pay market but no more. I don't know. Maybe I better pick out the bulls. Yer let me know if they got any for sale. Maybe swing by the TL and check with them."

"Will do, boss," Jake said. Inwardly, he was pleased with the outcome of that minor confrontation. He did not really want to be slowed down by trying to control and move bulls. And he did not know bulls anyway. Johnny didn't volunteer either.

"Okay," Walt said, "good luck to yer" and turned and walked back to the office.

"Johnny, can yer cut out a good packhorse and put it in the barn? We'll load the pack in the mornin'. Prob'ly be pretty light. Is there a tent we can use?" Johnny nodded *yes.* "Okay, can yer handle that? I'll check

24

with the cook for the chuck. All right? All right."

"One thing," Johnny said. "Looked like for a minute there, yer was 'bout to cross ol' Walt. Ain't a good ideer. He's mighty tough and quick and strong with his fists."

"Oh, I wasn't gonna cross him. I only wanted to make sure he knew how important it is to check down to the southwest. If he said no, well, he's the boss." Jake grinned at Johnny and draped an arm over his shoulders. "Now let's get geared up. What a yer say?"

In the bunkhouse Johnny was again vocal about Jake's plan, and Jake was watching reactions. And again, it was Scruffy who was not acting natural. Jake tucked that away in his mind. He was suspicious. There probably was a spy in the crew, and it was looking more and more like Scruffy might be the culprit.

Next day, Jake and Johnny were out the gate before dawn. It was pitch black, and looking back over the packhorse, Jake thought he saw someone hurry from the bunkhouse to the barn. Couldn't be sure.

On the second day out there was no sun, but it was warm and still. They swam the horses across the North Fork of the Wichita River, rode for another five miles to where

25

they climbed up a ridge, and looked out over the land. Jake pushed his hat back and said to Johnny sitting his saddle next to him, "Figure we're north of L Bar range. What a yer think?"

Johnny pushed his hat back and said, "Yup. Over thataway to the south yer can barely see the South Fork of the Wichita. It sort a marks the north border of L Bar range."

"Out here is where I think those rustlers be holdin' up. They could steal from the Flyin' XC and the L Bar. Make up a pretty good herd for a drive to the army forts in New Mexico. Or down south toward El Paso or even north to Colorado. Could even be L Bar hands. They's a little settlement a mile or so from the L Bar headquarters. They could get provisions there."

"Yup, and who might that be a cummin'?" Johnny posed as he backed his horse down the hill to reduce his profile on the top of the rise. Jake followed his lead and looked in the same direction. "See him out there a little over a mile, headin' southwest?"

"Yep. Let's put a glass on him." They both retrieved their spyglasses and focused on the rider. "Can't be sure, but it looks like Scruffy," Jake said.

"Oh, it's him all right. He's the onliest

one around that rides a Palouse horse. Says he got it from a Nez Perce injun in the Oklahoma Territory. See the dark body with a white rump and black spots? That there is a Palouse horse. Not a bad stock horse."

"Let's follow him and see where he's headed. We can ride this ridge until it plays out."

They followed, trying to stay high so they wouldn't lose sight of him while remaining well back. They never closed to less than a half mile. As the day wore on, the sun broke through the clouds, and with the sun in their eyes it became more difficult to keep Scruffy in sight. But they didn't lose him, and, toward sundown, Johnny stood in his stirrups and pointed. "Smoke," he said. It was soon obvious that Scruffy was headed straight for it.

"Yeah, I see it," Jake said as he recognized the plume of campfire smoke rising straight up about two miles out. "Sure enough, it's them. Let's work our way down that draw, circle around, and come in from the south. We'll reconnoiter their camp and jump 'em after they bed down."

"What's rekanoter?"

"It's a military term for scout."

"Oh. How many you reckon there are of 'em?"

"No ideer. Probably at least two, and Scruffy makes three. That's what we'll find out when we reco — er, scout them."

"What if there is more than three?"

"Then we take 'em all. That's why we're goin' in while they's sleepin'. Gotta be careful though. They prob'ly have a guard posted."

"What's posted?"

"Another military term. Means a armed feller stayin' awake and watchin' out for intruders."

"What's intruders?"

"Don't yer know nothin'? We be the intruders tryin' to git in they's camp and attack 'em. That's a intruder. A feller who's goin' in somewhere he ain't supposed to be."

"Never had no book learnin'. Can't read or write 'cept for my name. I can sign my name pretty good. Put a lotta curlicues on it like I seen in a catalog. But I can shoot hell outta this rifle and pistol. That's fer sure."

"Well good, cuz yer might git yer chance tonight."

They made their way around to the south and stayed in the little red-walled arroyos while they moved in ever closer. The smoke was their guide. In the still air it was rising high before it spread out and formed a flat and wide layer so that it looked like a mushroom. When they guessed-ta-mated they were close, they found a game trail leading up the side of the arroyo. They followed it to the top of the low ridgeline and saw that, before they might have a clear line of sight to the camp, they had to get over one more plateau. It looked ugly with its sides of rugged red gullies peppered with mesquite. So, they rode parallel to it. As they neared the far edge, they dismounted and tied off the horses to mesquite bushes. Then they crept to the top and out to the edge on their bellies. There below them was a small valley of green grass surrounded on two sides by rough red hills and by the plateau they were on that was more densely covered with scrub. There looked to be about fifty head of cattle grazing in the valley. Jake put his glass on the cattle and said, "Uh-huh. There they are. The big *S* on the neck and the *L* on the side. Those are L Bar cattle."

About a hundred yards almost directly below them was the camp tucked into a grove of cottonwood trees. They put their glasses on the camp and saw that it was well established on the edge of a small pond, probably spring fed, with a little stream flowing out and down the valley. There was a rough corral of wood rails within which stood the Palouse horse. More horses were out in the meadow. There was a shelter made of wood poles under a roof of boards, probably to store provisions, and two wide fire rings of stone. One was for heat that had saddles and bedrolls around it and the other for cooking with an iron spit and a pot hanging from it. The cooking fire was the source of the smoke.

There were five cowboys standing in a circle by the cooking fire. Scruffy was doing most of the talking and flailing his arms around for emphasis. One of the cowboys was pointing his finger at Scruffy and shaking his head *no.* Two of the others looked frustrated. The last one turned and walked to a saddle, pulled a Winchester from its scabbard, and sat down on the saddle with the rifle across his legs. He pulled the fixings from his vest and rolled a smoke. "See the one sittin' with the rifle across his legs? He's the one to watch. Prob'ly the most dangerous."

The light was going fast, and Jake concentrated on finding an approach to the camp. They were facing north, so he glassed the west side of the valley where he saw a cut in the steep hills. The rustlers would be expecting riders to only come from the northeast or south, so they could probably surprise them if they came in from the west. The plateau they were on top of sloped down to the southwest, so it should be easy enough to get over to that cut.

The little confab of cowboys in the camp broke up, and three of them went out to the meadow with ropes to catch the horses. Jake became concerned that the rustlers were leaving. So, they stayed where they were until it was clear they weren't leaving as he watched them put the horses in the corral. Probably planning an early morning departure.

It was twilight when they got to the cut. They came across a small spring on the way over there, so they stopped and watered the horses good while filling their own canteens. At the cut, the grass was good. They tied long ropes tightly to the mesquite and looped the other ends around the horses' necks and let them graze. Then they sat down for a meal of hardtack and jerky. They could smell the coffee and food cooking at the camp, and Jake said, "Smells good." They laid back and dozed off. When Jake's eyes blinked open, the moon was high. He could sense wide-awake-Johnny next to him.

"What if they start shootin'? What a yer

want to do?" Johnny whispered.

Jake looked over at him, studied him as best he could in the dim light, and probed, "Yer ever kilt a man?"

"Yeah. One. But he were far off. A rifle shot. Ain't never been in any kinda gunfight. But I kilt a lot of tin cans and rocks in my time," he said with a grin.

"Yer scared?"

"Are yer?"

"Yup. Only a fool ain't scared while he waits for the battle to begin. Started for me in the army during the war. I was just a kid then. Some mighty fearful times in that war. I'm kinda used to it. Besides, when the face-off comes, yer forget all about the fear and bear down on yer purpose and target."

"Wal, should we kill 'em if they start shootin'?"

"I'm hopin' we can get the drop on 'em before any shootin' starts, so we can talk with 'em. They could be L Bar hands out here for the ranch. But Scruffy being here makes that doubtful. Either way, I'd like to know if they are rustlers before they start shootin', so we're gonna have to be real quiet and snake their shootin' irons away from 'em before they wake up. But if some-how they should start shootin' before we can do that, wal, yer gotta protect yerself and yer pardner. So, shoot to kill. Don't make no never mind to me if they's dead or alive rustlers. Don't worry. Yer'll be fine." Jake smiled at Johnny, slapped him on the shoulder, and said, "Let's go reconnoiter."

There was a guard posted. Jake and Johnny had crawled to within sixty feet of the camp and were on their bellies watching for movement. The guard walked around the corrals and the cook fire, then squatted and fixed a smoke. He stayed there awhile and ambled back to the corrals. The horses nickered every time he came close. He spoke to them low and soft, and they quieted. Then he stepped away from the corrals and listened. The only sound was the faint gurgle of the stream, and the hoot of an owl and its flapping wings when it launched from a cottonwood on the other side of the pond. The guard went back to the cook fire, threw on a couple more sticks of wood, and sat against a boulder. The fire flared bright and warm. Jake was pretty sure it was the dangerous one he had picked out earlier, and it wasn't more than five minutes when the man's head started to nod. Jake waited, and presently the owl hooted again. The man jerked awake and listened for about two minutes before his head started to nod again. Jake waited a little while more.

There was plenty of snoring coming from around the other fire that was still burning bright.

"We gotta stay away from those horses, so they don't get nervous," Jake whispered. "Let's move in closer. Hope that dern owl don't hoot again." They crept to the side of the camp opposite the corral that put them behind the guard. "I'll sneak in and knock out the guard. You start liftin' their irons. Then we'll wake 'em up." Jake smiled.

Jake slinked around the boulder and slammed the butt of his pistol on the top of the guard's head. He fell to his side like a sack of flour. Johnny was picking up pistols and rifles off the sleepers, and Jake joined him. They piled all the hardware off to one side and stood between them and the cowboys. Johnny was working on the last one and having some trouble because the man was lying on his holstered pistol. Jake went over, rolled the man over, pressed his pistol against the cowboy's forehead, and put his finger to his pursed lips. He motioned for Johnny to guard the fellow, which he did with the muzzle of his Colt stuck in the man's neck, and in his other hand, he pointed the feller's pistol in the direction of the last three. Jake said, "Good mornin', boys. Time to rise and shine. Let's go," he said loudly as he kicked their feet.

Amid loud exclamations and surprise, they reached for their pistols and came up empty. They all came to their feet and stood still under the muzzle of Jake's six-shooter. "What the hell's this all 'bout?" one of them said.

"Wal, lorddy mussy. If it ain't Sour Billie Connell, and over there is his sidekick, Sweet Red Tilson," Johnny exclaimed. "Ain't seen the two a yer 'round here since yer got run off the TL, what? Two years ago?"

"Ain't no business a yers no ways anyways, Johnny Raymer," Connell said as he stared pure hate at Johnny. "Who's yer pardner?"

"That's Rawhide Jake Brighton who I was tellin' yer 'bout," Scruffy blurted out. Connell gave Jake a once over and then stared at him hard, but he blinked when Jake took a step toward him. "Watch out, Billie. He'd just as soon shoot yer as look at yer."

"Yeah, yer picked a pair to draw to, Scruffy. Y'all in the rustlin' business now, huh?" Johnny said with a scornful look.

"We ain't rustlin'. We hired on the L Bar and are bringin' critters up to this valley for the summer," Connell declared with indignation in his voice.

"That right?" Jake growled. "Git on yer knees all a yer."

"Please, Mister Brighton. Have mercy. Don't kill me," Scruffy pleaded in stark terror.

"Johnny, why don't yer hogtie them while I cover yer, starting with Sour Billie. While yer doin' that, let me ask yer, Sour Billie. To prove what yer sayin', yer wouldn't mind takin' a little ride down to the L Bar, would yer? But then. What's Scruffy doin' here?" Jake stepped over and pulled Scruffy by the shirt collar away from the others and rolled him in the dirt. Then he jumped on top of him and pressed his pistol in between Scruffy's eyes that were so big the whites were twice the size of the pupils. "Maybe yer'd like to tell us what's goin' on here, Scruffy."

Scruffy started to speak when Sour Billie growled a threatening warning. "Scruffy —"

"Yer can go to hell, Sour Bill. Yer all talk anyhows. Yer never kilt nobody. I seen this man, cold livered, kill Charlie Dalton not more'n a month ago. If I tell yer everthin', Rawhide, will yer let me go?"

"Let's hear what yer have to say."

"We done it all. We been stealin' beeves from all the spreads 'round here. Them 150

Flyin' XC yer brought in the other day? We stole 'em. Those critters out there right now they stole from the L Bar. Ugh!!" Scruffy grunted from the impact of Sour Billie's bull rush that knocked Jake off Scruffy. Then he dropped a knee into Scruffy's midsection. Sour Billie's hands were still tied behind his back, but he somehow had slipped the rope off his ankles. Jake jumped up, swung his arm in an arc, and smacked his pistol butt into the side of Sour Billie's head. It made a sickening cracking sound, and blood began to seep from Sour Billie's ear. He fell off Scruffy and started twitching on the ground. In a minute he stopped and was still, looking like he was dead.

The other two cowboys were still not tied up. Jake turned on them with fire in his eyes and snarled, "Any of yer want some a this? Just make a move, and I'll kill yer where yer stand." Their eyes were wide, and as they held their hands high above their heads, they shook their heads *no*. Jake turned and pointed his pistol at Scruffy, who had staggered to his feet. "No! No! No!" Scruffy screamed and fell face first in the dirt, out cold from a faint.

"All right," Jake said as he breathed deep and concentrated on cooling his temper. "Let's finish hogtieing these sons-a-bitches."

Then a moaning sound came from the guard near the boulder. "Better get him tied up, too," Jake said.

After they were all hogtied, they were sitting around the fire that was burning good from the extra wood Jake piled on it. Scruffy revived and was conscious. Johnny said to him, "Yer been at the Flyin' XC for what? Five years now? And been a good hand. How'd yer ever get hooked up with these varmints?"

"Gamblin'," Scruffy said and hung his head. "I got so far into Sour Billie, he said I had to work it off or he would kill me. So here I sit."

Four hours later, Sour Billie finally came to, but that was it. He couldn't talk or recognize his name, and his eyes were glazed over. Wobbly, he got to his feet but stood crooked and couldn't straighten up. He drooled saliva, drug his right leg when he tried to walk, and couldn't move his right arm. The guard whose head Jake had cracked complained of a bad headache but otherwise seemed to be all right.

"Glad yer boys are alive. I didn't want to go to no inquest. So now we can just turn yer over to the sheriff after we stop by the L Bar and let them know where they's cattle is. All righty. One at a time, Johnny, take 'em and git 'em in their saddles. I'll cover yer. Tie they's ankles to they's stirrups and wrists to the horns. This one here we'll have to tie to the saddle," he said of Sour Billie. "Let's tie up all the horses in a string."

It was tricky, but Jake and Johnny working together managed to get their prisoners halfway to the L Bar by sunset. They made camp in a grove of post oak beside a small stream. They faced each one of the prisoners to a tree in a hugging position and tied their hands on the opposite side of the tree. While Johnny cooked the chuck, Jake kept a watch on the prisoners. Scruffy moaned, "What's gonna happen to me, Rawhide, since I confessed everthin'?"

"Wal, what a the rest of yer boys have to say? Yer confessin'?" They looked at each other with inquiring eyes. Who would break first?

"Wal," Sweet Red talked first, "since Scruffy done tolt yer supposedly everthin', reckon it's his word 'gainst ours."

"Uh-huh," Jake said. "Wal then, guess we see what the boys at the L Bar have to say. If yer're for sure workin' for the L Bar, then I reckon Scruffy's a liar tryin' to save his own skin." Jake held up his hand to stop Scruffy's protest. "But —" he looked hard at the four of them each one individually and took a sip of his coffee. "If Scruffy's tellin' the truth, then I reckon yer onliest chance is to try and make a break for it tonight. But" — he again stared them down one at a time — "if yer try to run, I'll kill yer." He let them chew on that for a minute or two. "And I'm sure yer heard about Johnny's skill with shootin' irons. So, he'll kill yer, too." Each time he said the word *kill,* he emphasized it.

"Yer heared a Huntsville, Texas?" They all shook their heads *no.* "Any a yer ever before been convicted of rustlin' or some other thievin' or robbin' or like that?" They all shook their heads again. "Wal, Huntsville is where the state penitentiary is located. It's where yer boys are gonna be locked up for a long time. But I hear they just put in programs where yer can be leased out to work on a farm. So, yer can have yer pick. Confess now and maybe yer'll git on one a them farms. Or, fight it and spend the next ten years behind bars. Yer choice. Yer choices are run and git kilt. Deny yer guilt and go to prison. Confess and work on a farm."

They were quiet a long time looking back and forth at each other, and then the dangerous one, who wasn't so dangerous anymore with a busted head, said, "Oh, all right. We done it. Now kin I get a smoke?"

"Damn yer hide, Tony," Sweet Red said and shot Tony a disgusted look.

"That's two-to-two cuz I don't think ol' Sour Billie over there will ever be right in the head again." Jake smiled.

"Yeah, we done it," the other cowboy whose name was Rusty said.

Sweet Red twisted and fidgeted against his ropes, and Jake said, "That's three to one."

"Damn yer all to hell. Yer give a feller no choice."

"That mean yer done it like Scruffy said?"

"Yeah, yer dirty bastard," he shouted. "Look what yer done to my pard. He's as good as dead. Someday I'll catch up with yer and kill yer for it."

Jake smiled and shrugged. "Not if I kill yer first." Scruffy shuddered.

They made it to the L Bar the next day without incident, camped there for the night, and left in the morning under a clear sky with a cold driving wind at their backs as they headed east for Seymour. Jake was in the lead with a rope to the prisoners hitched up in single file, and Johnny rode drag with the packhorse on a lead line. Jake kept up a steady lope as he figured it was cool enough for the horses to hold the pace for a good long while. About halfway along on their ride they came to a sharp hairpin bend in the Brazos with a gentle sloping bank. There was a small seasonal creek emptying into the river. He stopped there to rest the horses, and after he tasted the water for salt, he let them drink. The last half of the ride, he followed the river right to Seymour. It was a thirty-mile ride from the L Bar to Seymour, and Jake was determined to arrive before supper time so he wouldn't have to get the sheriff out of his house. And he made it. They rode into Seymour on Reiman Street straight to the courthouse about three in the afternoon. He came into town that way to avoid attracting a crowd. But with a show of five men tied to their saddles, it wasn't long before people were hurrying over to the sheriff's office.

"Howdy, Sheriff," with a tip of his hat Jake said as the lawman with one of his deputies stepped out of his office onto the porch. Johnny was busy keeping the horses controlled.

"What're yer got here, Rawhide?"

Jake slid off his saddle and hurried over to the sheriff, stood next to him, and in a low voice said, "Sheriff, I'm workin' undercover. These outlaws and Johnny don't know I'm a stock detective. I'm workin' at the Flyin' XC. So . . ."

"Gotchyer," he said quietly and then louder, "wal, that is a humdinger. Yer say Walt Guthrie sent yer out after these fellers?"

"Yep. That's my pardner, Johnny Raymer. He's a line rider for the Flyin' XC. All these fellers confessed to rustlin', and we caught 'em red handed with stolen L Bar cattle. I reckon yer kin take their horses off our hands, too?"

"Reckon so. I'll impound them official-like."

" 'Cept the Palouse," Johnny said. "Scruffy, yer want us to take him back to the Flyin' XC for yer?"

"Be much obliged," Scruffy said and hung his head.

"That one slouched in the saddle on the roan, he's in pretty bad shape. He took a pretty good wallop to the head," Jake said.

"Yeah, and that sumbitch right there did it with a pistol whippin'. Nearly kilt him," Sweet Red yelled out, looking around the group of bystanders for sympathy. He was met with stern indifference.

"What's his name?" the sheriff asked.

"I'm told it's Sour Billie Connell."

"Well, I'll be. Didn't recognize him with

43

his head all swollen up like that. He unconscious? He got run off the TL for suspected rustlin' a couple a years back. Thought he left these parts for up north. Wal, come on, Bert. Let's git these outlaws behind bars. Rawhide, y'all have to come in the morning and write out affidavits. And I'd be much obliged if yer'd take them horses down to Quincy and tell him they're impounded by me."

"Will do, Sheriff. Thank ye."

After they got the string of horses corralled and had taken care of their own horses Jake said, "Wal, see yer later, Quincy. We'll be over at the Brazos if anybody's lookin' for us."

"I ain't yer seketary. So maybe I'll tell 'em and maybe I won't."

Jake waved his hand over his head as he and Johnny ambled out of the barn.

"I'm fixin' to have me a drink or two, a bath and a shave, some supper, and a visit with a friend a mine," Jake said grinning as they crossed the dirt street. "Yer got any money?"

"Nah. Didn't figger on needin' any."

"Wal, I figure old Walt'll be willin' to reimburse us our expenses when we tell him we caught five rustlers who was workin' Flyin' XC range, and that one a them was

Scruffy. So, I can lend yer some money and collect from Walt. But, just in case Walt ain't feelin' so generous, you'd still have to pay me back outta yer wages. Is that fair?"

"Wal . . . sounds fair enuff, but I think I'll just cook up some sowbelly and beans with ol' Quincy and bed down in the hayloft."

"Suit yerself. Let me buy yer a drink anyway."

"I'll take that, long as yer purty sure Walt'll, what'd yer say, reburse yer?"

"Yeah. Pay me back. But even if he don't, this one's on me."

"All righty. Thank yer."

Jake bought him another so Johnny had two drinks, then left the saloon, upon which Jake hefted his saddlebags and rifle from the floor, and Gracie took him by the hand to lead him upstairs into the heating room. It was warm and a little steamy as there were plenty of water pots on the stove heating for the tubs. Business was likely to increase in about an hour or so.

"Hello, Desideria," Jake said with a smile to the cleaning lady who tended to the water pots, kept the fire in the stove stoked, and cared for the towels and general cleanliness of the tub rooms.

"Hola, Señor Jake," she said seductively

45

with a flashing smile and flutter of her eyelashes.

"All right, all right," Gracie said. "Which tub is ready, Desideria?"

"Numero dos, just for my handsome Jake."

"I'll take it from here. Thank you, Desideria."

Jake shrugged and smiled again as Gracie took him by the arm over to the tub room. They went in, and before she shut the door, Gracie looked back at Desideria with a visual warning not to interfere. "I'll call you when we need more hot water. I expect there to be a lot of splashing." She grinned with a sparkle in her eye and shut the door.

He dropped his saddlebags, hung his pistol and ammo belts on a wooden peg, leaned his rifle against the wall, sat on a small bench, and Gracie pulled off his boots and his socks. He stood, shrugged out of his suspenders, and dropped his pants while she unbuttoned his shirt. Then he stripped off his union suit and stepped into the tub. "Whew. That is nice and hot. Ahh," he groaned as he slipped under the water. Gracie wrapped his head in hot towels, to which Jake sighed. After a few minutes she lathered him up and stropped her razor. In no time, with deft strokes, she removed his stubble and cleaned off the excess shaving cream with one of the towels. She trimmed his mustache with a pair of scissors and clipped around his ears and the back of his neck. Then she held a mirror for him to inspect her work.

"Very nice," he said approvingly. "Where'd yer learn to shave like that?"

While she cleaned up her shaving kit she said, "My daddy were a barber in Decatur. Learnt everthin' from him."

"So, yer was a respectable lady then?" Jake said with a grin.

"Not 'xactly. My Pa made his real money in a shack behind the barber shop."

"You?" Jake's face took on a clouded look.

"Yep. Me and anuther girl."

"Son of a bitch," he growled. "How old were yer when he started yer?"

"I were thirteen. My ma died the year before."

"How long — ?"

"Three years."

"What happened to — ?"

"We had a fallin' out, and I ran away. Made it to Henrietta on my own. Got a job in a laundry. Met up with a whiskey drummer. Went to Fort Sill with him. I learned the business end of my trade and went out on my own. A particular madam didn't like

47

that and ran me out. I ended up here with Alex. Been here since he opened. That's it. Not very interestin'."

"So, yer nineteen, twenty?"

"Just turned twenty. But what yer so interested in me for. I ain't nothin' but a saloon whore."

He smiled and gazed at her with soft liquid eyes that gave a look of deep endearment. "I like yer," he said lovingly. Gracie blushed and, with a bashful while somewhat mischievous smile, squeezed a sponge over his head. She soaped up his back, chest, and arms, then down his stomach and into his groin.

"Hmmm. Not real interested, huh?" She grinned lusciously at him.

"Due course, my love."

She massaged him a few strokes, and when she had a reaction she got up and pulled off her shoes, threw her dress off over her head, and took off her corset. "Ahh, that feels better," she said as she turned naked to face Jake. "See if this interests yer," she cooed as she stepped slowly toward him with her pretty blue eyes sparkling.

He stared at her petite, white nudity, rosy-red nipples on ample breasts, thin waist, and curvy hips as she came closer and closer. Then she vaulted over the edge of the tub and into the water with a splash and a scream. They laughed together and got down to business. "I guess yer interested now," she whispered in his ear with a couple of nips at his lobe.

In the morning at sunup, he sat up in the bed and spun around to set his feet on the floor. Gracie was still sleeping like a little kitten. He fished out from his saddlebags a clean union suit and socks, put them on and the rest of his clothes, too. A five-dollar gold piece he left on the dresser. He picked up his boots, hardware, and coat and crept out of the room. At the bottom of the stairs, he put on his boots and coat and strapped on his pistol and ammo belt. The saloon was empty, and Alex was nowhere in sight. He eased out the door and into the street, where he crossed to the livery and found Johnny and Quincy in the office drinking coffee.

"Yer two had any breakfast?"

"We're drinking it," Quincy said as he raised his tin coffee cup.

"Wal, let me give ol' Jasper a good brushin', then I'll buy y'all breakfast."

After breakfast, Jake and Johnny went to the sheriff's office. Quincy came along to pick up the paperwork for the impounds.

"Yer have paper and pencil?" Jake said to the sheriff. "I'll have to write the affidavit for both a us, and Johnny can sign it. He can't write."

"Sure. Yer can sit down over here." He pulled out a chair at a small table for Jake.

"Can yer sign this receipt for the rustlers?" Jake said as he handed him his receipt book.

They finished their business and rode out of town headed north. Toward the end of the day, they came to the Wichita, swam across, and in a few miles made camp at a small spring. In the morning they had only ridden two miles when in the distance to the north, they saw a dust cloud. They pulled up and had studied the situation for a few minutes when Jake said, "Might be rustlers. We need to investigate." As they came closer, they came across Flying XC hands rounding up cattle.

"Yo! Bodie," Johnny called out as he rode up to Bodie Carter, another top hand. "Yer roundin' up already?"

"Yep. Walt wanted to get started," Bodie yelled back as he rode up to meet them. "We got prob'ly 'bout fifteen thousand calves to brand and anuther ten thousand steers and cows to cut out for market. Roundin' up the whole herd at the Coman-che Creek big pasture."

50

"Where yer gatherin' at?"

"Just the other side a Beaver Creek."

"We'll join in the fun. C'mon, Jake, let's ride out to the east. Sound right, Bodie?"

"Yep."

"Can yer put up this here Palouse and our packhorse?"

"Shore. Ain't that Scruffy's horse?"

"Yeah. It's a long story."

They loped off across the low rolling plain that was closely dotted with short scrub of green and purple hue popping up over a gray-green blanket of blue gama grass. Here and there large green patches of buffalo grass claimed the wetter soil. The sun was up about midway between the east horizon and the noon zenith. The flies were already buzzing and the mosquitos starting to swarm. So, they kept moving and swatted at the annoying fly or mosquito that hovered around their faces and then attacked.

A mile out, they found twenty head of cows with calves and steers who were grazing in a large depression that was about a mile wide and two miles long. Surveying the area, they could see more critters spread over the depression, so they rode to the opposite side and started working the cattle. Jake popped his whip and kept yelling, "Hiya, hiya, get up, get up." Johnny swatted his rope against the animals and his own leg, yelling and whistling.

They got about a hundred bawling head bunched and came together to talk for a moment. "Yer got the point this time," Johnny said. "Just keep us headin' northwest until yer hit Beaver Creek, and we'll figger what to do when we git there."

Jake tipped his hat, touched his spurs to Jasper, and reined him over to the steers that were on the edge of the herd nearest the direction they wanted to head. Jasper came up against a steer and pushed him. Promptly, he was rubbed up with green cow pucky from another steer. It got on Jake's leg and under his chaps. "Had to happen sooner or later," Jake muttered. But they got the bunch moving, and about an hour before sundown they arrived at Beaver Creek. The cattle immediately started to drink, and before they let the horses drink, Jake jumped down and scooped up a handful of water to taste.

"Beaver Creek ain't salty. It's okay," Johnny said. Then he called out, "There they are," as he pointed due north. " 'Bout two miles out. See 'em?"

The cattle lined up at the creek as if they were at a trough, so when they were ready, Johnny rode up and down the line whooping and hollering and slapping his rope to chase them out of the creek. Then Jake picked them up and chased them farther from the bank and held them away until Johnny got all the rest chased out. In less than an hour, they had their bunch in with the rest of them that Bodie and his crew had gathered. There were now over a thousand head in the bunch, and almost all of them were Flying XC. Some of them were TL probably brought in by Johnny and Jake.

A few minutes after they joined up with Bodie and were still in the saddle talking, Walt came riding up. He rode right up to them and reined in at the very last moment. Then he sashayed his horse around so he could face them all. A stiff west wind was blowing, and the back of his hat tipped up when the wind caught it. Would have blown off if he didn't have his stampede string cinched down tight. The sight of Walt almost losing his fine nutria fur Texas sombrero made the rest of them instinctively tighten their own stampede strings. Everything else that wasn't tied down, chaps' bottoms, coats, manes, forelocks, bandanas, was flapping in the wind, and a little dust haze was developing.

Walt nodded his head and said, "Howdy,

boys. See yer two made it back. How'd it go?"

Johnny blurted out, "We caught five red handed with a bunch a L Bar critters. They was the ones stealin' XC beeves. Turned in them rustlers to the sheriff in Seymour." He waved his arm and hand up in the air and said with a look of conspiracy, "And yer'll never guess who was one of 'em." He waited for someone to proffer a guess as more cowboys came up to make a group of seven. No one ventured forth.

Walt shrugged his shoulders and said, "Wal, who was it?"

"Scruffy!" Johnny said loudly.

"Scruffy?" Bodie said as all the cowboys looked one to the other in disbelief.

"Yup. Said he got into poker debt with Sour Billie Connell. 'Member him? Wal, Scruffy said Sour Billie made him work off what he owed by rustlin' with his gang. Confessed to stealin' the Flyin' XC critters me and Jake brought in ta other day. I got his horse. Asked me to take care of it for him."

"All right. Good job. Maybe that'll stop the bleedin' for a while. Meanwhile, how much yer got cleared, Bodie?"

"All the range south of Beaver Creek up to the Wichita."

"All right. I told Sticker y'all were here, so he's 'spectin' yer to bed down this herd here tonight and run 'em into Comanche Creek tomorrow. Take about a day. Yer got enough men to start roundin' up north a Beaver Creek?"

"I got fourteen men here, countin' Johnny and Jake. So, I can run seven in with this bunch and send out seven onto the range."

"All right. Tomorrow start clearin' north a Beaver Creek up to Buffalo Creek, east to the Wichita. Hold 'em on Buffalo Creek at Stevens Creek. Send a couple a men acrost the river to see if any a them squatters got any stolen beeves. TL's workin' down from north of the river and east of Stevens Creek. They'll join up with yer all, and yer can drive in the whole eastern herd pickin' up the rest a 'em along the way like usual. Sticker'll be bossin' yer. TL's started, and the L Bar ain't started yet. TL'll be roundin' up east a Seymour as usual and the L Bar southwest, as usual. So, I want to get everthin' in so I can send crews down to pick up our cows with they's calves. Got 'bout twenty thousand head at Comanche Creek right now. Crews are roundin' up and drivin' in from the west and the south. Y'all gotta handle the east. Savvy?"

"Yes, sir, boss," they all said in unison.

"All right. Now I need a fresh horse."

"Take Scruffy's Palouse," Johnny said eagerly.

"Nah. He's too good a stock horse. Yer got that buckskin mare with the three stockings here. Yeah? All right. I'll take her."

"Yer want some coffee and chuck, boss?" Bodie said.

"Nah. I'll change out my saddle and git back out on the range. Gotta go west. Gonna have a headwind." One of the cowboys came riding up leading the mare by looped rope. In five minutes, Walt was in the saddle, tipped his hat, and spurred the mare into a lope heading west.

"Bodie. Me and Johnny can check the squatters fer yer. I run into one a 'em a little while back," Jake said.

"All right. Much obliged. Now let's git some chuck."

The wind blew through the night. The cattle were unsettled, and the cowboys had to work hard to keep them close. They changed shifts every two hours, and all of them night-hawked the whole night. Seemed to Jake like he just got to sleep, and he was being awakened to go out to the herd. Mercifully, though, the wind subsided right before sunup. Jake stroked Jasper as he unsaddled him and slipped him a piece of

56

hard candy. He talked to him and praised him for his hard work, but now it was time for him to rest. So, he left Jasper with the small remuda and saddled up a bay mare with a black mane and tail. Johnny took the Palouse. By sunup the crew had the herd moving north. Seven cowboys stayed with the herd, and the other five peeled off to the east.

Jake and Johnny followed Beaver Creek east on the north side but straightened their route rather than twist and turn with the flow of the creek. In about ten miles they came to the Wichita and found a place to swim across. On the other side not too far off they could see a line of dirt farms along the river each on a homestead of 160 acres. The farmers were out plowing with single- or two-horse rigs. There wasn't a lot of money in corn or cotton, and most of them were merely scraping by. Riding along they took note that some of the farms looked well kept, and others looked run down. They hadn't gone too far when they came across a hollow with a small running brook that had a hovel of sod huts arrayed haphazardly with all sorts of junk in the yards, pigs, and chickens. Barefoot children, too. Little girls in thin, dirty dresses and boys in dirty bib overalls running around all over the place. Dirty old men sat on the porches in rickety chairs with whiskey jugs at their sides and were whittling wood with jack-knives. Younger dirty men were tending to chores of sorts. Scraggly older women in dirty, thin dresses appeared to have their work, too. All the men and women, even the children, froze and stared blankly when Jake and Johnny walked their horses in. As they passed by, more than once, young women and older girls appeared in the soddy doorways and lifted their skirts or dropped their tops. They called out, offering themselves for fifty cents.

Jake saw a side of beef hanging in a wood shack that was so poorly built it looked like it was about to collapse under its own weight, let alone under the added weight of the beef. He thought about searching for the hide to check the brand. But then, who would he arrest? He didn't say anything. And standing in front of the hut next to the shack, watching them as they rode by, was a boy in dirty bib overalls. Jake reined in and stopped. He glared at the boy, and the boy glared back. "Yer made it home, eh?" Jake said tersely. The boy didn't answer. "Yer know horse thieves always swing at the end of a rope, don't yer? They hang and they's necks stretch 'bout a foot. They's eyes pop out as they choke to death. Is that what yer want?" Jake snarled through clenched teeth. The boy turned and disappeared in the hut. Jake drew his pistol and spurred the sorrel back away on an angle to the door of the hut, calling out at the same time, "Watch out, Johnny! He might be after a gun. Yer watch our backs. I'll watch the door."

He didn't want to kill the boy, but he would if he came out with a weapon or started firing from inside the hut. Slowly, concentrating completely on the hut door, he eased the mare back, and Johnny eased away, too. The whole miserable bunch of squatters were drifting their way, and Johnny yelled, "Y'all stay back now. We ain't a gonna shoot. Just stay back." They kept coming and looked like they might be picking up pitchforks and axes and such. The boy, Lester, stuck his head out the door and screamed, "Yer kilt my uncle. Yer lucky my pa and brothers ain't here. They got guns and would kilt yer dead!" Jake blasted two shots into the sod next to the door, reined the mare around, and spurred her off at a gallop, angling on the run so the soddy was between him and the dirt family. Lester ducked back inside as soon as Jake fired. Johnny boomed three shots into the dirt in front of the mob, and they scattered to take cover while Johnny spurred the Palouse after Jake. They ran the horses for a half mile, then slowed to a trot.

"Whewee!" Johnny exclaimed. "Fer a minute I thought we was gonna die and get et by them trash."

Jake laughed and said, "That boy and his kin tried to steal Jasper. They made a big mistake trying to steal ol' Jasper." He slowed the mare to a walk, and Johnny slowed, too. "Yer know," Jake said contemplatively, "I coulda hanged that boy as a horse thief right there in front of his whole family. Maybe I should've to set a warnin' to them." He paused for a minute. "Nah, I ain't that mean."

"They'd a probably just et him and gone on about their thieving ways without even a thank you ma'am." They both laughed and spurred the horses back to a trot.

After following the winding Wichita River all day and riding in and out of farmyards and small ranch yards they finally reached the junction of Buffalo Creek at sunset. They swam the river back across to the west side and headed northwest. It was about another four miles to the Stevens Creek junction, and there was a lot of mesquite to dodge along the way. So, just as the cook was starting to clean up, they came in for their chuck but had to suffer the rebuffs of cookie. After supper they sat around the campfire smoking and listening to the cowboy chatter about the roundup. Jake lasted about an hour before bedding down. He had the second shift for night-hawk duty.

Next morning, Bodie was ready to start moving the rounded-up herd west. It was another calm, cloudless day. They had a couple thousand head rounded up and expected to pick up another two thousand along the way to Comanche Creek. So, by sunrise the cowboys were heading them up and moving them out. The point rider took up his position. The rest of the cowboys moved around the herd whistling, yipping, yahooing, slapping quirts, flapping loops, and snapping whips. Slowly, they pushed them together to make up a sea of brown, white, and black splotches, and horns galore. The lead steers started following the point rider. Then Bodie and the two drag riders started pushing the rear cattle into the herd in the direction of the point rider, and the great sea began to move.

When all the critters were walking in the right direction, Bodie pulled off the drag and rode up to Jake on the right flank and Johnny on the right swing. They were still close enough that he could be heard by both. "Keep 'em in tight," he yelled. "I don't want a long line to spread out on this flat ground. I don't want any quitters to git away. They should be more cowboys here by noon." Then he spurred his horse and galloped him off to circle around the point and give the same instruction to the left outriders. After that, they could barely pick him out through the dust as he rode up a low hill and stopped to watch the drive. The herd was moving as it should, and he rode down to join up as the second point rider. The dust was billowing, and the cattle were bawling. In about an hour, the critters settled in, and the sea changed shape into a wide river of cattle ten abreast and a half mile long. It made its way up and down the low rises of the rolling plain in pretty much a straight line. More dust, and it was warming up. More cowboys were showing up, and they went right to work rounding up more cattle on the range and running them in with the herd. The river of cattle was getting longer, and two cowboys joined in on the flanks of the herd.

Jake was up on Jasper again, and he let the savvy stock horse basically have his head and do all the thinking for him, and the work, too. By mid-morning, Jake was disgusted. He had his bandana tied around his face and his hat pulled down on his head. He was continuously swatting flies, and it was getting warmer, so the fly swarm continued to increase around his head. Last time he drove cattle, he was riding drag with Johnny at point, and the dust and the flies were just as bad, but he was making money on those cows. He wasn't making any money here. The XC was paying him so it looked like he was employed, but the XC was a member of the association, and his services were a member amenity. The things he had to do while working undercover.

By noon the range boss, Sticker Joe Spurlock, and two more cowboys showed up. He rode up on a low mound and observed the herd. It was moving good. There were cowboys bringing in more cattle, as many as fifty to a bunch. They looked like they were doing well, but he apparently didn't like the long river of cattle. He sent the two cowboys to the drag with orders to move up the stragglers and rear critters to force the herd into a more oval shape, broad in the middle and tapered at each end. More cowboys rode in, and he put two on the flanks and set the rest out to round up more cattle.

Jake noticed all the management activity

but gave it no never mind. He was wondering if Sticker would call a midday halt to rest cattle, horses, and cowboys. He did not.

By mid-afternoon the warmth and the rhythm of Jasper's walk felt like that of a baby's cradle gently rocking in front of the hearth, and Jake was dozing in the saddle. Suddenly, Jasper jumped to the right and lunged forward. Jake flew out of the saddle but managed to hold on to the saddle horn and quickly vault himself back upright. He looked up to see that Jasper was chasing a big brown and white steer that had quit the herd and bolted away right in front of him. He pulled his whip off his right wrist and put it in his teeth, clenching down tight. Then he loosed his rope and loop and began to twirl at the same time as Jasper jumped a small clump of sage, which Jake took in stride because he was standing in the stirrups. He leaned forward with his coiled rope in his right hand and Jasper's reins in his left. As they came up on the running steer, he twirled his loop one last time and tossed it right over the steer's head. He missed. Jasper kept chasing the steer, and as Jake was recoiling his rope, Sticker Joe galloped up on his horse and dropped a loop over the steer's horns. He cinched it up tight and then let some slack into the rope. Jake held

Jasper up a little figuring he would drop back and heel the steer with a loop to its hind legs. He waited for Sticker Joe to pull his rope tight, but instead Sticker flipped his rope over the steer's flank, spurred his horse to run up parallel to the steer, and pulled in the slack so that his rope was low and tight around the steer's hindquarters. Then he cut forty-five degrees away from the steer, which twisted its head back and lifted its legs out from under it. The animal flipped over in a vicious twisting somersault and landed on his back with a loud grunt in a cloud of dust and his legs kicking in the air. He got to his feet facing back toward the herd. Dazed and confused he staggered off in that direction. Sticker Joe pulled his loop off the steer's head and swatted him on the butt. He continued on and meekly rejoined the herd, where he apparently acquiesced to be part of the group, for he worked his way in toward the center and behaved after that. While Sticker recoiled his rope, he trotted his horse over to Jake.

"What's yer name, feller?" he said in a loud and belligerent tone.

"Jake Brighton."

"Wal, Jake Brighton, that's what we call bustin' a steer. If yer want to stay on the Flyin' XC payroll, yer better stay awake in that saddle and learn to rope. That quitter ran right out in front a yer. Lucky yer got back in the saddle quick. Yer savvy?"

"Yes, sir."

Jake was now more than disgusted. He was pissed. He had been riding all day next to a bunch of stinking cows, choking on dust, swatting flies, all after a night of fitful sleep on the ground night-hawking, and now he got dressed down by an old buzzard who probably didn't know the first thing about detective work and probably loved this cowpunchin'. Well, Jake wasn't a cowboy, but, darn it all, he would have to act like one if he was to stay undercover. He would put his foot down though and would have to balk if they wanted him to go on the long drive to market. There had to be some other way. He just wasn't going to do it. For the rest of the afternoon, however, he stayed alert, because that crusty old range boss was riding all around the herd shouting orders, and it seemed he made it a particular to come by Jake more than the other cowboys.

An hour later and Sticker Joe came galloping by. He slowed his horse to a trot, and as he went by, he yelled, "Push 'em west. Turn 'em west. Want to stay away from Long Creek or they'll smell the water and run for it. We'll go close by the settlement."

Jake started popping his whip and urging Jasper into the herd. In and out they went and back and forth in coordination with the flank riders behind him and the swing riders in front. Slowly the herd turned to the west, and a half hour later, Sticker Joe came by again shouting, "We're gonna turn 'em north agin, so give 'em slack." Amazingly the cattle on the flank started to follow the swing and flank riders on Jake's side. He started to think maybe there was method to this madness after all.

Johnny dropped back to join up with Jake for a bit. "We're about five miles out," he said loud enough for Jake to hear him over the noise of the herd's sixteen thousand hoofs pounding the ground, swishing through the grass, and crunching the low scrub brush. Not to mention the bawl of one or another of the critters, which seemed to initiate a chorus of bawls as others joined in so that it was a constant rumble. Johnny reined his horse in close to Jasper's side and shouted, "Clouds buildin' in the northwest. 'Bout two hours a daylight left. That's why Sticker didn't want to stop for dinner rest. Got to get into Comanche Creek and git these critters settled in with the rest of the herd before the light's gone."

Jake pulled his pocket watch, flipped the lid, and checked the time. " 'Bout five thirty right now. What time's sunset?"

"Don't know. Probably around eight."

"Who's that Sticker feller? Where's he come from?"

"He's the range boss."

"I know that. Where's he from, and why they call him Sticker?"

"Wal, the legend is that he was born on the range way northwest of Austin. When he was 'bout three years old his ma and pa were kilt by Comanches. He got away on the back of an old cow that ran into the woods, and the Comanch didn't see her. Swam her across the Colorado where she joined a herd a wild longhorn, and he lived in the herd for a month, suckin' on that cow's tit. A rancher named Spurlock rounded up the herd and took him in on a spread on the Brazos. Adopted him. Give him his name. He fought Comanches and was cow boss on the ranch by the time he was sixteen. Walt and him been pards for over forty years."

"Why they call him Sticker?"

"Wal, the story is when he was a young cow boss, there was a bull on the spread that of a sudden went crazy. He couldn't be roped, and he was crashin' the fence in the lots and gorin' and chasin' everthing and everone in sight. Wal, after 'bout a week a that, Sticker had enough. He walked right up to that bull. Stared him in the eye. The bull froze, and Sticker twas 'bout to shoot him when he saw a big ol' mesquite thorn stickin' out right behind the bull's eye. Wal, he tied that bull to the corral post and fence. Cut out that sticker. Spread axle grease on the wound and sewed it up. When he was done that bull was so happy, he licked Sticker's hand and followed him around like a lovesick puppy ever after. And that's how he got the handle Sticker. Stuck with him ever since." Johnny stared at Jake with a look of mock challenge as if daring Jake to scoff at the story. Jake just looked askance at Johnny and smiled.

"Kind of old. Is he really that tough?"

"Yer ain't no spring chicken yerself." Johnny grinned. Jake ignored the comment. "He's second only to Walt Guthrie, and Walt's the toughest man in all a Texas."

"Walt ever a Texas Ranger?"

"Don't know. But I think he was a Texian in the Mexican War and might a been a ranger in the big war cuz after the war he was drivin' cattle and fightin' Comanches with Charlie Goodnight and Oliver Loving. Goodnight was a ranger, I hear tell."

"Loving?"

"Yeah."

Jake twisted in his saddle and looked behind him. "Here comes Sticker. Yer better git on back up to the swing, if yer want to stay on the Flyin' XC payroll." Jake tried to look tough and then laughed.

A half hour or so before sunset they came in with their herd of four thousand to the Comanche Creek big pasture of the Calhoun range that was about six sections of grassland set against the banks of Comanche Creek and Long Creek where the creeks joined and ran ninety degrees to each other. Jake was amazed at the sight of the herd of forty to fifty thousand head of cattle spread out over the range but still held in a fairly compact bunch by the cowboys out on the edges of the herd. The cattle roamed within the cowboy barrier down two miles to the south of China Creek and three miles to the west of Long Creek. Some stayed bunched up, but for the most part they browsed and grazed separately but close to each other. He counted four chuck wagons, one each next to each creek and one to the south and one to the west. There were two fires burning at each camp that he assumed were one for cooking and one for heat. Cowboys were bringing in dry mesquite firewood on sledges dragged behind their horses and dropping them at the campsites and at other locations. There must have been a hundred or more cowboys working the roundup, and most of them were in line for their chuck at the wagons. He could smell in the air a mouth-watering blended aroma of coffee brewing, biscuits baking, meat sizzling on the spits over the cook fires, and beans simmering in the large hanging pots.

Once Bodie's crew got the herd turned out to the main herd they, too, headed for the nearest chuck wagon. Jake was hungry like he had never been hungry before except for Andersonville. Of course, that was near starvation. This was just plain old work and fresh air hungry, and he intended to dig in heartily. While he was standing in the chuck line listening to Johnny tell tales of their adventure in the squatter hollow Bodie came by and called out, "Give me yer ears, boys. Y'all hear now. Kin yer hear me? All right. Walt's called an all-hands meetin' over at the Comanche Creek camp startin' in one hour. So y'all git yer chuck down and lope on over there soon as yer done. That's all."

All the cowboys' horses were tied off to a hitching rope in one long line. It was dark, but Walt had a fire roaring at the camp that

71

cast a circle of light for a goodly distance from the center of the fire ring. He stood in the light, tall and straight while he watched the cowboys come up to the fire. On either side of him stood Sticker and Xavier Calhoun. "All right, boys, move in close so's I don't have to holler. Kin y'all hear me good in the back there? All right. Every year I call this here meetin' cuz I don't like repeatin' myself." He did not smile. "First light tomorrow we start brandin', so y'all that's been assigned to the irons better roll outta yer sacks and have them fires goin' and the irons hot and ready to go long before dawn. Yer cutters move into the herd as soon as yer kin see good enough, and yer ropers be waitin' on 'em, too. I dern well better see things a hoppin' when I start my rounds. We be brandin' a thousand calves a day so plan on workin' dern hard. We don't stop for no weather neither, so tie yer slickers to yer saddles and keep 'em handy. Lookin' like it might be rain tomorrow. I'm castratin' all the little fellers 'cept for about a hunnert, so keep yer knives good and sharp. If yer got one that looks like it'd be a good bull let it go but no more than say ten at each fire pit. Git them branded calves back with their mamas as soon as yer kin, and turn 'em all out to the west. I hate all that bawlin' so help 'em out. Lotta outfits just let 'em roam around bawlin' away lookin' for they's mamas but not here on my crew. So, keep an eye out to remember what cow goes with what calf. After brandin' we'll cut out all the steers and yearling heifers and the culls for market. Yer top hands pick out the culls. Yer know which ones they are. 'Specially any open two-year-old heifer. Bodie, yer gotta find Buckwheat and keep him away from the main herd. Don't nobody be cuttin' out ol' Buckwheat. He's our lead steer on the drive, and he is a dern good one. 'Course we ain't got as far to go this year. And on that note Mister Calhoun wants a word or two." He turned to his right and motioned for Xavier Calhoun to take over.

The ranch owner was attired in clean khaki pants tucked into polished brown riding boots that were mounted with silver spurs, a white shirt and dark-brown tie in a four-in-hand knot tucked into a smooth, light-brown leather vest, and a nutria fur hat with a brown silk band. He was of average height and build with very keen and alert eyes. Slowly, he twirled a braided rawhide quirt in his hands as he casually looked over the bunch of hands, moving his gaze from left to right. "Looks like a mighty

fine bunch of cowboys you have here, Walt."
He nodded his head up and down in approval of his own statement and passed an approving smile all around, which was returned by almost all the cowboys. "Well, boys," he began. "It's another year, and here we are at roundup again. As Mister Guthrie said, we are not driving the herd to market as far as years before because we are not driving to Dodge but to Fort Worth." He waited for the murmuring to subside as the surprised cowboys looked one to the other. "Yes, I have contracted with one of the new stockyards there, and we will be driving southeast over mostly unfenced range to Jacksboro and then right down the stage road to the rail yard in Fort Worth. I have all the permissions in place, and we will only have to cut one fence if we put it back up after the herd goes through, which I have promised to do. Mister Spurlock will insure that is done, right, Sticker?" Spurlock responded with a casual salute. "Next year we'll probably drive the long, long thirty miles to Wichita Falls." He paused to let the chuckles subside. "You know the railroad arrived there a few months ago, but they don't have a stockyard and loading chutes yet. So, we're headed to Fort Worth. All right. Y'all know the Flying XC reputation

for treating its cowboys good. So, in continuation of that tradition, I have arranged for two nights of rooms at the Right Hotel in Fort Worth for each man free of charge —" A collective whoop went up from the cowboys. Jake smiled but remained silent. "You will collect your wages at the end of the drive and find your own way back here to the ranch. I advise you to stay out of the Hell's Half Acre district, but that's up to you." A lot of snickering and joking went around but ceased quickly as Walt and Sticker glared fiercely at the cowboys. "If you ranch hands are not back here in a week, we will assume you are not coming back and will hire hands to replace you. Y'all that signed on for the roundup and the drive are on your own after you are paid. All right. That's all, Mister Guthrie."

"All right. Thank yer, Mister Calhoun. One more thing. John Lytle'll be bossin' the drive as usual. Since it is such a short drive, he'll have other herds waitin' afterwards, so if any a y'all want to sign on with him, be my guest. Any questions?"

One cowboy piped up, "Couple a questions, Walt. Just to be sure, yer said turn the branded calves and their mamas out to the west?"

"Just a minute there, young feller," Sticker

Joe said. "Guess yer ain't been around cattle operations much, and we kin let it go this one time, but, to you and the rest a yer cowboys, this is *Mister* Guthrie. Yer got that?"

"Yes, sir."

"And this is *Mister* Spurlock," Walt said. "But to answer your question — that's right."

"And yer said cut out all the steers for the drive and not just the two year olds?"

"That too is correct."

"Wal, ain't that a little odd? Usually, most outfits leave the yearlings to fatten up on the range for anuther year."

Walt glared hard at the cowboy and started forward but stopped when Sticker gently tugged the back of his shirt. Jake noted that, apparently, he changed his mind and original purpose.

"Not in the habit of 'splainin' myself to a no-account cowboy. But since y'all are so eager to learn — the reason we're sendin' all the steers to market is because we only got 'bout a 150 miles to go, and they ain't likely to lose much weight on the way. Plus, prices are real good right now. That help yer understand," he said and then smiled slightly. "Any other questions?"

Jake thought he could hear a collective

sigh as tension seemed to ease. "All right, then. Let's bow our heads for a word a prayer." Walt waited for the end of the audible swish of all the hats pulled off their heads at the same time. "Lord, keep us all safe and give us good weather while we round up, brand, and drive yer critters to market. Thank yer. Amen." And they all said, "Amen."

"Roll out, boys. Cookie's got the coffee boiling and biscuits in the dutch ovens," Bodie said three times as he went around the camp. It was still dark, and there was no light in the east. One by one, the cowboys threw back their quilts and yawned and stretched, jammed on their hats, pulled on their boots, put on their coats, and amid jostling and cajoling went to the camp latrine. They came back to the big coffee pot and poured each other coffee and made up a queue for morning chuck. The branders didn't wait. They saddled their horses and rode out to get their fires stoked up to make a good bed of red-hot coals. They straggled back, got their chuck, and went right back out. By the time morning broke, clouds covered the sky in a solid gray blanket, and the wind was kicking up from the northwest. As the light in the east increased, Jake pulled his coat collar tight around the bandana tied to his neck. He sat on Jasper watching the herd as one of the twenty outriders whose job it was to keep the herd together.

All around the herd, cowboys waded in and cut out cows and calves, bunched them up, and drove them over by the branding fires, where the calves were caught at their hind feet by ropers and dragged across the ground over to the branding fires. That's when all the bawling from separated calves and mama cows began and went on through the whole day. The cutting horses and their riders ran back and forth, dipping in and out to keep the cows and calves separated. Dust kicked up by all the moving animals in the grass and sage made little hoodoos all over the range. At the fires, the ropers' horses kept the ropes taut while the cowboy roper jumped off his horse and grabbed the calf's front legs to stretch out the critter in preparation for the hot iron of the Flying XC brand. The branders pressed the irons to the calves' sides, and odors of burnt hair and flesh filled the air as the irons scorched through the hair giving off a swirl of smoke before the sizzle of flesh gave off less smoke. Another cowboy carefully and quickly sliced out the testicles from the scrotums of the boy calves and tossed them into a bucket for cookie to prepare rocky mountain oysters. Then the calves were released to find their mamas in the bunches of cows held by other cowboys, who moved the bunches off to the west as soon as all the cows and calves were reunited. And this dance of toil — the dust, the sweat, the bawling cows and calves, and the smell of burning hair and flesh — went on all day long without pause. There was no rest for the cowboys until daylight was gone.

As Jake sat in the saddle on the east side of the herd and munched a biscuit, he saw Walt loping toward him and quickly stuffed the biscuit in his coat pocket. He didn't know if he was allowed to eat while outriding, but he wasn't taking any chances. "Mornin', Walt, er Mister Guthrie," Jake said with a smile as the boss rode up and reined in facing him.

"Mornin'," he said with no smile. "How yer likin' this cowpunchin'?"

Jake immediately dropped his smile and said, "Barely tolerable. And since yer asked, will yer be needin' me for the drive to Fort Worth?"

"Heck no. Even though we're sendin' almost every head to market when the market herd leaves, there'll still be anuther fifteen thousand cows and calves and anuther four hundred bulls out on the range. Yer and Johnny are my line riders. I need yer both to stay here and protect the herd. This is a time when rustlers think they's got a 'vantage because the crew is off on the drive. No, sir. Yer stayin' here."

Just as he said the last, a cowboy rode up and reined in about ten feet away from Walt. He said in a voice that Jake recognized as a challenge, "Hey, boss. How come yer got me on the herd. I signed on as a roper." It was the cowboy who was questioning Walt last night. He stared hard at Walt, who then handed his horse's reins to Jake, kicked his left leg over his horse's neck, slid down to the ground, stomped over to the cowboy's horse, reached over its neck, grabbed the rein out of the cowboy's hands, whipped his quirt around the horse's left rear hock, pulled hard on the rein and the quirt, twisted the horse's neck back, held his hoof up, and threw him to the ground, which caused the cowboy to escape being crushed only by kicking loose his stirrups and jumping away from the thrown horse. The horse rolled away and got back up as did the cowboy, only to be met with Walt's fist smashing him between the eyes. He dropped to his knees, holding his nose, and fell forward headfirst as blood filled his hands. In a few seconds, he came to, stood, and swayed side to side as he tried to collect his balance. "What'd yer do that fer! Yer broke my nose!" he said angrily.

Walt took two steps toward him and shoved him hard. The cowboy flipped back and landed prone on the ground with a loud grunt. "Yer don't learn real fast, do yer? Told yer last night, I ain't in the habit a answerin' to a no-account cowboy. Yer know Sticker sets out the men for the jobs in the roundup. But I do the hirin' and firin'. Yer made one mistake too many. Yer can go see Sticker and pick up the wages due yer. Now git off my range." Jake fancied fire and smoke coming from Walt's mouth as he slashed the cowboy with his fury.

Walt turned his back on the cowboy and stomped toward his horse. The cowboy, who was still laid out on the ground, managed to get up on one elbow and glare pure hatred at Walt's back. He wiped his bloody hand on his pant leg. Jake drew his pistol and reined Jasper around ninety degrees. Sure enough, the cowboy pulled his six-shooter and lifted it to aim at Walt's back. Before he shot, Jake blasted him with two forty-four slugs to the chest that slammed the cowboy back into the dirt.

Walt crouched and held his arm over his head as his horse shied and side-hopped away from the muzzle blast. He spun around and saw the cowboy jerk twice, his boots kicking. In a matter of seconds, he was still, and an expanding pool of blood oozed out from under him. His pistol was in the dirt next to him. Walt looked at the pistol, at Jake, and back at the pistol and back at Jake, and raised his hand, slapped it against his thigh, shook his head side to side, and said, "Much obliged."

Jake said, "Yer welcome. 'Course now we got to go into Wichita Falls to open a JP inquest."

"I ain't got time fer that. I'm in the middle of roundup. Let's just plant him out here on the range."

"I expect there'd be too many witnesses fer that to work," Jake said as he motioned with his head for Walt to look over his shoulder to see the cowboys that were galloping toward them.

"Damn," Walt swore and spat.

"But yer kin write out a affidavit, and Mister Calhoun can witness it. I'll take that and the body to the sheriff. Should be enough for the JP."

Walt looked up and said to the first two cowboys to arrive, "Ben, Lonny. You two git that body on his horse and cinch it down tight."

"What happened?" Ben said with his eyes wide as silver dollars.

"He — what's his name?"

"It's Riley Durbin," a third cowboy said after he had ridden up and sat his saddle for a minute looking at the corpse. "He and me rode down from Greer County to sign on fer this here roundup and drive."

"Yeah. That's right, I remember now," Walt said with a suspicious eye to the cowboy. "What's yer name agin?" Two more cowboys showed up. "Y'all git back to work," he said gruffly with a wave of his arm to the two new arrivals. "I'll tell y'all what happened at campfire tonight. Now go on. Git back to work." Then he turned and glared at Durbin's friend.

"Andy MacDonald."

"He got any kin yer know of?"

"Yep, his whole family's up at Fort Sill. They work for the army. So's my family. We grew up together."

On hearing that, Jake, who was still in the saddle, reined Jasper around to get a more direct line of sight at this MacDonald feller.

"We went out together 'bout four years ago to become cowpunchers. I ain't much surprised by this. I reckoned Riley would get hisself kilt someday. He had a temper, and he didn't know when to keep his mouth shut."

"He ever kilt anyone?" Walt said.

"Nah. He's been in more than his share of brawls. But he ain't never kilt no one that I know of."

"Wal, he just tried to shoot me in the back, but Rawhide shot him first."

MacDonald shrugged his shoulders and said, "Like I said. It don't surprise me."

"All right. Wal, Jake's gonna take his body to the sheriff in Wichita Falls. I 'spect yer can give him names of his kin so Jake can send a wire."

"Yes, sir."

"All right. Ben, yer got that corpse cinched on tight? All right. Y'all kin git back to work now. Yer boys cover for Jake. He's gonna be gone awhile. All right, Jake. Let's go roust Xavier. He should be in his tent at the Comanche Creek camp if he ain't ridin' around yet."

About that time Sticker rode up. "What happened here?" he called out as he jumped out of the saddle.

Walt pulled off his hat and slapped it against his thigh. "Aw, that dumb-ass kid that was proddin' me last night tried it agin. I threw him and his horse, but he wasn't quittin'. Fired him. Still wouldn't quit. Tried to shoot me in the back. Rawhide here shot him first."

Sticker looked from Walt to Jake to the body to the pistol and then back to Jake with a curious look on his face. He studied Jake for a minute and then vaulted into the saddle and rode off.

Walt stepped into the saddle, leaned over, and picked up the reins of Durbin's horse. When they came to the camp Jake said, "Walt, do yer think I could ride on out to the line and start lookin' fer rustlers instead a comin' back to the roundup when I get back from Wichita Falls?"

"Reckon I could spare yer. Ain't likin' this here cowboy work, huh?" Walt grinned and slapped Jake on the back. Jake was surprised because Walt was never that friendly to anyone. 'Course, Jake did save his life.

CHAPTER TWO:
MORE RUSTLERS AND . . .
MARY JANE

It was well past sunset when Jake tied off Jasper and Durbin's horse to the rail in front of the plain brown box and strip building that had a crude hand-painted sign for Sheriff. The street was dark, empty, and quiet. The only sign of life he saw when riding into town was around the two saloons that were canvas tents with board fronts.

"Evenin'," Jake said to the deputy inside. "I got some business for yer. Man been shot and killed out on the Flyin' XC spread." He went through the details, and the deputy took possession of Durbin's body and horse. "All right then. You'll petition for a JP inquest tomorrow mornin'? Okay. Evenin' to yer," Jake said as he tipped his hat and went out the door.

He found a shack and corrals that was the livery and fed, watered, and bedded down Jasper, then he walked down the dirt street to the nearest saloon. He strode over to the bar, dropped his saddlebags on the floor, and leaned his rifle against the bar front.

"Where's a feller git a bath around here?" Jake asked the bartender as he downed his first whiskey.

"Wal, right here. Out back," he said with a smutty grin.

"Alls I want is a bath. Gotta git this cow stink off a me. Then I'll have a beef steak supper and a place to bed down. Yer got any rooms here?"

"Got cots out back, too."

"That'll do."

In the middle of the night the clouds opened, and it was raining in the morning when Jake went out to meet with the sheriff. In his slicker he walked up the muddy street to the sheriff's office, and together they went to appear before Judge Howard. Sitting behind a table the judge listened to Jake's story and read Walt's affidavit. He looked down his nose over his rimless glasses at the sheriff and said, "Did you examine the corpus delicti?" He drew the last two words out in a long drawl.

"Yes, Yer Honor."

"And did it match up with the story?"

"Yes, Yer Honor. I didn't see nuthin' suspicious."

"All right then. In view of the testimony, especially the written affidavit of Walt Guthrie witnessed by Xavier Calhoun, my judgment is that the cause of death of Riley Durbin was a justifiable homicide at the hands of Jonas V. Brighton in defense of another person. So be it." He wrote the decision on an official death certificate in two copies, signed them, and handed one to Jake.

"Your Honor, this is his next of kin information given to me by his friend. They're up at Fort Sill. And could I have one more copy of the signed death certificate for Mister Calhoun's files?"

"All right." He wrote out another certificate, signed it, and gave it to Jake. "Sheriff, you take care of the notification. In the meantime, you better get that body in the ground."

Jake tucked both death certificate copies inside his vest, shrugged into his slicker, tied on his hat, and went into the rain. He saddled up and right off headed for Xavier Calhoun's house to deliver the certificate. Walt told him that Xavier would probably be leaving soon for his mansion in Denton, so he thought it best to hurry. Rain was letting up so he spurred Jasper into a lope.

When he arrived late in the afternoon at

the white Victorian style house, he stepped up onto the broad covered porch lined with intricate railing and balustrade and scraped the mud off his boots on a scraper outside the front door. He stomped off the loose pieces and twisted the handle of the rotary doorbell. He heard light footsteps approaching the door. The door opened, and a fierce looking young woman said, "Hold it right there, buster. Don't take another step." Jake saw right off that she was attractive like women who aren't quite gorgeous but pretty. She was a few inches shorter than him, trim, and nicely endowed.

"I have a document for Mister Calhoun. My name is Jake Brighton. I think he's expectin' me."

"You won't have a thing if you track mud on Mister Calhoun's Persian rugs. Now you just sit down on the bench out there and take this here brush." She handed him a bristled scrub bush. "Make sure you clean it *all* off. I'll check them before you come in."

Jake obeyed and felt like he had cleaned his boots pretty darn good. He opened the door and stood in the threshold. "How do these look?" he asked tentatively. "Maybe I should remove my boots and walk in my stocking feet," he said with a wry smile.

"Let me see," she said as she walked over to Jake. "Turn around and raise your boots one at a time so I can see the bottoms. Uh-huh. I guess they look clean enough."

"Well, I aim to please," Jake said with a grin. "If I may ask, are you married?"

She smiled and showed him a row of nice white teeth. When she smiled, she was far more attractive. She held his gaze with glacier-blue eyes, and Jake swore he saw sparkles in them. "Why do you ask?" she said.

"Well, I was gonna say that if you are not, maybe we might picnic some Sunday soon."

Still smiling, she said, "I am married. Name is Mary Jane Walton. My husband is the local blacksmith hereabouts and farrier at the ranch. We live here in the back, and I keep house and cook for the Calhouns."

"What a coincidence. I used to be a smithy, too."

"Well, you aren't now." Jake did not even hear Xavier Calhoun walk up, so taken was he by Mary Jane, and when Calhoun spoke it startled him, but, fortunately Xavier was smiling. "How'd it go?"

"Oh, fine. Judge ruled it justifiable homicide. I brought you a copy of the official death certificate," Jake said as he pulled the document from his vest and held it out to Xavier.

"Wonderful. Thank you. Good day, Jake, and, again, thank you for what you did. Walt is the heartbeat of this ranch." He smiled again, turned, and walked back into the house.

Mary Jane followed him but stood for a moment by the door before she shut it and smiled so coquettishly at Jake. Then she was gone. Jake was smitten so bad his toes were tingling. He vaulted into the saddle and spurred Jasper into a gallop out of the settlement. Rain pelted him, and mud from Jasper's pounding hooves sprayed him, but he did not care. He had to work off the heat of passion. Never before had he felt such an effect of a woman. She was pretty, she was sassy, she was firm of character, she seemed intelligent and fun loving but responsible, prudent, dutiful, probably a loyal wife but — she flirted with him, or at least he thought she did. He slowed Jasper to a lope and thought over the situation. Was he crazy? She is married and Calhoun's housekeeper. To have her, they would have to run to another state. Or she would have to divorce her husband, and he would have to quit detective work. What if her husband wouldn't give her a divorce? And what if she doesn't even want me? Crazy. I got to

91

get her out of my mind. And so, on he rode trying not to think of her. It wasn't working. It kept rolling over in his mind while he rode well west and north of the roundup. When he got to the ranch, even while he washed, dried, brushed, fed, and watered Jasper, she was a vision always on his mind.

He trudged into the bunkhouse. It was empty. In the cookshack there was a Chinaman stirring a large pot on the stove. Jake came up behind him and said, "Whatcha cookin'?" The fellow jumped off the floor and clanged the metal spoon against the side of the pot. He began to jabber angrily in Chinese, spun around, and shook the spoon at Jake.

"What you do? Clazy cowboy. I whack you good with spoon. Scaling old Chan." He frowned and shook his head side to side.

"Sorry. Sorry," Jake said. "I thought you heard me."

"Cooking good Chinese chicken noodle soup for boys working in lain. They like. You like?" He quit frowning, looked more pleasant, and tossed the spoon into the pot.

"Sure. Chicken noodle soup sounds good. I'll have a bowl."

"*Chinese* chicken noodle soup."

"Oh, yeah. All right. Yer say yer name is Chan?"

"Changming Da Chan. It mean vely blight and intelligent." He smiled and bowed thirty degrees at the waist with one hand folded over the other held out in front of him. "So, I vely smat. You cannot tlick me." He frowned again but with a look of warning. "Everyone call me Chan."

Jake laughed and then covered his mouth with his hand but kept chuckling.

"Why you laugh, cowboy? I make no joke."

"Sorry. I meant no disrespect. It's just that the way you said that was like a leprechaun."

"What lep-le-kan?"

"It's a tricky elf of Irish superstition."

"What Ilish?"

"People from Ireland. One of the British Isles. You know, over across the Atlantic Ocean."

Chan carried a steaming bowl of soup over to the chow table and set it down with a spoon. "You sit and eat. I not know any Ileland. I not know Atlantic Ocean. I know cook, clean, washing. Work hard. Save money."

"That's good. I read in the newspaper there's a lotta Chinese lookin' for work down in El Paso now that the railroad from California's been connected to the railroad on to San Antonio. You know anything about that?"

"I on work for Cental Pacific. I come here after that. Been here all time. I have lelatives in El Paso."

"Uh-huh. Soup's good."

Jake had been out west for a week, just him, Jasper, and the packhorse. He only found a few stray heifers with the Flying XC brand, and he drove them to the meadow where he and Johnny had turned out the bunch of heifers they recovered from the Sour Bill rustler outfit. He was a little north of the North Fork of the Wichita in the southwest quadrant of the open range around the Flying XC when he saw and smelled mesquite smoke and heard what sounded like a steam engine chugging. Except it wasn't the heavy pound of a steam locomotive. It was more of a rhythmic whir. He rode closer and over a ridge into a large and thick juniper forest to indeed see a steam engine huffing and two men working around it. The steam engine he recognized as a Tozer like the ones he had seen all over the Kansas and Missouri farmland. The boiler was painted black and set on a frame that had wagon wheels and a tongue for towing. The flywheels and piston mechanism on top of the boiler were green. A tall, ten-inch-round black smokestack rose from the end of the boiler that had the tongue for towing. A wide belt ran from the big flywheel to a flywheel on a machine that was spiked into the ground behind the steamer. The machine was a rail that had a sled on it, and through a combination of reduction gears, a chain, and a levered cog, the sled pulled logs into a big steel wedge at the other end and split them like a machete through a watermelon. Jake sat in the saddle and watched the men work. They did not notice him until he rode closer, and one of them looked up, saw him, and looked at a rifle propped against one of the steamer wheels. Jake raised his hands and said, "Whoa now. I'm Jake Brighton, a line rider for the Flyin' XC, and mean no harm."

The man studied Jake for a good long minute, then reached for a valve on the steamer to reduce the flow of steam and slow down the machine. He walked over, and Jake dismounted, leaving Jasper and the packhorse to graze on their own. "Name's Martin Smith," he said as he held his hand out for a shake. "This here is my brother and partner, Ed. What can we do for yer?"

"Wal, nuthin'. I'm hereabouts ridin' the line lookin' fer strays and rustlers and came across y'all. Whatcha doin'?"

"We're here by right of open range. We

ain't doing anything wrong or illegal. We're just makin' fence posts out of this juniper grove."

"Yeah, I know yer on open range. I got no quarrel there. That's a humdinger of a machine yer got there. Ain't ever seen one like it. Who yer makin' the posts fer?"

"Whoever wants to buy 'em. We figure there's gonna be a lotta fencin' goin' on around here, so we're splittin' up a supply of posts to sell to the ranchers. We was workin' for a feller around Paris. He had three a these machines. We bought one, a steamer, and those two mules over there. Then we come out here."

"How much yer sellin' the posts fer?"

"Ain't figured that out yet. The feller in Paris was selling 'em for a nickel a post. Just don't know yet."

"Yer cuttin' those juniper logs all by yerself?"

"Yep. Just me and Marty." The other brother spoke for the first time.

"Wal, I come 'round here regular. Can I bring yer anything?"

"Nah. Much obliged. We're pretty well provisioned," Marty said as he nodded toward a canvas tent off a little way from their work site. Jake looked over toward it and noticed a big stack of fence posts probably about six foot high and ten, twelve foot long.

"Wal, good luck to yer." He tipped his hat and went to retrieve Jasper and the packhorse.

Later that evening he rode into Seymour. The sun had just dropped over the horizon, and there was a long red afterglow over the southern prairie. Maybe it was the mystique of the wash of red over the country or who knows what, but Jake was feeling a little devilish. He walked Jasper right into Quincy's barn trailing the packhorse behind him. Quincy ran out of his office screeching and shaking his fist over his head. "Damn yer hide, Jake Brighton. Yer know I don't allow no mounted horses in the barn!"

Jake stepped down from his saddle, took off his hat, and placed it over his heart. "Why, Quincy, I am real sorry. I plumb forgot. Can yer forgive me?"

"I'll forgive yer all right after yer pay the penalty fer disobeyin' the rules," the little bald feller said with his hands on his hips, legs spread apart, and jaw jutted out like a pouty child.

Jake laughed heartily and said, "That's a good one, Quince. Hah hah."

"I mean it. Don't yer give me no trouble now."

Jake's grin slowly faded. "Now, yer know yer can't do that unless it's in the contract we made."

"Yer mean the verbal contract we made where yer said yer would abide by the rules."

"Sure, but yer never said what the rules were. 'Course, I know yer don't like nobody mounted inside the barn. I was just feelin' impish and was twistin' yer tail."

"Impish, plimpish. The rules is posted." He nodded a look behind Jake, who turned and saw a sign in dim light back in a corner of the barn that listed all the rules of the barn.

"Wal, cain't hardly see it tucked back like that."

"Don't matter. It's a dollar fine."

"A dollar?!" Jake questioned loudly.

"Yep. But see'in how it's yer first offense, I'll set the fine aside. This time and only this time. Now git yer damn paint in a stall, and the other one, too, and groom 'em, feed, and water 'em before I changes my mind and banishes yer from the premises."

"Humrumpf. Kinda high-falutin ain't yer?" Jake said under his breath as he walked Jasper and the packhorse to empty stalls. And now Quincy had put him in a foul mood.

■ ■ ■ ■

"Somebody's bein' a real grouch," Gracie said as she wrapped Jake's head in a steam towel.

"Ah that Quincy got his hooks into me 'bout his rules. And I was only joshin' him. Then come to find out yer ain't whorin' no more. How'd yer expect a feller to feel. I'm particular 'bout the girls I get with, and yer the only one in this town I want to be with."

"Ah, that's sweet. But I am engaged now, and I want to be true. I want yer to be happy fer me."

"Oh, I am, Gracie. But it's gonna be lonely without yer." He gave her his bedroom eyes look. She smiled but looked away quickly. "Now don't yer try and tempt me, yer devil."

"Nah. I wouldn't do that. Respect yer too much. Who's the lucky feller?"

"His name is Robert Corrigan. He's downstairs. We're gonna have supper. Why don't yer join us?"

"What's his business besides stealin' my favorite girl?"

"Stop it now, yer scallywag." She gave him that cute little scolding look he liked so much but never told her. "He sells thorny wire. We knowed each other since we was kids in Decatur. He knows all about me and what happened. Says there's gonna be a lotta wire sold hereabouts, and we're gonna be rich."

"Hmm. I heard somethin' like that once already today."

"Like what?"

"Like there's gonna be a lotta fencin' done around here. Sure, I'll have supper with y'all. Buy yer a drink, too." He smiled and winked at her.

Jake set his knife and fork on his plate that was empty except for a scrap of t-bone. He shoved the plate away from him, emptied his beer mug, and wiped his mouth and mustache with the large red and white table napkin he had tied around his neck. All through supper, he had been listening to Robert Corrigan extol the virtue and value of barbed wire and the coming prospect of the effect of fencing on the cattle industry in northwest Texas. He was a lively young man, full of vim and vigor. By his talk and manner, Jake easily recognized him as an educated man and saw that Gracie hung on his every word. She dismissed the men that came up to her, soliciting; as if they were flies, she shooed them away from her. Jake smiled proudly at Gracie and it made her blush a little.

Jake queried, "Cigar and brandy?"

"Why, yes. That would be grand." Robert smiled graciously, and Gracie looked curious.

Grand? Jake hadn't heard that since Missouri. "Alex!" Jake called out, then to Robert he said, "You been back east to school?" Robert was about to answer when Alex came up beside Jake. "How were the beef steaks?" he asked confidently.

"Excellent," both Jake and Robert said simultaneously.

Alex smiled like a snobby New York waiter and said, "What else can I get you."

"Two —" He looked inquiringly at Gracie who turned her head slightly side to side. "Two of your finest cigars and brandies."

"Excellent," Alex said and wheeled away.

"St. Benedict College in Atchison. It is a boarding school my parents sent me to."

"Ah. You are a Catholic then?"

"Yes."

"I was baptized in the Church, too, but I haven't been very good ever since," he chuckled, as did Robert.

"Me either, I am afraid. But soon I will have a better part," he said as he patted

Gracie's hand, to which she smiled demurely.

The cigars and brandy arrived. They lit up and took their first sip. "Back to barbwire," Jake said. "Will you be selling anything else?"

"Yes. I have options with the Deere Company and Flint, Walling, and Company — they manufacture the Star windmills — and other companies to develop outlets and market farm implements and windmills. As I said previously, with fencing going in, water availability will be less abundant, and ranchers and farmers will need to drill their own wells."

"How much are you selling the wire for?"

"It goes for two dollars per thousand-foot roll."

Grace said, "Jake yer sound as edecated as Robert. You been foolin' me all along?" She smiled slyly at Jake.

"Maybe just a little," he said and winked at Robert.

The next morning as the sun was rising, Jake stepped out on to the porch of the Brazos and took in a few deep breaths of the crisp air. There were only a few clouds in the sky, so he figured it would be a dry and warm day. He walked across to the livery and through the big barn doors that Quincy already had open. Usually not one to hold a grudge, he called out, "Yo, Quincy. You here?"

"Right up here," came the reply from the hay loft.

"I'll be ridin' out this mornin'. So, I'll repack the one horse and saddle up Jasper."

"All right. Just leave the twenty-six cents on my desk. See yer next time around."

"Yup." Jake went into the office and left two two-bit coins on the desk with the idea that the extra money should smooth Quincy's ruffled feathers.

He was about two miles out of town headed west with the intent to ride further west and then turn north to Vernon to look up Wes if he was around. Then an idea popped into his head, and he started thinking about fencing. Robert was probably right about the coming closure of the open range. That's what Ole Olsson and Don Bayliss were talking about down at the Circle Bar B Ranch. Only makes sense for cattle to be fenced in so they can be better managed. Ranchers don't have to hire as many cowboys. They can control the grazing and recovery of the grass and browse. Protect their water rights. Keep cattle in. Keep others out. Sounds logical. But who's going to do the fence installation? Cowboy crews? Or a professional fence company?

At camp that night by firelight, he sat with his coffee and started listing costs with a pencil and a little notebook he kept in his shirt pocket under his vest. It was less than an hour when he slapped the pencil down on the notebook and stared into the dark thinking about what he had figured up. If a crew of five men and a foreman could install three hundred feet per day of five-strand fence it should cost about $11.25 per day for labor and material including posts, wire, and miscellaneous other items. To get started, a feller would need tools, a wagon, two draft horses with harness, and miscellaneous other items for a total cost of, say, a $250.00 grub stake. Figuring a six-day work week it would take 81¢ a day to recover the initial investment in one year. So now the per-day cost is $12.06, say $13.00 to be safe. Now if a feller charged 6¢ a foot to install the fence that would be $18.00 per day, which would make $5.00 per day in profit or $150.00 per month, which is double his current salary. He whistled, and Jasper pricked his ears forward. "Oh. Sorry, Jasper. Didn't mean it for you," he said and then, "Got to see if Wes would be interested in goin' in halfers on this. Sure, we know all the ranchers and could get contracts, starting with the Flyin' XC."

Mid-afternoon Jake trotted Jasper and the packhorse into Vernon's main street. He got them settled in at the lean-to livery and parked his saddle and pack in the locked tack shed. Gave the livery man two bits and, carrying his rifle and saddlebags, walked to the small hotel and checked in. After depositing his gear in his room, he walked to the nearest of the four saloons in town, which was already well packed with all sorts of fellers. At the bar, he had a quick drink while he covertly surveyed the room in search of Wes, who would have stood out. Wes was tall and lanky but muscular through the shoulders and arms. Most notable though was the overgrown yellow handlebar mustache on a face that was craggy and bronzed from years on the range. And he was fully a rugged Texas cowboy, full of bravado and good humor. But Jake didn't see anyone like him in that saloon. He did the same at the other three saloons in town and came up empty. He walked by the sheriff's office and jailhouse and peeked in the window. The office was empty. He looked around the town for Wes's horse maybe hitched somewhere. He was a copper-red bay gelding with striking black points named Noble. No Noble. So, seeing as it was getting on to supper time, he walked back to the hotel dining room. By the time he was halfway through his meal of pork chops and potatoes, in walked Wes, all washed up for supper.

Their eyes met, but neither one nor the other gave any indication of familiarity. After Wes sat down at another table, Jake began to slowly rub his cheek with four fingers as if he were contemplating something. He was communicating to Wes that he was in room four. Wes got it and rubbed his chin with a thumbs-up. Then Jake finished his supper, got up, and left for his room.

Thirty minutes later there was a light tap at his door, and he let Wes in. With wide grins on their faces, they shook hands and slapped each other on the shoulder. "What're yer doin' here?" Wes said.

"Wal, I took a chance you'd be here instead a out on the range. I want to talk to yer 'bout somethin'."

"Yer got lucky. I just got here today from the panhandle. The cowboy strike fizzled out, and Jim sent a new man up to replace me. Now, I'm back down here, and you and me can work this whole northwest region. You undercover at the Flyin' XC and me roamin' 'round like I usually do. Pards together agin. Just like Loving wanted us to before the strike." He grinned. "By the way, Jim wants a report. What'd yer want ta talk to me 'bout?"

"Wal, write this down. Here's my report." He waited for Wes to get out his notebook and pencil. "Since yer went north, me and Johnny Raymer recovered two hundred head and brought in Sour Bill Connell and four other rustlers. Since then, the Flyin' XC ain't lost any cattle." He pushed out his chest and snapped his suspenders. "Whatta yer think a that?"

"Not bad for a shave tail." Again, he grinned.

"Not bad, he says. What'd yer do?"

"Oh, not much. Just brought in Alamosa Bill and put in my voucher for the three hunnert-dollar reward. Caught Slippery Wayne Jenson, a known horse thief, with three stolen horses. Brought in him and the horses. That's 'bout it." For the third time he grinned.

"How come you didn't hang him right there and then if he was a known horse thief?"

"Weren't no tree or pole around. Had to bring him in. 'Sides, I thought there was a reward out on him, too."

"Wal, it's good fer yer that yer got some extra money."

Wes squinted one eye and furrowed his brow. "How's that?"

"I got a proposition fer yer."

"What's that mean? I wish yer'd quit usin' them five-dollar words."

"It means yer can invest in the Northwest Texas Fence Company and make a lotta money."

"Yer mean like buy in?"

"Exactly. Here it is. Yer and me are fifty-fifty pards in a new company that's gonna put in all the fences in northwest Texas. You put in $125.00, and I put in $125.00 and leave the rest to me. When we have our first contract, we make $150.00 a month profit, $75.00 each. That's as much as our monthly salaries, or mine anyway. In two months, we each got our $125.00 back, and the rest is gravy after that."

"Who's gonna do the work?"

"Yer know Chan, the cook at Flyin' XC?"

"I seen him. Don't know him."

"He's got relatives in El Paso that been let go off the railroad cuz it's done, but they need work. So, we get Chan to send for six of 'em. One's gotta speak English and be the foreman. We pay him a buck-fifty and the others a dollar a day."

Jake went on to explain the plan to Wes, and when he finished, he said, "Wal, how's it sound? Are yer in?"

"We don't gotta do nuthin'? We can keep on detectivin'?"

"Yep. Except get customers. But yer know all the ranchers, so that shouldn't be a problem. Walt's got me ridin' the line on the west and south and Johnny on the north and east. So, on my routes every month I can always collect from our clients, take the payroll to the crew, and pay for the material, and catch rustlers, too."

"Sounds too good to be true, and yer know what they say 'bout that."

"Wal, I gotta put it all together first. I know that Xavier Calhoun is surveyin' his east property line right now for fence, so I am goin' to propose a deal to him right off. Then we'll see if it'll work. First though, I gotta see if Chan can get some relatives up here. We need that cheap labor."

"All right. Count me in. But I won't git the reward money for a couple a months."

"That's all right. I'll loan it to you, interest free. Hah, hah, hah," Jake laughed. Wes chuckled, still a little wary.

Wes changed the subject. "I'm headed west to MC range tomorrow. Duane Down says he's losing cattle and ain't got the crew to track the rustlers down cuz he's in the middle of roundup." He paused, continued, "He's the cow boss for the MC workin' for J. D. Duross. He's the manager for the Maguire brothers. They's a big outfit runnin' the MC brand on the range around the north and middle forks a the Pease River. I think they are all Irish. Maybe we can help him out. Yer wanna come along?"

"All right. But I gotta git over to the Flyin' XC dern soon to git our enterprise a goin'."

"Uh-huh. Wal, we better git bunk time. Ride out at dawn. All right?"

Duane Down sat straight and tall in his saddle. He barely acknowledged Jake and Wes as they trotted the boys up to him, then slowed to a walk and reined in about ten feet away. He glanced at them, then back to observing the cutting out and branding of calves. The detectives had ridden twenty miles, trotting the boys most of the way, and Jake was a little put out by Down's seeming indifference. So, he took on an attitude of nonchalance as he looked around. He stared up into the sky. It was another clear day with deep-blue sky and puffy snow-white clouds. "Almost feels like you could touch them clouds," he said. The sun was still low in the east and, facing east,

Down had his hat pulled down low over his eyes.

Finally, he spoke while continuing to gaze straight ahead. "Trailed the herd here three years ago and turned them out to the range. Should've been about five thousand calves. I can see already we're short. Probably about a couple hunnert. Rustlers are thinning me out, and I ain't got the crew to go after 'em. Think y'all can help me out?" Then, at last, he turned his head and held his eyes upon them.

"We'll do our best, Duane," Wes said. "Which way you think they're runnin' 'em?"

"West. I found some sign two days ago. Looked like about fifty head. It's over that-away about ten miles." He looked in the direction he spoke of. "Haven't had rain. You can't miss it. Looks like about fifty head. Mixed. Steers, cows, and calves. But there's gotta be more they got. For me to be two hunnert short right now means they got more from before now."

"All right. We got a lotta daylight left. We'll get goin'. Cut that trail and follow it out," Wes said as he started to rein Noble in that direction but stopped when Jake eased Jasper up close to Down.

Jake held out his hand and said, "Name's Jake Brighton." They shook hands, and Jake continued, "Ever think about fencin' your range? Might help slow down the rustlers."

"Been thinkin' about it. Right now, though, I need my beeves back."

"Understood," Jake said and tipped his hat. "We'll get 'em."

When they went by the herd, Jake took note of the MC brand. He remembered seeing it in Loving's book. "That's a pretty good brand, ain't it?"

"Nah. Pretty easy to run a rocker under the *M* and *C* or run a bar through 'em. Call it the rockin' MC or bar MC. If anybody questioned it, a rustler could hold up a phony bill a sale and a buyer'd prob'ly take 'em. Hard to say. Wouldn't get by a good brand inspector."

As they trotted the boys west, side by side, Wes said, "Tryin' to sell fencin' already, eh?"

"Might as well. Competition's only goin' to get bigger."

"What competition?" Wes looked over at Jake with a little frown and no smile on his face. "Thought yer said there weren't no competition."

"That's what I said. There ain't no competition now, but there will be. That's why we gotta move fast."

"Uh-huh."

They didn't talk much after that. Jake

sensed that Wes might be feeling a little squeamish about the fence company. Wes would probably feel better when the cash started to come in. And, with that, Jake's thoughts went mainly to the myriad of tasks required to set up the business.

After a few more miles of tracking, they both at the same time reined in the boys. "Whoa," Wes said. "Now would yer look at that. They think they's real smart trying to sweep out they's trail. Not a very good job. They's prob'ly jest draggin' some brush behind 'em. Still easy to follow, eh?"

"Yep. Where do yer think they's headed?"

"Wal, they can only go so far west, and they'll be into the dry mesa of the Llano Estacado. Not enough water there for cattle. So, I don't think they'll go there. Sooner or later, they gotta turn north or south to the markets in Kansas or in Texas prob'ly at Abilene, or they could go all the way to the army at El Paso. Right now, though, they's probably hol' up at a camp somewhere along the Pease River is how it's lookin' to me."

"Uh-huh."

Another eight miles of following the trail of the dragged brush, and they both at the same time saw the movement on the ridge to the north of them and then smelled the mesquite smoke. Whatever it was that moved up on the ridge disappeared. "C'mon. Let's make tracks fast. I think they spotted us," Wes said.

They spurred the boys into lopes and in another couple of miles saw the smoke. They eased up closer to the top of a small hill and got out the spyglasses. "There they are," Wes said excitedly. "See 'em? A little to the south a the river? Looks like they got about three hunnert head there. Lotta cows and calves. They's runnin' a hot iron on the brands. See that?"

"Uh-huh. I count three, but there's the one ridin' guard out there somewhere. He knows we're here. Can't wait around. Gonna have to charge 'em. What a yer think?"

"Yep. Let's split up. Come at 'em from two sides. Yer take the south, and I'll take the north. Try and rope 'em if yer can. Sound all right?"

"Yep."

Jake and Jasper loped off to the left, and Wes and Noble went to the right. When they were about two hundred yards out, Wes gave the signal, and they spurred the boys into a full gallop.

One man sat a horse with a taut rope on a calf. Another man held the calf stretched

114

out on the ground, and the last feller was applying the running iron to the calf's hip. Smoke from the fire and from the burning hair and flesh of the calf swirled round the two men on the ground and obscured them from sight. The detectives had raced about 150 yards when a rifle shot rang out from the south. The two men stood up, and they all looked but for a brief second in the direction of the sound of the shot and saw the detectives charging down on them. The man on the horse dropped his rope and spurred his horse around to run away. The other man ran away to the north to a saddled horse, and the third appeared to be so flustered he danced in a circle. When he finally ran, he was knocked silly in a collision with Jasper, who was in a chase after the mounted man.

Jasper ran down the other horse, and Jake dropped a loop around the rustler as soon as he was in range. Ol' Jasper came to a skidding halt, and the rustler was jerked out of his saddle, landed hard on his butt, grunted, and rolled over on his side. His horse kept running. Jake jumped out of the saddle, ran down the rope through the dust kicked up by the horses, and lashed the rustler's hands behind his back with a piggin' string. He was about to hogtie him when a whining bullet sizzled through his shirtsleeve and gouged out a crease in the dirt. Jake dove behind his prisoner and rolled him over on top of himself to provide a cover. The rustler screamed in pain as another bullet splashed into him. He screamed again and hunched over on the ground. Jake tried to pull his pistol, but his gun hand was trapped underneath the rustler's body and the holstered pistol covered likewise. Jasper was pulling the rustler away from Jake, and Jake struggled to keep from being exposed. He peeked over the body to see a renegade Comanche ten feet away, running at him and howling a war cry. He had a rifle in his left hand and a knife in his right. The Indian jumped, and Jake threw the body off and reached for his pistol. But he knew he was too late. He looked up into the black eyes of the renegade warrior and saw death a comin' and knew he was a dead man. He grimaced and prepared for the stab. The knife went up and flashed in the sun, but instead of plunging down into Jake's chest, it fell to the ground, and Jake saw a half-inch hole appear in the renegade's forehead. At the same time, he heard the crash of a gunshot, and the back of the Comanche's head blew apart. He twisted grotesquely in the middle of his airborne jump and landed in a heap next to Jake.

Jake turned around and saw Wes thirty feet behind him sitting astride Noble with his rifle across his lap. Jake crossed himself and jumped to his feet. He picked up his hat and slapped the dust off his shirt and pants. He shoved a boot under the rustler, who was delirious and moaning. Jake rolled him over, squatted, and pulled open his shirt to see blood flowing from the wound. "Better say yer prayers. Yer ain't got long," Jake said flatly. Then he walked over to Wes and held up his hand for a shake, "Thanks, pard. Now, I owe yer one."

"Ah, twern't nuthin'. As I said afore we'll probably be scorin' back and forth if we are detectivin'." He grinned. Jake couldn't quite get up for a grin. He looked down at his hands to see that they were trembling a little.

"That one might count as two. It was that close. I thought I was a goner."

"Wal, here. Have a snort a this." Wes reached back into his saddlebag for a dull tin flask. "Normally, I keep this for cleanin' wounds and dullin' the senses when sewin' up wounds and sech as that. But in this sit-chashun, looks like yer qualify." Again, he grinned as he handed Jake the flask. This time Jake managed a grin. It was hard not to be affected by Wes's dry wit and humor. Jake took a pull off the flask and handed it back up to Wes, who said, "Guess I'm a little rattled myself. Better have some medicine to calm my nerves, hah, hah, hah." He took a big swallow, wiped his lips on his sleeve, recorked the flask, and put it back in his saddlebag.

"Wal, where'd we end up," Jake said. "These two are dead. What about the feller yer chased?"

"Aw, I missed and got him around the neck. Ol' Noble broke the feller's neck like snapping a twig. Didn't have no time to slacken the rope. So, he's dead. What 'bout that other feller."

"Let's go see." They mounted and trotted the horses back to the branding fire and found that the last rustler apparently hit his head on a stone in the fire ring when he bounced off Jasper. Dried blood was on his ear and caked in a line down his cheek. He was dead, too. "Wal, guess they all wasn't so lucky," Jake said.

"Yep. Wal, now the work begins. Let's git these bodies hung up high in that oak over there so's the varmints don't git to 'em. Then let's catch their horses and git 'em hobbled. After that we can sit by this nice fire they left us, and have a cup a coffee and some chuck. In the mornin', we gotta round up the critters and drive 'em back to the MC."

It was a clear night and warm enough for the detectives to sit in their vests and shirtsleeves, lean back against their saddles, and stare into the fire. They had already downed their chuck, cleaned their tin cookware, plates, and eating irons, and were smoking their cigars over cups of coffee. Wes was idly stirring the fire with the running iron the rustlers left behind. Jake was brooding, and Wes didn't interrupt until finally he couldn't take it any longer. "What a yer stewin' 'bout?" he said.

Jake looked up from the fire and glared at Wes. "Ain't gonna do it no more," he said with challenge in his voice.

"What?" Wes spread his hands wide, cup in one hand, cigar and running iron in the other, and surprise all over his face.

"Rope a fleein' bandit."

"How come?"

"Too easy to git kilt. If I didn't chase after that rustler, I coulda shot that renegade and then shot the other feller. Wouldn't a come to a hairbreadth of gittn' kilt today. If yer wasn't there I'd be pushin' up daises right now." Jake stood up and paced around the fire, waved his arms about, and glared at the ground. "If like today I know fer sure they's rustlers and I can't git the drop on 'em like me an Johnny Raymer did, then I am a gonna shoot 'em by God. Without question. Specially if they's runnin'. That says guilty all over it. Yer know if yer chasin' 'em they can always stop, turn, and shoot yer or yer horse. No, sir. I don't like it, and I ain't ropin' no more bandits. They run, they's gonna git shot." He sat back down and folded his arms across his chest.

Wes said, "Wal, I guess I like to live a little more dangerous than yer. And I give 'em a chance at justice. More sport in it. The courts can judge 'em I always say. Guess it makes me feel good to bring 'em in alive. Oh, I ain't agin shootin' 'em if there ain't no way to catch 'em. If they's shootin' at me, I'm a gonna shoot back."

"Yeah, wal, that renegade was sure as hell shootin'. See this here shirtsleeve? Nuther two inches to the right an' I'd a prob'ly lost this arm. Then, let me ask yer. Yer ever had death's hot breath on yer face?"

"What'd yer mean?"

"I mean that damn crazed renegade Comanche was right on top of me, and I knew I was gonna be kilt cuz I couldn't git my pistol free. I knew it as sure as I see yer there. His knife flashed in the sun. That's when I saw the little devils. In the flash. They were laughin' and dancin' cuz I was gittin' kilt. Thank God yer were there. When yer shot him and the knife dropped to the ground, the little devils disappeared. That's what I mean. No, sir. Never agin'."

Wes remained quiet for a couple of minutes and then said, "Wal, there was a time onced when I came pretty close. Feller had the drop on me. Ten feet away. Pistol pointed right at my belly. Mine still in my holster. He was a known killer and was gonna shoot me sure."

Jake waited a minute then said, "Wal, what happened?"

"Oh. When he cocked his revolver, I pulled my pistol an' dropped to one knee. Leaned far to the right. His shot whizzed by my ear, and I shot him in the groin. He died the next day."

"So, yer didn't have death's hot breath on yer face. More like ten feet away. Was yer skeert?"

"Nah. Can't say I was. Little shaky afterwards. What 'bout yer?"

"Same. Seems like when I am in the heat of the battle I git real serious like. Bear down and determined. Yer know what I mean. Ain't no time to panic. That's what gits most men kilt. Prob'ly why this time I knew I was being kilt but wasn't skeert cuz there weren't no time. It was too fast. No time to think 'bout it, like I am now. I was hoppin' mad at those little devils. No, sir. Never agin'. And what 'bout that renegade. He was the one we saw on the ridge. Sure got down to the camp quick. He was the one fired the warning shot. Wasn't he? Yer figger he was a renegade left from Indian Territory and joined up with these fellers?"

"Yep, probably so. It was his first shot at yer what fouled my concentration when I heard the shot. I had just tossed my loop. Naturally, I turned to see what the shot was, and the loop fell around the feller's neck. He was already on his horse a runnin'. Wal, Noble pulled the rope tight, and that was the end a that feller. I saw that renegade chargin' his horse down on yer, so I dropped my rope and turned Noble to try an' stop the charge, but he was gainin' too fast, so I got as close as I could and set up for the rifle shot. By the time I had a bead on him, he was on yer, and yer know the rest."

Jake grinned at Wes, slapped him on the knee, and said, "Next time try not to take so long." He chuckled, and Wes did, too. "Wal, that's enough fer one night. I'm hittin' the hay." He tossed the dregs of his coffee into the fire and pulled his tarp over himself. Wes stared at the fire for a while longer, then he, too, rolled over and bedded down for the night.

Long about noon, Jake had the point and Wes the drag along with a string of the four horses and bodies of the rustlers. It was a lot of work for the two of them to keep three hundred head gathered and moving. They were constantly chasing quitters. Jake would go after a quitter, and the bunch would slow down, spread apart, and start grazing. So, he had to bunch them up again and snap the whip to get them moving. Wes would chase a quitter, and the same thing would happen, plus he had to re-catch the body-laden horses each time. They were tired, so they stopped for a break.

As they sat in the dirt and ate their jerky and hardtack, Wes said through a mouthful, "Tomorrow yer ridin' drag. It's only fair we should split it up."

"Don't think so."

"What?" Wes was incredulous.

Jake nodded his head to the east, and Wes turned to look behind him. There were three riders heading for them, and one of them looked like Duane Down. He rode up to them, reined in, and jumped from the saddle. He marched over to where the detectives were standing, held out his hand to shake theirs, and said, "Good job, boys. Looks like y'all recovered about three hundred head and eliminated four rustlers. Good job. What happened?"

They told him the story, and when finished Wes said, "Thought yer couldn't spare any cowboys from the roundup to go after this bunch."

"Well, I didn't think I could, but it's lookin' like we are ahead of schedule, so I thought we would trail you for a few miles to see if we could help. Looks pretty much like you don't need any help though." He smiled at them and doffed his hat as well.

"Wal, thank ye fer yer words, but this is a mighty lively little bunch. It's gonna take all of us to hold 'em together and make any time."

"All righty. Are y'all ready to head out now?"

Jake said, "Yes, sir. We're ready to get going. Mind if Wes and I take the swings?"

"Absolutely not. I'll ride point, naturally." Again, he smiled.

"Oh," Wes said. "Afore we get goin', we need yer to sign these receipts for the outlaws and the cattle for Jim Loving's records. After we get this bunch back to yer herd, Jake and me will take the outlaw bodies to Vernon or —"

"That is mighty good of you. I am sure that as bad as they were, they still have a mother somewhere or, if not, then other kin."

Later, Down said they could take the bunch from there when they were about eight miles from the main herd. Jake and Wes tipped their hats and loped off toward Vernon. There was about two hours of daylight left. "Dern. I was hopin' Down'd go along with just plantin' these four out on the range. Oh, well, let's trot 'em all the way so we don't gotta camp tonight," Wes said.

"Fine by me. Should get to Vernon before seven," Jake replied as he consulted his watch. "That's if one of them horses don't go lame or break down."

"They look to be pretty sturdy," Wes said.

Next morning after the JP inquest was over, Jake saddled up Jasper and headed out for the Flying XC. He arrived at the bunkhouse in time for the noon chuck. Most of the crew was gone on the drive to Fort Worth, so only a few cowboys were in the chow hall. Jake didn't know any of them, so he sat by himself. After he finished eating, he moseyed into the kitchen and found Chan. He sat at a small prep table and said, "How you been, Chan?"

"Fine. Thank you. How Mista Blighton?"

"Fine. Fine. Say, Mister Chan, I need six men to build barbwire fencin'. One of them has to speak English to be foreman. Think any of your relatives in El Paso might be interested? I'm payin' a dollar a day and a dollar and a half a day to the foreman."

Chan carried a pot over to the pump over the sink and started pulling on the pump handle. "Yes," he said. "Chan have lelatives. Need work."

"Do yer think they would come and work here for me and my partner, Wes Wilson, if we paid their travel expense?"

"Already say they need wolk. Yes. They come if Chan say so. I am Changming Da Chan, head of Chén family in Amelica and Macau." He folded his hands in prayer fashion and made a one-quarter bow. "At selvice to you," he said and smiled politely. "Chan lequire nolmal five pacent commission on his service." He bowed again and smiled.

Jake was silent for a couple of minutes as he contemplated the offer. "Five percent of what?"

"Of all cost. Includes Chan's management

of Chinese coolies."

Then Jake smiled also and said, "Sounds fair. Shake on it." He held out his hand.

"What Chan say good. Not Chinese custom to shake hands." He smiled.

"All right. My word is good, too."

He bowed again. "Chan send out today."

"How will you do that?"

"Have cousin in Velnon. He send one of his boys with letta from Chan."

"All right. But don't send the letter until I tell yer. I have to get some work under contract first. I'll let yer know as soon as I got it."

The next morning after breakfast, Jake headed straight for the office looking for Walt. He wasn't there but he found him in the barn. He was watching a feller file down a foreleg hoof of a red mare. Jake made enough noise so they could hear him coming. Walt glanced his way, then turned his attention back to the farrier work.

"Mornin', Mister Guthrie," he said cheerfully.

"Mornin'," Walt returned without looking up. Jake waited and idly watched the farrier work. When he finished filing, Walt handed him a horseshoe, and the farrier sized it to the hoof he held between his bent legs.

127

"Gonna take a little re-sizing," he said as he dropped the horse's hoof to the ground.

"Josh Walton, this is Rawhide Jake Brighton," Walt said.

"Glad to meet yer," Jake said as he held out his hand.

"Likewise, but my hands are awful dirty," Walton said as he rubbed his palms on his apron bib. This was Mary Jane's husband. Jake looked him over keenly without being obvious. He was older than Jake had assumed and not as tall and sort of a humdrum looking feller to be hitched to one as pretty as Mary Jane.

"Ain't afraid of a little dirt." They shook, and Walton turned to the forge. "Can I talk with yer a minute, Walt?"

"Sure. What's on yer mind?"

Jake edged away from the farrier shop toward one of the stalls. Walt naturally followed. "Me and Wes Wilson are thinkin' about startin' a side business puttin' in fencin'," Jake said as he watched Walt's reaction. Seeing no objection, he explained his plan. "Mister Calhoun's surveyin' the east boundary for fence, and I want to approach y'all with an offer to do the work. What do yer think?"

"Ain't thought 'bout that much. Where yer gittin' the labor?"

"Chinese outta El Paso. They finished the railroad, and they need work."

"Good ideer. What 'bout the wire and posts?"

"I got sources lined up."

"Don't see no hitches long as it don't confound yer detective work."

"No, won't let that happen." Jake looked seriously at Walt. "So, yer don't object to me talkin' to Mister Calhoun 'bout it?"

"Reckon not."

An hour later, Jake had Jasper tied off out front and was stepping up on the porch of the Calhoun house. It was a clear, dry day, but he checked his boots to make sure they were clean. He removed his hat. A slight breeze tossed his hair a bit, and with a slightly trembling hand he twisted the lever on the doorbell. As he waited for an answer, he unconsciously rotated his hat in a circle. His armpits felt damp, but he had washed earlier in the morning and didn't have any stink about him. Hopefully, Mary Jane would answer the door. He couldn't decide whether he was nervous about the proposition he had for Calhoun or seeing Mary Jane. He suspected the latter. Sure enough, the door swung open, and there she stood as pretty as ever. Jake could not help himself. His heart fluttered, and his throat went dry. He was hesitant to speak because he was sure he would croak and stammer.

Then she smiled, revealing white but not quite perfectly straight teeth. It was a smile that next to her face was the prettiest thing he had seen in a long time. "Why, Mister Brighton. What brings you here?" Her unspoken suggestion that it was to see her was obvious in the way she spoke and held her body and batted her eyes at him. And suddenly he realized she was playing him. The little scamp. He smiled big and inwardly chuckled. He didn't feel as nervous anymore and admired her all the more for her playfulness.

"Why, Missus Walton, I am here to see Mister Calhoun and maybe feast my eyes on your natural beauty." That got her. He laughed inwardly as she blushed a little, but her smile only increased.

"I do believe you are flirting with me, sir."

"You do believe correctly, madam."

"Well, I declare. I never —" she said and stood aside, still smiling. "Right this way. You may have a seat in the parlor while I see if Mister Calhoun is available. Are your boots and clothes clean?"

"Yes, ma'am." He watched her retreat down the hall and wasn't sure, but he thought she might even be sashaying a little.

Then she turned into a door and was out of sight.

It wasn't long and Xavier Calhoun came down the hall and entered the parlor. He held his hand to Jake as he came in.

"Hello, Jake. How goes the detective business?"

"Hello, sir. Yes. Quite well. We've arrested or killed eleven rustlers and recovered over five hundred head of rustled cattle. At least a couple hundred of them Flying XC cows. Not to mention the strays we brought in."

"That is quite commendable for such a short period of time. What has it been? Two months? I understand one of the rustlers was from our own very crew."

"Yes, unfortunately that is true."

"Well, what is it you want to see me about?" he said as he motioned for them to sit down.

Jake went through his pitch, and Calhoun listened intently. When Jake finished Xavier said, "Very interesting. I can see the benefit to farming out the work instead of using my own crew. I was going to retain five to ten men for fence building, but at six cents a foot their cost would exceed that." He stood and retrieved a humidor from a bureau drawer and offered Jake a cigar. They lit up and he said, "In fact, I plan to fence the big pasture, cultivate it, irrigate it, and grow hay. We will put up duck canvas stack covers to store the hay for winter feed. Water will come from weirs in Comanche Creek and Long Creek to flood the pasture. That allows me to decrease my winter mortality and put more weight on the beeves for market. Plus, I am not liking the lack of rain we have had so far this year. Last storm of any size was two months ago and none since. Usually, we average at least a storm a month. Range might dry up." He paused and puffed his cigar and studied the glow of the burning end for a few seconds. "Stored feed will be a good idea. And I am thinking about digging wells with windmills pumping out water. One a the reasons I decided to sell all the yearlings this year. Better to get something for them rather than lose them if a drought turns up. When do you think you boys will have your crew ready?"

"Shouldn't take more than a month to get the men up here from El Paso. In the meantime, I will procure the tools, horses, wagon, posts, and wire to be ready when they arrive. And it just so happens that my wire supplier is also a Kenwood windmill dealer. I could have him get in touch with you if you'd like."

"Yes, do that. What's his name?"

"Robert Corrigan. Nice young fellow. From Decatur, Texas, but educated at a boarding school in Atchison, Kansas."

"All right. Have him wire me. Meanwhile I'll bring the surveyors over to lay out the line for the pasture and when you finish the pasture you can move to the ranch boundaries. So, six cents per foot, minimum three hundred feet per day. Agreed?"

"Agreed." They shook hands, and the deal was sealed.

CHAPTER THREE: FENCING WARS

Jake rode back to the bunkhouse, gave Chan the go ahead, packed up his saddlebags, tied them and his bedroll, tarp, and slicker onto his saddle, and headed for Vernon to give Wes the news. He arrived at the hotel about mid-afternoon to find out that Wes was up at Doan's Crossing. So, he high tailed it up to the Red River crossing much used by trail herds.

He let Jasper take a long drink from the stock trough, then tied him off to the rail in front of the store. There was another small adobe with a porch next to the store on one side. He presumed it to be the storeowner's residence. On the wall of the other side of the store that was exposed to view for a long way was painted in two-foot-high, black capital letters on a white background: DOAN'S STORE. He slipped Jasper a piece of hard candy and walked into the store. There were a few women slowly moving from one small counter to another and surveying the merchandise on the wall shelves as they gabbed away. One man was looking at some tools in a corner, and the young shop clerk was behind the main counter. Jake walked up to him.

"Howdy," he said with a pleasant smile. "I'm lookin' fer Wes Wilson. Yer know him? Seen him?"

"Sure. I know Wes," the young man behind the counter said.

"Have yer seen him? Know where he might be?"

Then the climate changed as the young man carefully looked Jake over. He stared into Jake's eyes for a moment and apparently did not like what he saw. "Who's askin'?"

Jake had a decision to make. This feller was rightfully suspicious and protective. There would probably be no chance of convincing him that Jake was on the up and up unless Jake revealed his identity. But that would expose him and ruin his cover. He decided it was worth the risk. After all, time was wasting. Jake needed to find Wes and get back out on the range. So, he leaned in close to the feller and lowered his voice to almost a whisper.

"I am a stock detective like Wes. We're

partners. I work under cover, and I shouldn't be tellin' yer this, but yer look like a righteous feller so I am lettin' yer in to make yer an assistant. Are yer up fer that?" Jake looked at him intently, serious. And then he smiled and winked. "Yer can keep eye and ear open here and tell me or Wes if yer see or hear anythin' suspicious about cattle rustlin' or other crimes."

"Do I get a badge?" the feller asked with a look of interested excitement.

"Wal, can't do that right now. Yer gotta have special trainin' to be sworn in as a detective, and there ain't a spot available right now. But . . . when a spot comes open and yer been a assistant to me an Wes it'll go far for yer as top choice to fill the spot. Like I said, prob'ly shouldn't be tellin' yer all this. What a yer say?"

"Wal," he said like he was keeping something secret. "Sounds interestin', but I better talk to Wes first."

"That's a good feller. I like the way yer thinkin' already. Don't take nuthin' for granted. I'll tell him when I see him. So, I am gonna go meet up with him. We got work to do on some special information I just come across, and we gotta git it done afore sunset. I'd tell yer what it is, but I don't know fer sure yet if yer can be trusted." Jake dropped his gaze to the floor and traced a circle with the toe of his boot.

"I can be trusted. He said he was goin' down to the river crossing. Probably to check brands. Is that the information yer got?"

"Yep. Got a whole herd a stolen beeves all with altered brands comin' in directly. I'll check back with yer to see if any cowboys came into the store sayin' anythin' 'bout it. But I gotta hurry and talk to Wes." He said the last as he was walking out the door.

"I didn't get yer name," the feller called after him just as Jake untied Jasper, vaulted into the saddle, and rode off at a lope, pretending he didn't hear him.

There were two herds of about two thousand head each waiting on the dry, sun-drenched range. A bigger herd sloshed through the reddish-brown water and gravel on the bars in the river to reach the Oklahoma Territory side of hard-caked, light-brown mud banks.

Jake saw Wes on the Texas side sitting in the saddle atop Noble with one leg hooked around the saddle horn. He had in his hands Loving's brand book, a pencil, and a Gray Eagle ruled tablet. Jake saw him squint against the glare of the sun on the water as he looked out over the sheen of the crossing. Like a hawk he searched out and checked every brand on every flank he could see, making notes as they passed directly in front of him clomping to the water's edge.

The critters bawled in deep throated bellows as they splashed into the water, pushing and shoving against each other. A thin cloud of flies hovered over them all, buzzing around in and out of the critters' noses, eyes, ears, and pucky caked rears. The cowboys slapped their ropes and called and whistled and chased up and down the line of cattle. Water sprayed out from their horses in sheets as they ran through back and forth. As the herd crossed, it churned up the water and mud into a roiling mass of reddish-brown slop. On the other side, the cowboys hurried the cattle out of the water, across the dried mud flat, and into the grass and low scrub of Oklahoma Territory. As Jake rode up to him, he looked upriver where Wes was staring and saw another herd about a quarter mile up starting across the red gravel.

"Git on that herd up there," Wes yelled and pointed upstream. "Check every brand, and git the name of the outfit and its trail boss. Hurry! They's startin' acrosst."

Jake waved and put Jasper into a gallop with red mud splashing his chaps as Jasper ran upriver. He reined in at the same time as the lead steer was stepping into the water, followed by the old matrons of the herd. He got out his book and found the brand that was on the cattle he was observing. It was XL on the side. The brand was registered to T. F. Maxwell out of Stephens County. Jake watched the whole herd splash across and made a mental head count. When the last cow came to the riverbank he chased after a cowboy on the drag, caught up to him, and hollered, "Where's your trail boss?"

"Who wants to know?" came the sour reply in between whoops and whistles at the cattle. Jake called back, "Stock detective of the Stock-Raisers' Association of North-West Texas." His cover was getting mighty thin out here on the river.

"Too late now. We're already acrosst the river and in Oklahoma Territory," he yelled.

"That don't matter. The stockmen's association I work for has mutual agreements with Oklahoma associations. Yer hidin' somethin'?"

The cowboy shrugged his shoulders and shouted back, "Nah. Far as I know we're all legit. He's over there on the bank sittin' on that gray mare, white hat and shirt. Brown vest. See him?"

"Yep. Thanks." Jake walked Jasper through

the red water across the river and trotted up to the trail boss. He came at him from the west, and the sun was low so the boss, already facing west, had his hat pulled down to shade his eyes and then squinted at the rider coming up to him. He sat tall in the saddle, had a bushy salt and pepper mustache that was stained with tobacco juice and at least a two-week beard stubble. He didn't move. Jake slowed to a walk and reined in when the horses' noses were about five feet apart. Jasper wanted to get closer and nose the mare, but Jake held him back. "Howdy," Jake said loudly with a slight smile. "Name's Jake Brighton. Detective for the Stock-Raisers Association of North-West Texas."

"That Jim Loving's outfit?" He spoke in a strong, low voice with a heavy Texas drawl.

"Correct."

"What can I do for yer, Detective?" He spat a stream of tobacco juice to the ground.

"Wal, I inspected yer herd as it crossed. All the brands look good and above board. Looks like a well-managed herd. Jim wants us to collect information for the association's records. So, I reckon this is T. F. Maxwell's herd outta Stephens County, right?" Jake wrote that on his tablet.

"That's right." He watched Jasper ease

closer to the mare. "That ol' Jasper?"

"Sure is. How'd yer know?"

"Did some contract work for Loving a few years back. He's a dern good horse. Yer take care a him."

"Yer can count on that. Mind if I ask yer how come yer ain't trailin' to Fort Worth or Abilene?"

"They ain't got enough stockyard. Pens are all filled up or under contract."

Jake entered the information in his tablet. "How many head yer got?"

" 'Bout three thousand, give or take."

"Where yer takin' this herd?"

"Place called Chadron Creek, Nebraska. Outfit called Dakota Stock and Grazing Company. Mister Maxwell sold the whole herd to 'em at a dern good price."

"Wal, soon enough I guess there'll be plenty a pens at the railheads closer by."

"Reckon so," the trail boss said and spat.

"Sorry. Can I have yer name fer the record."

He paused and glared into Jake's eyes only to be met with the natural challenge in Jake's ocular expression. Seemingly satisfied he said, "Bartholomew P. Cummings." He watched Jake close for any reaction. Apparently not seeing any unfavorable reaction, he continued, "Most folks call me Bart —

Boss Bart."

Jake wrote that down in the tablet and then looked up and said, "My formal name is Jonas V. Brighton. Most folks around here call me Rawhide Jake Brighton." He stared steady at Boss Bart, who gave up a blink and a little sag in his mustache. Then he spat.

"Heared a yer. Keep up the good work." He tipped his hat, reined the mare around, and spurred her off to catch the herd. Jake held Jasper still and said out loud to himself, "Guess we both got funny names, formally and informally."

The detectives finished the inspection of the last two herds as the sun dropped below the western horizon. There was a massive bright-red afterglow that spanned the sky from south to north as far as the eye could see. Jake sat on Jasper for a few minutes and admired the view. Upriver, the water course made a bend turning out of the west to the south, and with imagination it appeared that at that bend the Red River blended with the afterglow suggesting that the headwaters were somewhere there in the red expanse.

"C'mon. Let's get a drink," Wes yelled to Jake.

■ ■ ■ ■

At the bar after Jake explained the whole fencing plan to Wes, he said to Jake, "Yer see the brand-new hotel they got here in Doan's Crossin'?"

"Yup. We better get us a couple a rooms afore they sell out. Don't make no never mind anyway. My cover around here is gone out the winder."

"What're yer sayin'?"

"I had to reveal myself, not my name, just my job to the young feller at the store. Promised him he could become our assistant if he told me where yer were. Checking the herds, anybody who wanted to could see I'm a detective. Besides, what's the matter with yer? Ain't yer excited about the fencing contract?" Jake tossed back his drink and turned to stare at Wes.

"Sure. A course I'm excited. I jest got a lot on my mind with all these herds comin' through and so on. Rustlers prob'ly havin' a hay day out on the range with all the cowboys out on drives. Don't fergit, we're range detectives first afore we're fence builders."

"Wal, I think I can do both, so I'll do all the work and make yer rich, pard." He

143

grinned at Wes and slapped him on the back.

"Wal then, mister . . . whatta they call 'em, tycoon? Yer kin buy me nuther drink. Hah, hah, hah." And he clapped Jake on the back.

A few minutes passed as they chatted when Jake said, "I do need to get back out on the line for the Flyin' XC. I'll make my way down to the North Fork of the Wichita and follow it to the main river and cut over to Seymour and pick up a wagon and team, take on a load of posts, and haul 'em up to the Flyin' XC headquarters."

"What 'bout the wire?"

"Gonna order a shipment from that young Corrigan feller. Have it drop shipped at the train depot in Wichita Falls."

"Sounds right by me, pard."

A week later, in the late afternoon, Jake trotted Jasper up the Oregon Street extension, turned into the thick, sunbaked dust on Main Street, and pulled up to the barn at the livery in Seymour. He dismounted saying, quietly to Jasper, "We don't want to get fined" and led him into the shade of the barn interior. "Yo, Quincy," he called out.

Quincy popped his head out the office door and said, "Wal, look what the cat just drug in. Two fine fellers who roam the range and enforce the law." He walked over to Jake and said, "Four a them fellers yer brought in is already on their way to Huntsville. That Sour Bill is done in I'm afeared. He went to a special sanitarium, I think that's what they call it, in Dallas."

"Sorry to hear that, but yer know what they say. Live by the sword, die by the sword."

"Uh-huh. Wal, what a it be this time. Same as always?"

"Yeah but, depending on how it goes, we may not be here very long. Yer know where I can buy a wagon and a team a draft horses?"

"Sure do. Old Jacob Lee down at the smithy's shop has two wagons for sale and" — he gave Jake a sparkly smile — "I know right where I can fetch a couple a plow horses fer yer."

"How much?"

Quincy rubbed his palm across his chin and said, "Reckon it'll probably be 'bout eighty bucks each."

"I'll pay seventy and not a dime more." Jake did not smile.

"Wal, let me see what I kin do. When do you need 'em?"

"Tomorrow, if yer kin. Meantime, I aim to git ol' Jasper here comfy. Then, I'm gonna git a bath, shave, supper, cigar, couple a drinks, and bed."

"All righty. Why don't yer close the barn door when yer done, and I'll go see 'bout them horses." He left quickly. Jake knew he would probably buy the horses for a hundred bucks and sell them to Jake for a hundred and forty bucks, which was fine because that is what Jake had budgeted and that's the way the horse-trading business was anyway.

Jake stepped up to the bar in the Brazos. Alex stood with his back to the front tending to something or other, but he saw Jake in the mirror. He turned around and said, "Hello, Jake. How are you?"

"Just fine. How about yourself?"

"Fine. Fine."

"Gracie here?"

"Nope. She ran off with that Corrigan fellow. I think they went to Henrietta."

"Leave a forwarding address?"

"Yes. I have it right here." He turned and took a piece of paper from the backbar and handed it to Jake.

"I'll be right back. I have to send a wire."

He went to the telegraph office and wrote out his telegram for Corrigan:

REQUIRE 100 SPOOLS BARBED WIRE 100 LBS STAPLES. TWO DOLLARS PER

SPOOL. HALF ON ORDER CONFIRMA-
TION HALF ON DELIVERY. DROP SHIP
WICHITA FALLS TRAIN DEPOT. CON-
FIRM WIRE BY NOON TOMORROW TO
BRIGHTON AT SEYMOUR.

Back at the Brazos he said to Alex, "You're still selling baths, ain't yer?"

"Oh yes. Desi is in charge now." He grinned and winked.

"Desi?"

"Yes, Desideria. I shortened her name now that she is in the business. She looks pretty good. You should go see her."

"She was always pretty."

"You should see her now. I shoulda put her in the business long ago. She's a natural. Brings in good money."

"Who's tending the bath house?"

"She is doing both for now, until I can find another woman to do the work."

"She ask you to start whoring or did you ask her?"

"She asked me. I think she was doing it on the side down at her adobe anyway."

"Wal, maybe I'll go see her. She busy now?"

"Nope. You're the first today. She's popular, too. Lively, I guess." He grinned.

"Gimme a shot." He downed it and went

upstairs.

"Señor Jake!" Desi exclaimed as Jake stepped into the bath house and she turned at the sound of his entry. "My handsome hombre. I did not know you were coming, and I am so, so, so glad." She flashed a cheery white smile surrounded by full ruby lips and stared at him with dark, shining, eager eyes that were made up more and far more accentuated and expressive than before. The dress she wore was far more provocative than the standard blouse and skirt she wore before. It was a fine red cotton with lowcut bodice that displayed her deep cleavage. Her black hair hung to one side of her face, and she had a red carnation on the opposite side in her hair. All in all, she glowed, ready for fun and excitement.

"Hi, Desideria," Jake said with his own smile.

"Oh, I have news for you, Señor Jake. I am Desi now. Gracie is gone, and now I am here to take her place." She moved to Jake, laid herself out on his side, and caressed his back and stomach down low. "I always wanted you so much, and now we are together," she said as she breathed heavily into his ear and nibbled the lobe.

"Let me git a bath and shave first. Yer can

148

do that, right?"

"Certainly. For you, anything."

After Jake was bathed and shaved, he sloshed out of the tub, and Desi wrapped him in a big red towel and rubbed him down good. Then she took him by the hand and led him to a room two doors down. "This is my room now," she said coyly.

Jake glanced around the wooden room to see a nice bed with a white spread and wrought-iron headboard, a brown wool rug under it centered on the room, a bureau and mirror on one wall, a tall wardrobe on the other, and on the fourth wall a draped window with a chair, table, and lamp in front of it.

"Looks like you've improved your lot in life." He grinned.

She took him by the arm and tossed him on the bed. He did not resist, and the towel fell open. He was ready. Desi stepped back and slipped the dress off her shoulders and let it fall to the floor. She was naked. Jake gazed at her golden-brown, unblemished skin and her dark-brown nipples on silver-dollar size rosettes. They appeared to be a perfectly symmetrical pair. Why he thought of that he could not tell. She was a tad plumper than Gracie but also shaped like an hourglass. Desi did not give him long to admire her. She kicked off her shoes, jumped on top of him, and started wiggling around on him like a little puppy, licking and moaning.

Afterward they were spent. She was nestled into Jake with her head on his shoulder and her face near his. "I love you, Señor Jake," she whispered.

"Uh-huh," he said as he sat up and swung his legs off the bed. "Let's get some supper." He did not look at her to see her disappointment.

Jake had already been over to the livery before breakfast and fed Jasper and the other horses there for Quincy. After having finished his breakfast, he stepped through the arched stone portico of the hotel onto the boardwalk and lit a cigar. It was another clear morning, and it was warmer even with the breeze. Then he crossed the street and started walking to the blacksmith shop.

He ducked inside the shop, and, following the ringing, he walked to the back where a man was hammering a hot steel tire onto a wagon wheel. As Jake walked up, he poured cold water on the tire, and it sizzled as clouds of steam rose. Jake watched and determined that the smithy knew what he was doing. He looked up at Jake and nodded his head. Jake waited for the steam to subside and then said, "Howdy. Name's Jake Brighton." He held out his hand for a shake. They shook, and the smithy said, "Jacob Lee. Let me finish settin' this tire, and I'll be right with yer." A few more bangs with the hammer and he seemed satisfied.

"Quincy Brown up at the livery said you might have a wagon for sale."

"Yes, siree. Got two a them. Right out back here." He led the way. "One's a Conestoga, and the other's a Studebaker freighter. I completely rebuilt 'em. New tires, springs, axles and put on steel skeins, brakes, and that Conestoga has a new tongue. Made it myself. Extra beef on it. Replaced bad boards on the sides and all new beds. Hinges all fixed up like new. Painted 'em. Heck, they might as well be brand new."

"I like that Conestoga. Gonna need the high clearance cuz we'll be drivin' off the road out on the range. If yer have the cover, I don't want it. How much yer want fer it?"

"Yeah. Ain't got the cover. Wal, let's see. I could let that one go fer, say, sixty bucks."

"I'm startin' up a business, and I got fifty bucks budgeted for a wagon. I can't do more. Can yer see yer way to fifty?"

"Wal . . ."

"How long yer had this wagon?"

"It's been a while."

Jake kept quiet and let him stew on it for a minute or two. Then he held out his hand for a shake and said, "Deal?"

"All right. Reckon so."

"Providin' a course, it's in the shape yer say it is."

"A course." And they shook on it.

"Good. Now we need to get that wagon up on blocks so I can check it over. Make sure it's as great as yer say it is. I'll help yer." He gave him a friendly smile.

Once they got it up on blocks, the first thing Jake did was to check all the wheels for wobble to make sure the hubs were good and tight on the skeins. Then he took each wheel off to check that the skeins were in fact steel, not wood and well-greased. Everything else he could observe without taking anything apart. He looked closely at the tongue. It indeed was new and bigger than the original. That would be good for going across rough country with a load of juniper poles or wire on board.

"It all looks good. I need to go higher on the sideboards and tailgate. Say two feet. Think yer could do that fer, say, three bucks?"

"Reckon I could."

"Could yer do it today?"

"Could, if the lumber's sawn down at Baker's."

"All right. I'll come back later this morning. See how yer doin'. Quincy is supposed to be chasin' up a team of plow horses for me."

"Plow horses? 'Twas a farmer come by here a week or two ago. Had a team of good lookin' plow horses he was sellin' for eighty bucks includin' harness. Said he had to sell out and git on the train back to Indiana. Some kinda family trouble."

"Where's the farm?"

"Think he said it was 'bout five miles west a town on the river."

"What's his name?"

"Don't recall that."

"All right. Well thanks. If yer could just make me up a receipt I can pick up the wagon maybe later today." Jake counted out fifty-three dollars in notes and held them out to Lee.

"Done is done as done is." Jacob Lee grinned.

Jake walked back up to the other side of town to Quincy's livery just in time to see him ride up bareback trotting a beautiful Belgian with a near twin on a lead behind him. The horses were a matched pair of large dapple-white geldings, at least eighteen hands tall, thick boned and as stocky as a bull. As Jake walked up to Quincy, he couldn't help but admire the magnificent animals. And he took special note that both horses were fully harnessed for pulling.

"What're yer think a these big beauties?" Quincy said with a beaming radiance on his face as he slid off the big horse. Jake opened the barn door for him, and he led the team in and tied them off each to separate rings on separate posts. "And lookee there, I got all the harness, too, that I can let go for ten bucks additional."

"They are magnificent," Jake said as he gently ran his hands over each one, checking their legs, eyes, ears, and teeth, cooing as he went. "What're their names?"

"This here is Joe, and that's Jeb. Joe's got the darker rump."

"How old?"

"Eight years old. Been farmin'."

"Uh-huh. I like that they ain't got feathers and their spats are short. We're gonna be out in the scrub a lotta the time, and I don't want to be all the time brushin' the burs outa 'em," Jake said as he stroked their ankles, one after the other. "All right. I'll take 'em fer a hunnert twenty bucks includin' the harness," he added.

Quincy immediately turned sour as his radiance disappeared to be replaced by surprise and then anger. He kicked the dirt floor of the barn, clenched his hand into a ball, and with fire in his eyes, hooded over by a heavy brow, he shook his fist at Jake. In a loud squeaky voice he said, "Dag nab yer. I know'd yer was gonna hornswoggle me. We shook on a hunnert forty, and there weren't no talk 'bout harness."

"Wal, yer the one's that's doin' the hornswogglin'. First, we never shook. Second," Jake said as he, steadily staring into Quincy's angry eyes, slowly stepped closer and closer to Quincy, who back stepped for every step Jake took. "I know yer never paid more'n eighty bucks for them horses includin' the harness. When I said a hunnert forty I figger'd yer fer forty dollars profit. That's what I'm allowin' now. And that's a good amount a profit fer a day's work. Yer can take it or leave it. But if yer leave it, I guess yer'll be out eighty bucks and have to feed them hay burners for a long time cuz they shore don't look like no saddle or buggy horse to me." Jake waited. It was quiet in the barn as Quincy turned the proposal over in his mind. Finally, Jake said, "Yer want a make me out a receipt fer a hunnert twenty includin' harness before I lower the amount?"

Quincy kicked the dirt again and said, "Oh, all right."

"All right. Now yer being sensible," Jake said. Quincy said nothing and stomped off into the office. Jake was still caressing Joe and Jeb when he noticed Jasper had his head out of his stall and was nickering to Jake. "Oh, I ain't forgot about yer, Jasper, ol' boy. Yer still my favorite." He gave Jasper a piece of candy and stuck one in his own mouth.

Quincy came out of the office and handed Jake his receipt, which Jake read and, satisfied, stuffed in his shirt pocket inside his vest, then handed one hundred twenty dollars in notes to Quincy. "Just to show they ain't no hard feelin's I'm a gonna pay yer to board these big boys."

"Hurumph. What makes yer think I only paid eighty bucks includin' harness fer them horses?" Quincy said.

"Jacob Lee told me that farmer was by his place offering to sell 'em for eighty bucks includin' harness."

"Wal, I only paid seventy bucks. How's that grab yer?" He puffed up his cheeks, made an *O* with his mouth, and opened his eyes up like saucers as he stepped back and said, "Oops." Then he ran up the hay loft ladder, and his cackling laugh floated down after him.

Jake stood for a moment staring after him, then shook his head and turned to go out the barn door. His next stop was the general store to buy feed and supplies. Then he checked at the telegraph office next to the store for a wire from Corrigan. It was there waiting for Jake, and the order was con-firmed, so he paid the telegraph agent a hundred dollars in notes to wire out plus three dollars for the wire and the cash transfer fee. He was feeling pretty good about things, and if the wagon was ready, he was ready to head out.

The sun was directly overhead, and the wind was still steady out of the northwest, but that didn't hinder the flies as they were thick and buzzed around Jake's head while he hitched up the team to the wagon. He tied his bandana around his head to keep the sweat from blurring his vision. His shirt was soaked at the armpits and in back. He could feel the drip of sweat down his legs under his pants.

Jacob Lee had made fast work of the sideboards, but since Jake wanted to leave right away there was no time to paint them. With a wave to Jacob, Jake called out, "Hey, Joe, Jeb, giddy-up." And he gently slapped the reins to their backs. With a little lurch they were off to the general store, where Jake loaded up his feed and supplies. Then he went to the livery, saddled up Jasper, and led him over to where he tied him to a lead rope at the side of the wagon up front. Jasper was too proud to eat the dust of the other horses, or so Jake told himself. And in a trail of dust kicked up by the hooves of Joe and Jeb and the wagon wheels they pulled out of town headed northwest.

The next day he rolled into the Smiths' post-making plant in the late afternoon and made a deal for two hundred posts. By the time they got them all loaded, the sun was fading fast, so Jake decided to stay the night with the Smiths. It was beneficial for him because he learned much about fencing. As soon as the sun was up the next morning though, Jake was rolling out of their camp. He had already crossed the Wichita at a shallow gravel bed with an empty wagon. So now with a pulling weight of close to two thousand pounds he could roll right on in to the Flying XC headquarters and did not have to contend with any river or creek crossings. Joe and Jeb were pulling fine, almost effortlessly unless they had to go uphill. If he couldn't find a way around the hills, on the way up or at the top Jake would stop and let the big boys have a blow so they could catch their breath and not develop any pulmonary difficulties.

Two days later and he was unharnessing the Belgians at the Flying XC barn. He had already unhitched and left the loaded wagon at the big pasture. Of course, he had to take care of ol' Jasper first and get him settled in. Then he turned to the big boys. Joe and Jeb attracted a lot of attention from the wranglers and cowboys as Jake washed them, brushed them, and put them in their stalls for water and feed.

"Howdy, Jake," Walt said as he walked into the barn. "Fine lookin' team yer got there."

"Howdy, Mister Guthrie. Yeah, they's hard workers, too. Pulled a couple thousand pounds thirty miles in two days."

"Yep. That's purty good. We'll be needin' plow horses to pull harrows in the big pasture. Got three teams lined up right now. A fourth would make things a quarter agin' faster. Think yer kin loan 'em to us?"

"Sure. Our pleasure. They been farmin' for most a they's life." He smiled as he answered.

"Our?"

"Me and the big boys. Joe and Jeb." His smile broadened into a grin.

"Okay. A couple a brand-new steel disc

harrows we ordered just came in. They's at the depot. And a seeder is due in on the nine o'clock train tomorrow. Think yer — *and the big boys* — could pick them up fer us?"

"Sure. Yer got a wagon don't yer. I don't want to unload my wagon and re-load it all over agin."

"Yep. Over there behind the barn. Two a them. Take yer pick. Then we can probably start diskin' day after tomorrow. One team per harrow. Start on the sides and work to the middle. Probably take nigh on to three months to git the whole pasture done with four teams workin'. 'Course, I guess we only got yer team so long until yer start fencing, huh?"

"Wal, I only really need 'em to pick up posts and wire. Yer give me a team a regular horses to pull wire and sech and yer can use the big boys to work on the pasture when I ain't usin' 'em," Jake said matter of factly.

"Wal, much obliged," Walt said with an appreciative smile Jake had never seen on him. "The boys 'bout got the weirs done. Onced the pasture is all disked and dragged we'll flood it and see what we gotta do for ditchin' and gradin'. Gonna try for one cut this year. Maybe two."

"Wal, yer becoming a regular old farmer, Walt." Jake grinned that contagious grin of his.

Walt smiled and said, "Don't tell nobody. Wouldn't want it to git out." He winked at Jake, and he could tell Walt liked him, probably because he saved his life.

Three weeks later when Jake was sitting at the supper table in the bunkhouse talking to Johnny Raymer, Chan caught his eye and motioned for him to come see him.

In the kitchen by the back door stood a young Chinese boy, probably fourteen or fifteen years old. "This Chenglei." The boy bowed. "He my cousin's son. He bling message. Men in Velnon. Want to come."

"All right. We'll ride out in the mornin'."

"One thing," Chan said. "Thlee have wives."

"Oh. Hadn't figgered on that." Jake gave it some quick thought and said, "Guess they's no harm in it. So instead a ridin', we'll *roll* out with a wagon in the mornin'." He grinned. "Yer know how to drive a team a horses pullin' a wagon?" he said to Chenglei. Chan translated and the boy nodded his head *yes* and spoke to Chan in Chinese.

"He say he dlive wagon at railroad. Do good job." Chan smiled big.

161

"All right. Guess we'll find out tomorrow."

Since his wagon was still loaded with posts and the Belgians were working in the pasture, Jake borrowed a wagon and team from Walt to take to Vernon to pick up his crew. Changlei handled the team well and obviously knew what he was doing.

Pulling an empty wagon, they could trot the team most of the way, so they came up on Vernon by noon. About a mile before town, they came to the small camp the Chinamen made. Changlei pulled the team and wagon around and headed them back toward the ranch. Jake stayed in the saddle, removed his hat, wiped off the sweat of his brow on his shirtsleeve, and looked up to the vast deep blue of a cloudless sky. He held his hat up to blot out the sun and shade his eyes while he gazed out over the horizon in search of clouds — any clouds. He gave it up and put his hat back on and then looked down at the Chinese. He walked Jasper up to the little group and scrutinized them closely. There were six men and three women, and, again what Jake hadn't counted on or even thought about, two of them were nursing babies. "Wal, I'll be hornswoggled," he said to no one. "Didn't think I was gonna be the patriarch of a whole family of Celestials." But he was overheard.

One of the men came over and stood before Jake. He bowed and said, "So sorry, Mista Jake. They best wolkers. Even women wolk. I Boqin He Chan. Cousin of Changming Da Chan and Changpu He Chan. I your foleman." He smiled big and bowed again.

Jake was speechless. He looked back at the group. They were all standing in a line with a very large man on the left with the rest of the men standing in rank to the right, ending with the women. Except for the women they all wore shabby, threadbare work clothes and scuffed up boots with worn-out heels and soles. They were clean shaven, and their black hair was short but in need of haircuts. The women wore more traditional well-worn black or dark-green Chinese jackets with stand-up collars and quilted pants. All three had long black hair in a single braid down their back. They all looked to be less than thirty years old and, each in her own way, appeared to be sweet and comely. Jake couldn't suppress his fondness for women as he smiled handsomely at the women, to which they smiled and lowered their eyes.

Their gear, arranged in neat piles around their camp, looked to be the least possible necessities one could get by with out on the range. He looked for a tent but did not see one.

"This Niu," Boqin said as he gestured to the very muscular, large man. "It mean ox." He smiled broadly. He went down the line and introduced each man and their wives. The one woman who did not have a baby was his wife.

"Do you have a tent?"

"No. We sleep under sky." He smiled again but not as broadly.

"All right. Changlei is the wagon driver. You probably know him."

"Yes. He my cousin's son."

"Is the whole Celestial nation all cousins?"

"Hah, hah, hah. You make joke, Mista Jake."

Jake smiled and said, "All right. Get your gear loaded in the wagon, and then y'all hop up there. We're going into town."

They rolled into Vernon, and Jake halted them in front of the general store. As he was tying off Jasper to the hitching rail, a little crowd of onlookers gathered on the boardwalk.

"What're them coolies doing here?" someone said.

Jake looked up to see if he could locate the speaker but could not.

"We don't need no chinks here in north-west Texas."

There was a low rumble of agreement from the little crowd. The man stepped forward and raised a fist at the folks in the wagon. Jake spied him. He was standing in the back of the group of onlookers. Slowly Jake stepped up on the boardwalk, and while never taking his eyes off the fellow, he moved through the crowd, separating them by the mere power of his presence. He must have seemed to them like a fellow whose way they didn't want to block. He stopped in front of the vocal fellow and said in a low growl, "I am Rawhide Jake Brighton, and these folks are my employees."

When the man heard that, his eyes opened wide, and he became fidgety. The crowd of people moved away from the two of them. Jake stepped closer so that he was but twelve inches away from the man, and he placed his gun hand on the butt of his holstered pistol. He speared the man's eyes with his hot, deadly stare and said, "Yer cause them trouble then yer causin' me trouble. Yer want to do that?"

"No sir. No sir. I heared a yer. Sorry, sorry." Unable to bear the ferocity of Jake's blazing, unblinking stare the man dropped his gaze to the ground.

"All right. All yer folks go on about yer business now. We got business here in this general store. And yer better not let me see yer face around these parts for a long time. Savvy?" he said to the vocal man, who immediately turned and hurried off the porch and out into the street. Jake motioned for Boqin to bring everyone into the store. Silently, the men jumped off the wagon. "Women, too," Jake said. And the women were helped off the wagon by the men. They all stood in a huddle beside the wagon. "C'mon," Jake said. "Let's go inside."

"Maybe betta we wait outside, Mista Jake," Boqin said.

"No. Yer come inside so we can get everyone fitted with new clothes and boots. Then we're goin' over to the barber shop and get haircuts."

"Please, Mista Jake. Be betta if you buy scissols and comb. We cut hail."

Jake studied Boqin for a minute and then decided he must have had some bad experiences at a barber shop. "All right," he said. "I'll do that. Now let's go inside."

Having seen the scene outside, the shopkeeper was waiting for them behind a counter. Jake walked up to him and said, "Howdy. We need to get these folks all new duds including hats and boots and whatever the women need for themselves and for the babies. The women can have their choice of clothes. They all need work gloves, too, and we need a large tent. Yer got one?"

"Yes, sir. The biggest I have is a twelve by nineteen army canvas complete with poles, stakes, guys, and guy ropes."

"How much?"

"I can let that one go for twelve dollars."

"Uh-huh. Need a tarp, too. Got any cots?"

"Yes, sir. Got those, too. Tarp'd be another dollar. Army folding cots of hardwood and canvas."

"How much?"

"They'd be a dollar two bits each."

"Wal, I'm gonna need ten. How much for a volume discount?"

"How about ten bucks for all ten?"

"Deal. Now how 'bout blankets?"

"Yes, sir. Would they be for use with the cot under the tent?"

"Yes."

"Then I recommend these in size eleven-four heavy-duty wool in gray."

"How much?"

"Two dollars each . . . but I could let ten go at eighteen dollars."

"All right. I'll take the tent, cots, blankets, clothes, hats, boots, gloves. And also, two fifty-pound bags a rice and ten pounds a tea if yer got it. And one a those Winchester repeaters in twenty-two rimfire caliber. And ammo."

"Yes, sir. Be ten dollars for the gun, and cartridges are forty cents per box of one hundred."

"All right, I'll take five boxes. Write me up a bill and be mindful I ain't one to be gouged." He stared hard at the shopkeeper.

"Yes, sir. I am fair and square in all my dealings. John Garner's the name." He held his hand out for a shake, and Jake took it with a strong grip to seal the deal.

"Jake Brighton's mine. Oh, and throw in a big bag a that hard candy yer got there on the counter. I'll be at the barber shop if yer need me."

"What flavor of candies?"

"We like orange."

"Yes, sir. I have that."

"All right, fine. Oh yeah. They're gonna need a comb and pair a barberin' scissors."

Jake turned to speak to Boqin. He gave him his orders on all the clothing and gear and told him the rifle was for him to hunt varmints to eat.

"But, Mista Jake," Boqin said. "You buy ten of evelthing. We only nine."

"Wal, I'll be comin' to visit regularly so I need a place to sleep, too." He smiled.

168

After his shave, mustache trim, and hair-cut, Jake came around the corner from the barber shop to see a commotion going on in front of the general store and drovers at the rear of Jake's wagon. They were in town probably with a herd outside town on a drive north. Three cowboys on horses were whooping it up while they had all of Jake's crew bunched up like cattle and were twirling loops to throw on them, no doubt to drag the Chinamen into the street. He took off running, and he was closing fast when the loudest cowboy threw a loop around Niu. The cowboy dallied his rope around his saddle horn and started backing his horse to set tension on the rope. It was a mistake. Niu set his feet and braced his body against a hitching rail. He began to reel in the rope and pulled horse and rider to him. When the horse was up to the hitching rail, Niu looped the rope around the horse's neck and tied it off to the rail. Then he lifted the loop off his body and with a deadpan face offered it up to the cowboy.

By this time Jake was on the scene, and just as the cowboy pulled his pistol, Jake jumped and struck a mighty blow with the butt of his own pistol right between the cowboy's shoulder blades. The cowboy dropped his pistol in the dirt and let out a wild yell. Jake grabbed the cowboy's belt and pulled him off the saddle, throwing him to the ground. The cowboy landed with a grunt, and Jake kicked him in the head, knocking him out cold. That was it for that one.

Jake spun in time to catch the loop about to fall around him. He threw it off and pointed his pistol at one of the other mounted cowboys who had his pistol out, leveled at Jake. Jake fastened his hardened stare on the fellow and, with the intense concentration of a stalking lion, slowly took three steps toward him. He was a kid. Couldn't a been more than eighteen years old. Jake took notice that the cowboy's pistol was not cocked, and there was a hint of tremor in his hand. The pistol might have been double action, but he doubted it. That meant if the cowboy cocked his pistol, he was dead, because while the boy was thumbing back the hammer Jake would be pulling his trigger. An instant more and the third cowboy was twirling his loop behind Jake. He was about to toss it when a loop dropped around him, and he was yanked from the saddle. Jake sensed something was happening behind him but did not take his eyes off the kid with the drawn pistol. He said in a low, calm voice, "Yer ever kilt a man, son?"

The cowboy didn't answer. "It ain't a easy thing to do. And it stays with yer the rest a yer life. I know cuz I kilt a few. Now. Yer see. Here we are in this Mexican standoff, but I got the drop on yer cuz this here is a double-action pistol. It means all I have to do is pull the trigger and it fires. Yer still gotta cock yer six-shooter. While yer doin' that I'll be killin' yer, and just so's yer know, I am Rawhide Jake Brighton."

When Jake said the kid's pistol wasn't cocked, the kid blinked. He snapped a peek at his pistol and then returned his stare to Jake. He sat in his saddle for a minute, then looked past Jake at his trussed-up partner. He holstered his pistol and said, "I'm gonna git a drink. Yer comin'?" The feller Jake kicked was coming to, and the kid dismounted, helped him up, and said, "C'mon, Tommy. Les' git a drink."

Jake took a quick glance around and saw that Wes was letting his rope go slack, and the other feller was releasing himself from Wes's loop. Then the three of them, leading their horses, walked up to one of the saloons. Jake and Wes stood side by side and watched them go.

"Kinda becomin' a habit, ain't it?" Wes said.

"What's that?"

"Me arrivin' right in the nick of time to save yer life or pull yer bacon outta the fire."

"Aw, look at 'em. They was all just boys. Off a drive havin' fun. They weren't gonna hurt nobody."

"Maybe so. But in a couple hours they's gonna be full a whiskey courage, and then they might hurt someone."

"Yeah. I prob'ly oughtta git outta town so I don't have to kill nobody. So, where we at — I owe yer one now?"

"Le's see. I saved yer in the Brazos and from the Comanche, and yer saved me from Jonesboro. So yeah. Guess I'll let it go at one." He slapped Jake on the back and grinned. "That our crew?"

"Yeah. C'mon over. I'll introduce yer."

"Boqin, this is Wes Wilson, my partner in this fencing company. And this big fellah is Niu. His name means ox."

"Uh-huh. I kin see that."

"Boqin is the foreman. He speaks English."

Boqin bowed with his hands folded in front of him.

"Wal, nice to meet y'all. Good luck with the work." He turned to Jake and said, "I'll be workin' 'round here and up to Childress so's yer know where to find me next time yer git in trouble." He grinned at Jake and jumped into the saddle. "Adiós, amigo," he said as he touched his spurs to Noble's side.

Jake arrived at the big pasture with his crew and saw that the Flying XC farmers had what looked like about five hundred acres disked up. The surveyors had the line for the fences set out, and it looked like everything was ready to go. He picked a nice site under a stand of cottonwood trees by Comanche Creek and told Boqin to set up camp there. The wire spools were piled up by the wagon with the posts in it just down from the campsite. He and Boqin looked over the survey line and the supplies, then Jake pulled back a tarp and showed Boqin all the tools. "We set camp up, put out supplies. Be up with sun," Boqin said.

"Good. Tear into it," Jake said as he smiled at Boqin. Then he rode off for the bunkhouse.

As spring gradually gave way to summer, the big pasture was sprouting green seedlings of grass to be eventually cut for hay. The fence around the pasture on two sides was all installed. Comanche Creek and Long Creek provided the barrier to the other two sides. Jake's crew was working on the eastern border of the Flying XC, and Jake had commissioned ten windmills for

Xavier Calhoun. He arranged for the purchases directly by Xavier from Robert Corrigan, Gracie's new husband. All together Jake was making a fair amount of money and was, with Walt's permission, socking it away in a locked box he kept in the ranch safe.

One warm evening in July, Jake was sitting by himself on one end of the porch of the bunkhouse with his crossed boots up on the porch rail. Crickets were chirping, and fireflies danced out across the lot in front of the bunkhouse. On the other end of the porch a pair of cowboys were making quiet, peaceful music, one with a harmonica and the other with a guitar. Several of the crew sat around them listening. The rowdy bunch was inside playing cards, and their bursts of cursing and laughter frequently disturbed the peace on the porch. But such was the life of the bunkhouse.

Casually he smoked a cigar and was mentally going over his Texas accomplishments of the last six months or so. Shared in the capture or killing of eleven rustlers and recovered seven hundred head of rustled cattle. He had already collected from Loving his share for the rustlers and the cattle. The fencing business was off to a good start, and now he was a windmill salesman, too. Lately though the detective work had gone dry, and there didn't seem to be any rustlers around. He was proud, though, that despite his extracurricular businesses he never slacked off on his detective duties and relentlessly continued to patrol the western and southern borders of Flying XC range.

"Whatcha doin', cowboy?" The voice was on his left side and a little behind him, just above a whisper. Jake dropped his feet to the floor, jumped out of his chair, and spun to his left. His right hand automatically moved across his waist to his left side to grab hold of his pistol, which was absent because, as was the custom, his pistol belt was hanging on a hook inside.

"Gol dern, Walt. You scared hell outta me."

"Wal, that's good then, huh?" He chuckled, and Jake joined in. "Mind if I join yer?"

"Heck no. Here. Sit right here. Want a cigar?"

"Don't mind if I do."

Jake pulled a fresh stogie from his inside vest pocket and handed it to Walt. As he did, he remembered his pocket pistol was still there in his vest pocket and hoped Walt didn't notice. Apparently, he did not. In the flare of the match when Walt struck it and held it to his cigar, Jake got a clear look at

Walt's face. He appeared to be calm. "Wal, still no rain. What's it been? Five months now?" Walt inquired idly.

"Reckon that's right."

"Good thing we're puttin' in those wind-mill wells. Looks to me like even the flow of the creeks is slowin' down below normal. That ain't good. Thanks fer brokerin' those windmills fer us. We're probably gonna need more." He smiled and puffed his cigar.

"My pleasure. Anythin' I can do to help."

"And turn a profit, eh?"

Jake immediately tensed up. He rolled his cigar to the other side of his mouth then back again. He breathed out slowly when Walt said, "Oh I cain't fault a man for grabbin' holt of opportunity when it comes along. So, more power to yer." He took another drag of his cigar and seemed to be absently gazing out over the lot. "We don't git enuff rain this year, next roundup we're gonna sell purtin near the whole herd, calves and all. Keep just as many bulls and cow-calf pairs as the big pasture can feed and that's it. Ol' Xavier's a smart feller. He hedges his bets real good. But I don't know 'bout that wire. Always liked the open range. But heck, I'm just an old bull past ruttin' ready to be culled. Yer heard 'bout the trouble to the east a us with the wire cuttin'?"

"Heard somethin' 'bout it. What's happenin'?"

"Wal, looks like the small ranchers that don't own any range are goin' out at night an' cuttin' the fences of the large landowners. Small ranchers say they can't git they's herds to water and graze, and if there's drought a comin', they's worried they's gonna lose they's herds. So they's takin' things into they's own hands and cuttin' the fences so they's cattle can git through to water and grass. But like us here on the Flyin' XC, big ranchers don't like it cuz we're tryin' to save our graze and water for our own herd on our land. Xavier ain't fencin' any land that don't belong to him. Some of the other big ranchers are, but we ain't. Anyways, I think yer oughta ride on down thataway and take a looksee."

"First thing in the mornin' then."

"Rode out thataway the other day. Yer crew's doin' real good. Makin' over four hunnert feet a day. Yer foreman, what's his name?"

"Boqin."

"Yeah, him. Said he thinks they can do five hunnert feet on the flat ground."

"Yep. They's mighty industrious. That's why I hired all Celestials. I think only

177

cowboys, when they's workin', work as hard as Chinamen. Honest, too. And honorable."

"Yep. Wal, I better git back to the house. My dearest wife, Millie, will be wondering where I got off to. I'll take this here seegar with me though. Mighty fine. See yer in the mornin'."

"See yer in the mornin'."

Jake was out on the range before sunup. He rode southeast with the wind at his back along the eastern border for four hours when he thought he saw the large tent. He pulled his hat brim down to shade his eyes, and sure enough there it was standing like a small temple by a grove of cottonwoods at the confluence of Beaver Creek and Turkey Creek. Glancing around as he rode up, he saw only one woman there washing dishes in a small tub of hot water. He stopped by her and from his saddle he smiled and said, "Where are the others?" Before she answered she returned his smile and bowed many times but looked like she was trying to figure out what he said. Jake heard the brief cry of a baby come from the tent. He figured she was left there to tend the babies and handle the camp duties. The other two women must be out with the crew. "Where are the others?" He repeated himself and tried to indicate other people and their whereabouts by making motions with his arms and expressions with his face. She probably guessed what he was asking and spoke in Chinese while she pointed down the fence line to the south. *"Xièxienǐ."* Jake said thank you, translating from his meager lexicon of Mandarin Chinese. She answered in Mandarin, *"Nǐshìshòuhuānyíng de zhǔ-rén,"* meaning "you are welcome, master." Jake smiled again and doffed his hat before he turned and rode off to the south.

In a mile he saw the crew working down in a shallow hollow. Several posts were laid out on the ground ten feet apart in a long line. Four men were turning two-man augers for postholes, so they were digging two postholes at a time. Boqin and the two women were setting the posts, shoveling in dirt, and packing it with heavy tamping rods. The Belgians, the wagon, Changlei, and Niu were nowhere in sight. He walked Jasper up near to Boqin, who saw him coming and had a wide smile as he walked toward Jake. Jake swung out of the saddle and let Jasper's reins drop to the ground. Jasper wasted no time nosing through the grass to find the choice green sprouts to crop. "Howdy, Boqin," Jake called.

"Howdy, *zhǔrén* Jake. What you do hele now? Not payday."

"There's been reports of fence cuttings out thisaway. Thought I'd come out and take a looksee. Yer had any trouble?"

"No, but a week ago men came. Ask us what we doing. I say, building fence. They say fol who? I say Lawhide Jake. They lide off." He smiled a toothy grin.

"Mmmm. All right. Let's go over the books, and then I'll take a ride up the line. Make sure everything's all right."

After Jake finished his examination of the books, he caught Jasper, mounted, and trotted him up back along the completed fence line. He had ridden about five miles when he saw a rider a long way out on the east side of the fence riding toward him at an angle heading southwest. He stopped and took out his spyglass. The first thing he identified was a Palouse horse, and thinking it was probably Johnny Raymer he waited the few minutes until he came into focus to confirm. He raised his arm and waved. Johnny waved back. When they met up, Johnny pushed back his hat and said, "Howdy, Jake. On the wrong side of the range ain't yer?"

"Howdy, Johnny." He didn't want to say that Walt had sent him over to snoop around, but it did raise the question: why did Walt send him? "Checkin' on my fencin' crew. Heard tell of some fence cuttin' goin' on. Yer seen anything?"

"Matter a fact, I was headin' fer yer crew to git 'em to make a fix. There's a gap in the fence on up 'bout a mile. Some varmints cut the wire and pulled out ten posts. Yer want a take a looksee?"

"Yep." They rode north and came to the hole in the fence. It was a good hundred feet wide. Jake stared at it for a minute, turning his head from side to side. He swung out of the saddle, grounded Jasper's reins, walked over to the damaged area, and looked down at the sign. All shod horses. He squatted and looked closely at a set of prints. One print showed a nail missing and a crack in the shoe of the right front hoof. Then he stood and looked around. Just like Johnny said, all five strands of the wire were cut, and the posts had been roped and pulled out. They lay strewn about the gap in the fence. He walked over to the south standing post and, grabbing it with both hands, shook it to see if it was loose. It was, and it was leaning to the south from the tension of the wire pulling on it. He walked across to the north standing pole and checked it. It was in the same condition except it was leaning north. But he cracked a slight smile because there was a wide and long swath of dried blood on the post. Somebody got whipped by snipped barbwire.

"All right. Gotta git the crew up here to fix this. Gonna lose a day's production."

"Wal, Calhoun's still gotta pay fer it, right?"

"Oh, yeah. I jest like to keep the crew movin' down the line. Let's go. Yer might as well tag along. Let's ride this sign out. See where it goes."

They followed the trail of four horses for about six miles until they came to Wolf Creek. It was easy enough to see where they went into the creek, but there was no sign of them coming out. Jake motioned for Johnny to come close. "You follow the creek north for one hour. If yer don't find anything in an hour, turn around and come back to this spot. I'll do the same thing to the south. But if yer find something stay there, and if yer ain't back here in two hours I'll head up yer way and find yer. Yer do the same thing fer me. Savvy?"

"Yep." They walked their horses into the creek and turned in opposite directions. It was a narrow creek, but four horses in single file could easily stay in the middle and off the creek banks. Jake worked Jasper carefully through the rocky bottom and in a half hour arrived at the confluence of the Wichita River. Well, not ever having been there before, it was new to Jake. He sat in the saddle and looked down the river and then up. They probably swam their horses down river with the current and who knows where they could have come out. He turned Jasper around, and they climbed the shallow bank out of the creek. They trotted back to where they left Johnny to find him already there.

"Find anything?" Jake asked.

"Nope. Came to where the water was just a trickle. Never saw any sign. Gave it up. Boy, this creek was a lot longer last year."

"No rain. Yeah. I came to the river and gave it up. Wal, we can probably still git a hot dinner at the camp. You like rice?" Jake grinned.

They came to the camp and were in luck. The crew was just sitting down for noon-time dinner. Jake pulled Boqin aside and told him about the hole in the fence. He finished with, "Yer'll have to make a splice wrapped to a set a H posts. When are Changlei and Niu due back?"

"Should be back today," Boqin said with several nods of his head.

"How come yer sent Niu along with Changlei?"

"He vely stlong, vely fast, and vely smalt.

183

He take cae any trouble."

"Have yer had any trouble?"

"Month ago two cowboys tly steal holses."

"What happened?"

"Niu scale them so bad they lun off," he said, and again the toothy smile spread across his face.

"Boqin. This shines," Johnny said, holding up his bowl of boiled rabbit stew with rice on the side. "What y'all call it?"

"Tùdùn."

"What's that mean?"

"Labbit stew," Boqin said with his toothy smile.

"Oh."

"Yer know, rabbit tastes pretty good roasted, too. But this is tasty," Jake said as he nodded his head and smiled all around at everyone sitting in the ring, especially the women who had prepared the stew. "Wal —" he started to say when he stood up and stopped in mid-sentence as he looked out over the range. Riders were coming in from the east.

Jake set down his tin plate of stew and went over to where the horses were tied to a rope hitch. He pulled his rifle from its scabbard. Johnny followed and did the same. The riders stopped a little under ten yards away and sat their saddles. Jake, Johnny, and

Boqin stood in front of the campfire with their rifles cradled in their arms. Boqin had the twenty-two in his arms.

"Howdy," the older feller of the four said in a gravelly voice. "Name's Seamus McCarthy. Own the Lazy Rocking M east a here. Whatch y'all doin'?" He was a big old Irish stockman with a wild salt and pepper beard and hair hanging out from under his hat. His face and hands were the color of burnt umber and wrinkled heavily by years in the sun. His nose was decidedly hawkish, and his deep-blue eyes were intense. He wore a cartridge belt over his shoulder and across his chest, and what looked like a big forty-five in his holster and a thirty-eight stuck in his waistband. Across his lap he rested his Winchester. Jake took an immediate disliking to the man. He gave the impression that he thought he was somebody.

"We're buildin' fence. What's it look like?" Jake spoke in a low tone, but loud enough to be heard by all. He glared at the old feller with a fixed stare of challenge.

The intense blue eyes took on a deadly stare. "Just tryin' to be neighborly, mister. Yer don't need to git all scratchy."

"What happened to that feller's arm?" Jake said as he nodded toward one of the cowboys whose shirtsleeve was torn and blood stained. Through the torn sleeve a white bandage could be seen.

"Mesquite sideswiped him. Look here, I ain't got time to dilly-dally. Now yer buildin' fence across range that's been open since the beginnin' a time. And that ain't right. I been usin' this here range fer over five years to graze and water my cattle. We always turned 'em out around this here Beaver Creek range, and nobody said nothin'. Now yer fencin' it. How's that?"

"Range is owned legal by the Flyin' XC, under proper deed for moren' five years. Years past, Mister Calhoun didn't mind sharin' the graze and water. Now his herd is a dern size bigger, and there is probably drought comin' on. He can't share no more. So, he's fencin' in."

"And fencin' us out. We cain't let that happen. Farmers keep comin', and they's fencin', too. Always chasin' the damn squatters off. Rustlers stealin' me blind. It's gotta stop." He glared at them, and it was quiet except for the creaking of the leather as he shifted his weight in his saddle. Jake tightened his grip on the rifle.

"It's all gotta stop," the old man repeated as he pulled off his hat and wiped out the sweatband with his red bandana. "Gonna have to run yer off, son."

"There's women and children in this camp."

"I don't see nuthin' but yeller skin."

"You come against this camp with women and children in it, yeller or not, then yer ain't no better'n a savage, and you'll be going against God Almighty, the code of the West, and me."

"And who are you, mister?"

"I am Rawhide Jake Brighton."

The old man blinked, and his eyes dulled out a little. The other three shifted in their saddles, and their gun hands moved closer to their pistols.

"I heared a yer. Yer a killer."

"That's right. And this is Johnny Raymer. Yer heared a his shootin' skills, too." There was more saddle creaking. "We're standin' here with our Winchesters. If yer move, we're gonna kill yer. Johnny, yer take the old man, and I'll take the young one that looks like him. Then if they don't turn tail, we'll take the last two. Boqin'll probably get one, too." Jake slowly shifted his feet around to take up a shooting stance.

The old feller sat silent for over a minute. "All right, we're leavin'. But this ain't over," he said at last.

They turned their horses and rode away toward the east. Jake waited until they were out of sight, and then he went over and squatted by the tracks they left. Johnny came up beside him and said, "I see it. Same cracked shoe."

Jake stood up and said low and slow, "We better sleep with our boots on tonight. If yer git my drift." Then he called out, "Boqin, let's tear down the camp, and when Chenglei gets here we can load up and move it down to the end of the fence line. In fact," he said as he shaded his eyes with the flat of his hand, stared down to the southwest, and saw a large moving dot weaving through the mesquite, coming across the prairie, "looks like they's a comin' now."

They got the camp moved, and Jake sent Boqin, Changlei, Niu, and one other man along with tools to mend the hole in the fence, and, as an afterthought, he asked Johnny to go along to provide protection. They got the job done and returned in time for supper. After the camp chores were done for the day, the crew sat around the campfire talking. Boqin, Changlei, Johnny, and Jake sat together in one little group, the rest of the men in another, and the women in the tent tending to the babies and other domestic duties. Four of the men were playing a table game with small tiles. Niu watched over the shoulder of one of them.

"What's that they's a playin'," Johnny said to Boqin.

"That Mahjong. Old Chinese game."

"Uh-huh. Well, do they wrap it up soon so's we can all git to our bunks?"

"Yes, Mista Johnny. You sleep my cot. Vely nice."

"No, no. Thas all right. I'll bunk out here under the stars with my head on my saddle like I always do. I like it better." He yawned big and stretched his arms over his head. Then he sauntered off to his saddle and spread out his bedroll. Jake went into the tent and took note of the sheets hung from the tent top to partition off separate spaces for the married couples. He spread his roll on his cot and heard Boqin speak sharply in Chinese. There were a few exclamations from the men, and they put away the tiles. In fifteen minutes, the camp was asleep.

But sure enough, long about midnight Jake woke to the sound of Jasper's loud warning neighs. He pulled back the tent flap and looked out into the moonlight to see Johnny already running for his horse. Jake grabbed his rifle and cartridge belt, and tore out of the tent. About a half mile to the north, he saw the riders silhouetted under the light of the flaming torches they held over their heads. They were coming fast, and the torches were streaming fire and flaring wildly to their front in the north wind that pushed from behind so that they looked like large fireballs on the ends of the torch shafts. The torchers galloped their horses three on one side of the fence and three on the other. Strangely, the thought ran through Jake's mind that they had cut the fence again, and production would be delayed again. He shook it off.

"Boqin!" he yelled. Immediately Boqin was at his side. "Have everybody pick up a shovel and start clearing the grass about a hundred yards to the north of the camp." He pointed north. "Out there. Do you understand?"

"Yes, Mista Jake. Make filebreak."

"Exactly," he shouted and just for a second looked curiously at Boqin. How did he know that?

By the time Jake got to Jasper, he was crow hopping against the hitching rope and making the big boys nervous. Johnny was riding bareback at a gallop to close the distance between him and the riders. Jake untied Jasper's hackamore bridle from the hitching rope, grabbed a hunk of Jasper's mane, and vaulted onto the paint's back. Jasper wanted to run from the fire, but Jake reined and spurred him around to catch up with

Johnny. Jake came alongside Johnny and hollered, "You take the three on the left. I'll take the others on the east side a the fence."

Jake veered off to the right and raced Jasper at a full run for about two hundred yards and then pulled up. He tied him to a fence post and ran up to the next post. There he laid the forestock of his rifle on the top of the post and started to take careful aim but paused when he was shocked and sickened by the sight of the riders torching the grass around the fence on both sides. He fired and knocked one back in his saddle, and he dropped his torch. It immediately ignited the dry grass. His horse turned and ran with him lurching in the saddle. He heard Johnny's rifle bark. A wall of flame quickly formed in front of the riders, and in the light of the flame they were well illuminated. Jake fired again and hit another one who had already tossed his torch. He flipped out of the saddle, and the third rider held back until the fire had advanced far enough to give him the cover of darkness. Jake could barely make him out picking up his partner and riding off to the east. There was no clear shot, but Jake fired six shots in rapid succession just the same. He thought he saw the rider jerk but couldn't be sure. Then he heard Johnny fire three more times, and there was a two-shot pistol report.

The orange/red flames shot twenty feet into the air in front of Jake. The fire was gaining speed and ferocity as it roared south in the stiff wind out of the north. It hissed and popped, and red-hot embers were swirling around like swarms of locust. He looked to the west for Johnny and saw him running on foot in frantic retreat from the fire. Where was the Palouse? Jake untied Jasper and vaulted onto his back again and spurred him to intercept Johnny. Jasper fought it, but Jake held him hard and ran parallel to the fire line, urging the big paint faster, faster. He talked soothing things into Jasper's ear, but Jasper wasn't buying it and strained at the hackamore. The whites of his eyes were flaring in the dark, and the combination of effort and heat from the fire were lathering him up. But he obeyed the rein and the spur. Johnny was slowing. Jake bellowed, "Johnny!" Then he swooped Jasper in beside him and held down his hand. Johnny grabbed it and in one motion pulled himself onto Jasper's back behind Jake. Jake let Jasper run away from the flames even as they singed his tail.

"I think I got two a 'em," Johnny yelled into Jake's ear.

"Me, too. Where's the Palouse?" Jake hollered back.

"Don't know. He got away from me."

In a minute they got to the camp, where everyone except Changlei was frantically shoveling and throwing dirt. Changlei about had the big boys hitched to the wagon. That was a good idea. Jake and Johnny grabbed shovels and joined in the melee of dirt throwing. Presently, Jake looked up, stared at the oncoming fire, looked at the meager fire break, and decided. "Boqin," he yelled. "Tell Changlei to pull the wagon over to the tent. Everybody throw their shovels in the wagon and get everything they can out of the tent into the wagon. We gotta git outta here. Fire's comin' too fast. It's spreadin' out all over. We gotta outrun it to the river."

Boqin called out his orders. In a cacophony of Chinese shouting back and forth, everyone ran for the tent. Changlei pulled the wagon around so the back was facing the tent opening. He hopped off the driver's seat, ran around, and opened the tailgate when the wagon started moving. He raced to the front of the big boys and caught their bridles to hold them steady. The whites of their eyes were now showing, too.

Johnny was making a visual search in every direction for the Palouse. "I don't see him anywhere," he shouted through the wind to Jake, who came up beside him. The wind was blowing against their clothing, flapping the sleeves of their shirts, flying their bandanas like flags in a gale, and bending back their hat brims. "We gotta run, Johnny, or we're gonna burn up," Jake yelled. Johnny nodded his head, and they turned to run for the wagon when of a sudden it was dead calm. A minute later the wind kicked up again, but it was swirling, turned direction, and blew hard out of the south. The moving wall of flame stalled and shrunk as the wind blew the fire back onto already burned-out ground where there was no more fuel. "Git the shovels," Jake hollered as he and Johnny ran back to the wagon waving their arms wildly. "Boqin! Boqin! The wind's shifted. We can beat down the flame. Git everybody back out there with shovels. Throw dirt on the flame. C'mon! Hurry! Hurry!"

The leading edge of the fire was a good five hundred yards long, but the crew attacked it like a precision drill team. As flame was snuffed out, they leap-frogged each other to extinguish still burning grass and scrub. One of the women brought out a bucket of water with three ladles that was drunk up quickly, and she ran back for more. They all sweat it out heavily in the heat of the fire and in the strain of the work. But they fought on. Nobody quit, and nobody was overcome by smoke inhalation as the wind remained in their favor.

After four hours of exhausting hard work in the inferno, Jake leaned on his shovel breathing heavily and looked around at the fire perimeter. He saw no flame except for several fence posts that were still burning. "Boqin," he shouted, "let's git water on them burning posts. See if we can save 'em."

After the fence posts were extinguished Jake called everybody to gather around. They formed a semi-circle before him, even the women with the babies, whom they gently rocked in their arms. Jake grinned. He looked like a scarecrow with the stark white of his teeth shining in his black, soot-covered face. "Look at the feller next to yer." Boqin translated. Gradually, grins popped out on all the faces, then Jake said, "Yer ain't Chinese no more. Yer Negroes." Boqin translated, and everyone was laughing. Jake let it run a minute or two, then he said, "Yer all fought hard and brave. I'm proud of yer. Yer saved the range. Thank you." He removed his hat and bowed slightly. Boqin had translated, and they all returned the bow. "And thank the good

Lord for changing the wind direction for us."

"Amen," Johnny said, and the crew repeated the amen.

While they were cleaning up and reorganizing, the sound of hoofbeats came from the north. Everyone stopped and looked in that direction. In the gray light of the dawn, they saw some twenty riders bearing down on them. Jake ran for his rifle. Johnny stood still and held his gaze on the riders. In a minute he called out, "That there is Walt. I know how he sits the saddle. And Flyin' XC crew."

Walt Guthrie and his cowboys pounded through the burn and kicked up a cloud of black dust behind them. Then they broke into the unburnt grass and stopped before the tent, where Jake and Johnny were waiting for them. "Howdy, boss." Both Jake and Johnny extended their greeting at the same time. Their smiling faces were still smeared and smudged from the firefight even after they had rinsed off with water. They both stood with their hands folded over the muzzles of their butt-grounded Winchesters and were a little puffed up, expecting a pat on the back.

Walt sat in his saddle and said, "Who started the fire? And don't tell me it was lightning cuz there ain't no clouds."

Jake's and Johnny's proud smiles immediately disappeared. "We was attacked," Johnny blurted out.

Walt swung out of the saddle and walked deliberately to face Jake and Johnny. "Who attacked yer?" he said. And Jake told the story, beginning with the discovery of the fence cut.

When Jake finished, Johnny added, "It was a miracle, boss. If that wind didn't turn, we would be crispy like a roasted rabbit fer sure."

"Uh-huh. Wal, thank the Almighty for that. We smelled the smoke and came a runnin'. If the wind stayed outta the north, the range'd still be burnin'. Coulda lost acres and acres a grass right when we need it bad now. Guess I gotta go have a talk with McCarthy." He turned to the cowboys who had dismounted and were milling around smoking and joking. "Y'all head on back to the headquarters and git back to work. Jake and Johnny got everything under control here. Turn Cactus Jack and that wagon 'round when yer come to it." He turned back to the two firefighters and said, "We loaded a wagon up with barrels a water, shovels, and setch. Guess we didn't need 'em. Yer and yer crew did real fine. Thank ye and thank them fer me. Now, yer boys come with me. We're gonna visit Seamus McCarthy. Watch yerselves 'round him. Thinks he's purty fast with a shootin' iron."

"We gotta catch my horse first. Can I use yer horse, boss? I don't think Jasper'd take to me."

"Hurry on up then. I ain't got all day."

In a half hour Johnny was back trailing the Palouse behind Walt's horse. He got the Palouse saddled and ready to go, and Walt said, "All right. Let's move 'em out." They crossed Beaver Creek, rode east, swam the Wichita, and rode through dry country for another six miles. Jake kept his head on a swivel watching for trouble and looking for water. He made a mental note that there wasn't a creek or spring anywhere in sight. He hefted his canteen and was glad he filled it before they left Beaver Creek. Just as a trickle of sweat made a thin trail down the side of his face from under his hat, they came within sight of ranch buildings set with cottonwoods around them. "That'd be the Lazy Rocking M," Walt said.

The closer they came, the more Jake could see of the outfit. There was a weathered barn with corral lots and two shacks, each with a covered boardwalk in front and an outhouse behind it. In front, a little away from the shacks, was a stone well wall with a windlass over it. McCarthy stood on one of the boardwalks in front of the door with his hands on his hips and his feet spread. He watched their every move. But he did not move an inch even the closer they came.

The three rode abreast of each other and reined in at the same time about ten feet from the hitching rail. "Howdy, Seamus," Walt said.

"Walt. What brings yer down thisaway?"

"Think yer probably know why."

"Don't know what yer talkin' 'bout."

"Yer don't mind if we have a looksee in yer bunkhouse then."

"Hep yerself. It ain't purty."

"Uh-huh. Johnny. Jake," Walt said as he nodded for Jake and Johnny to go over to the bunkhouse. Jake swung out of the saddle and kept an eye on McCarthy as he walked the short distance to the bunkhouse shack. He drew his pistol and slowly pushed the door open. The light was dim inside, but he could see a table on one end and six bunks in a line toward the other end. There was a man laid out on each of four bunks. Two had bandanas over their heads and the other two moaned laboriously with every breath. They looked like they were semi-conscious at best. Jake cautiously backed out and walked with Johnny over to Walt, who had dismounted and was standing in a face-off in front of McCarthy. "Wal?" Walt said while keeping his full concentration on McCarthy.

"Four men. Two are goners, and the other two are jist about there. All of 'em shot."

"What happened, Seamus?" Walt questioned.

McCarthy still had not moved. In fact, all that was moving of his person were his eyes and his brown bandana fluttering in the breeze. "If it's any a yer bizness, after we left yer camp" — he glanced at Jake — "we come back here to find horse thiefs trying to make off with my remuda. We got in a gunfight. Think they faired better'n us. But they ain't got any a my horses. Sent McKenzie to Wichita Falls for the doctor."

"Uh-huh. Yer know, Seamus, yer always was a good storyteller. An' they ain't no witnesses to say yer story ain't true. 'Cept me. Cuz, I know yer a liar, and yer lyin' now. Ain't yer?"

"Hell, no," he roared. "I ain't lyin'." Then he took on a menacing look. "It's jest like I said. An' if yer don't like it, I cain't hep it."

"Uh-huh. Wal, only a jackass would burn off graze, 'specially in a dry year like this one. Yer started that fire last night. So now

200

yer a liar and a jackass."

McCarthy's face began to turn crimson and his breathing more labored. His gun hand slowly drifted closer to his pistol butt.

"Go easy, now, Seamus."

"Yer callin' me a liar an' a jackass." He spat a stream of tobacco juice into the dirt.

"Yep, I am. But I was jist wonderin'. Yer ain't been a jackass since I know'd yer. So, why'd yer fire that grass?"

"Y'all are fencin' it off. That ain't right."

"Wal, it's more ain't right to burn off graze for no good reason, 'specially grass that ain't yours."

"I been grazin' that range for better'n five years, and yer tryin' to fence me out. My stock is out there right now. If I cain't have it, nobody can."

"So, see. Yer was lyin'. I know yer herd is out there. Matter a fact I was fixin' in a few days to gather them up and drive back across the river. But — ain't nobody gonna burn my range unless I say so. What 'bout the women and children yer put in danger?"

"Nothin' but yeller trash," he sneered, and just for a second, he looked to the ground to spit. At that instant, in a rage, Jake lunged and smacked McCarthy a good one right between the eyes with the butt of his pistol. The big man grunted, and his sharp blue eyes went dull as they rolled around in their sockets. He hit the boardwalk headfirst with a thud, and a little cloud of dust puffed out from beneath him when his body landed. He was out cold, and a trickle of blood flowed down from the bridge of his nose into his beard.

"He had no call to say that," Jake said in a quiet voice.

"Wal, throw a pail a water on him," Walt said. "See if we can wake him up and find out when he expects that doctor to git here. If he's a comin'. That McKenzie coulda rode off and ain't comin' back."

Johnny fetched a bucket of water from the well and splashed it on McCarthy's face. The Irishman groaned, sputtered, blew water from his mouth, and rolled over onto his side and rubbed his head. "Who done that?" he growled.

"Don't matter who done it. Now git on your feet. When's that doctor comin'?"

"Ain't gonna be no never mind fer yer, Walt Guthrie," he growled low like a threatening wolf baring his teeth. He feigned like he was groggy as he got to his feet, then suddenly jerked his pistol from his sash and shot Walt, who flew backwards from the bullet impact and landed on his rear, sitting up. Four shots exploded, and McCarthy's body shuddered four times as Jake and Johnny each shot him twice. He crashed to the floor, and the lifeblood drained out of him through the four bullet holes. He rolled on his back and with a wicked grin said, "See yer bastards in hell."

Walt jumped up, and his forty-five roared as he pumped two slugs into McCarthy's chest. That did it. Seamus McCarthy was dead.

Jake and Johnny looked curiously at Walt. He looked back at them, then down to the belt buckle for his pistol belt. It was broken, and imbedded in the belt buckle for his britches was a thirty-eight slug. He pulled out the mushroom shaped lead and held it up. "Ever onced in a while" — he held the slug higher and stared at it like he was inspecting a gold nugget — "a feller gits lucky."

"What'd yer say? I can't hear. My ears are all plugged up from muzzle blast, but I guess yer ain't been plugged," Jake said with a grin. Walt started laughing. Johnny and Jake joined in, and the crescendo grew until Johnny said, "Boss I ain't never seen yer laugh."

Walt said, "Yeah, wal, yer might never see it agin, so shut yer yap and slurp the cream. Savvy?"

"Yeah, boss. I got yer," Johnny said in between guffaws.

After a few moments, Walt stared at the slug and said, "Lucky it hit my buckles, an' lucky it was a thirty-eight. Any bigger an' it woulda blown right through the buckles." He put the slug in his pants pocket, then pulled off his hat and gently slapped the side of his thigh. "Wal, guess we better catch some a they's horses and saddle 'em. Then we kin tie on those bodies and haul 'em up to the sheriff in Wichita Falls. Best turn the rest a the horses loose. Ain't no tellin' when someone might be back to look after 'em." He turned and looked to the west. "Still gotta run his cattle back over the river, too."

Johnny came out of the bunkhouse and said, "Only one left, boss. One of 'em just gave up the ghost."

"Wal, if that McKenzie feller left here — when do yer think?" Walt said.

"Prob'ly couldn't travel very fast cuz a the wounded. So, if they got back here say four o'clock, he mighta got off around five," Jake said as he turned and looked north and took out his watch. "Two hours to Wichita Falls. Half hour to rustle up the doc. Two hours back here. Say nine thirty he should be back at the latest. It's eight thirty now."

"All right. We'll give it an hour. If he ain't

204

back by then, he prob'ly ain't comin'. We'll have to take that varmint in to town ourselves. He bandaged up good, Johnny?"

"Reckon so."

"I'll look at him. Got battlefield experience, yer know," Jake said as he walked off to the bunkhouse.

"Uh-huh. C'mon, Johnny. Let's catch some horses," Walt said.

Jake came back out to where Walt and Johnny were saddling five horses at the corral fence. "Don't look good for him, boss. He's gut shot and looks like he lost a lotta blood. Startin' to turn pale. I sealed up the hole as best I could but . . . I don't know," Jake said with a slightly worried look on his face.

"Yer think he kin travel?"

"Sure, it'd kill him."

"Uh-huh. Wal, I gotta git back to the ranch, an' I cain't leave him here alone." Walt rubbed his chin for a moment or two and then said, "Johnny, yer take the bodies up to the sheriff. Tell him what happened. If he needs my affeedavid, tell him I said to send a deputy out to the Flyin' XC to collect it. Jake, yer stay here and do the best doctorin' yer can. If he croaks, then yer take the body on up to the sheriff. Meanwhile, Johnny, yer can head back down here with the doc. If yer don't run into Jake, then keep goin' till yer get back here. Y'all savvy?"

They nodded their heads a little sheepishly. "Shame it had to end for them like this all because a one bad man," Jake said with disgust.

"Ain't that the truth," Johnny said.

"All right. Let's git movin'," Walt said as he swung up into his saddle.

An hour after they left, the feller slipped into the afterlife. Jake wrapped and tied the body in a tarp and struggled but managed to get it draped over the saddle of the last horse left beside Jasper. He shut tight the bunkhouse door and the door to McCarthy's shack and led Jasper and the other horse into the barn, where he found some oats. He slipped oat bags over their noses and started searching around the barn to see if there was anything useful to be had. There was a lot of junk, but all he found of use to him were two pairs of wire pliers/cutters. He grunted at the irony, stuffed them into his saddlebag, and took off the oat bags. He slipped a piece of candy to Jasper and led him and the other horse to the trough, where he dumped in some fresh water for them. They drank their fill. He filled his canteen at the well, stepped into the saddle, and reined Jasper around to head north with the horse and its sorry cargo trailing behind on Jake's rope.

A month later and the fencing crew was across the Wichita working its way down to the Archer County line, where the survey line turned southwest. Jake had just come into camp with the payroll and supplies money on his person. The work for the day was done. He was there an hour and sitting around the campfire, sipping tea while talking with Boqin, when he looked up and saw a rider coming in from the south. He and his horse were a silhouette in the sunset, and Jake could see he was trotting his horse as the wind blew sideways the dust kicked up by the hoofbeats. He was heading directly for the camp. Jake stepped over to his saddle and pulled his Winchester from the scabbard. He cradled the rifle in his arms and waited for the rider, who came right up to the camp with his horse at a full trot before he pulled back on the reins stopping not more than eight feet in front of Jake and Boqin. He dismounted, took two steps forward, and stopped three feet away from Jake.

He was tall and skinny, and he stunk. His clothes were threadbare, dirty, and stained. His beard was tobacco stained and full of bacon grease. His long hair was greasy, and his rancid breath was laced with a strong odor of whiskey.

He stood in a slouch and stared intently at Jake and Boqin. After a long few seconds, Jake was about to say something when the feller grinned and revealed a mouth full of broken and decayed teeth. Then Jake heard the hammer cock behind him. Right close behind him.

"Don't be turnin' 'round," the feller said as he pulled his grimy pistol from its scuffed and cracked holster. "My pard's got the drop on yer. He's a 'pache breed. That's why yer never heard nuthin' 'cept the hammer a his pistol. An' like the fools yer are, yer had all yer attention on me."

"I thought Apache were peaceable now. What a yer want?" Jake said.

"Wal, we all got our mavericks, ain't we. We's jest driftin' down from the Nation. Been down in Seymour and heared 'bout yer outfit here. Figgered yer got a payroll. That's what we want."

Out of the corner of his eye, Jake saw Niu peeking through the very narrow slit of the tent flaps. "Ain't pay day yet. Got no payroll," Jake said with blazing fury flying from his eyes to the devilish eyes of the drifter, who then slapped Jake hard across the face.

Jake bent under the force of the blow and instinctively started to reach for his pistol.

"Tut, tut, tut," the drifter clucked. "Don't be doin' nuthin' stupid." Jake withdrew his hand. "Now we can dance 'round like this all day, but I ain't a patient man. So's I jest as soon turn yer over to my pard here, who'll string yer up and start skinnin' yer alive 'til yer talk. And if yer got any women here we start with them first, after we finish with 'em a course."

"He said he will rape the women and then skin them alive," Boqin said loudly in Chinese which meant Boqin probably saw Niu, too.

"Shut up, chink," the drifter said and took a threatening step toward Boqin.

"All right. All right," Jake said. "It's in the tent here."

"Let's git it then. Yer lead the way." He motioned with his pistol.

Jake and Boqin turned to go into the tent, and Jake caught a glimpse of the other feller. The two drifters came up behind them, and all four started to move toward the tent flap. Two feet away, and Jake made like he was reaching for the tent flap when he yelled, *"Now!"* and dove to the right. Boqin dove to the left, and Niu charged through the tent flaps, wrapped his big hands around the

209

guns of the drifters, and raised them up high with the drifters still hanging on. A shot went off into midair when Niu ripped their guns down and out of their hands. He tossed the pistols away into the dirt and grabbed each of the drifters by the neck — one in his left hand and one in his right. He lifted them off the ground the full length of his raised arms and let them hang there. They choked. They kicked. They flailed. They gurgled. The Apache half-breed pulled a knife from his sash and tried to slash Niu, but Jake caught his arm and twisted the knife out of his hand. They clutched at Niu's wrists and kicked at his body. It was all no use. In two minutes, they quit twitching and hung limp and still. Niu held them up another thirty seconds, then he tossed them like rag dolls into a heap in the dirt. "Nobody will ever rape and skin our women. Never," he said fiercely in Chinese that Boqin translated.

Two hours later they had the grave hole dug down five feet and four feet wide. They rolled in the bodies, and Jake examined their rusted and dirty shooting irons. He threw in their pistols. "Surprised they even work," he said as he stomped his boot heel into the seat of the cracked saddle the skinny man had ridden, and his boot went through. "A couple a months' cowboying coulda bought him a new saddle instead a whiskey. Look here, Boqin. The Apache didn't even have a saddle. Jest a blanket with a cinch over it. Probably slept in it, too. Wal, let's throw it all in and cover it up. Be dark soon. Keep their horses in case we can use 'em. Better let 'em graze a week or so. They look like they could use some rest."

After the grave was covered and the crew was sitting around the campfire, Jake said and Boqin translated, "Niu, you did a very brave thing, and we all thank you very much for saving us from evil. They were bad men, and yer gave them what they deserved." He bowed to Niu, who returned the bow.

Another month went by, and after supper Jake was sitting at his usual place on the porch of the Flying XC bunkhouse smoking his cigar. Sun was hanging in the west but a good half hour before setting so Jake could see Walt as he walked up directly to him. "Howdy, boss," he said.

"Howdy." He stepped up on the porch and sat down in one of the chairs. "Thought you'd like to know. Just got word there was a meetin' in Henrietta between the Clay County ranchers and the fence cutters. Looks like the ranchers ownin' land agreed to take down and not fence acrosst land that ain't theirs and build gates for farmers and small ranchers to use. And the fence cutters said they'll quit cuttin' fence. How 'bout that? Hear tell there's rumblin' down at the legislature to make fence cuttin' illegal."

"Wal, that's good news. Irritates me when I have to rebuild fence I already built."

"Uh-huh. Cowboy came down yesterday from the panhandle full a news. Lookin' fer work. Said that McKenzie feller got kilt in Tascosa. Thought maybe the Rocking Lazy M would have an opening." Walt gave Jake a knowing look and smiled. "Wal, maybe things'll be more peaceful, for a while anyways. Let's celebrate with one a yer fine seegars." He cracked a rare grin.

"Sure. Here yer go," Jake said with his own grin to acknowledge Walt's friendly ploy for a cigar. He didn't mind. "What a yer hear 'bout McCarthy's ranch?"

"In probate. Mister Calhoun and Sticker Joe already rode it out. Boss might make a play for it. I hear TL's lookin' at it, too. But if the boss decides he wants it, I'll ride it out with Sticker, and we'll make our recommendation." He smiled shrewdly.

CHAPTER FOUR:
SNARING A MURDERING WEASEL

Jake continued to go about his range detective work and managing the fencing business. Sold a few more windmills and listened to the old-timers talking drought. There still had been no rain since March, and everyone was becoming edgy. Jake, however, was a little bored. He was tiring of riding the range day in and day out on a circuit from the Flying XC headquarters to the west, to the south to Seymour with a stop along the way to buy more fence posts, stay a night or two in Seymour, and then back the same way in reverse except when he went north once a month to pay the fencing crew.

Long about late August he was in Seymour. He hadn't been in town for two months, as he was keeping close to the southern border of the Flying XC range, which was several miles north of Seymour. He came in and stepped up to the bar at the Brazos. Three men conversed together at the bar. Another feller, looked like a drummer, was at a table gobbling his supper. And there was a small poker game of four men going on at one of the poker tables. Jake noticed there were no cowboys in the saloon.

"Hello, Jake," Alex said.

"Howdy, Alex," Jake said as he pulled off his hat and let it hang on his back by the stampede strings. He mopped his forehead and brow with his bandana and said, "Over a hunnert today. Lookin' a little slow tonight. Where's all the cowpunchers?"

"Probably out working. Getting ready for the fall roundup. Usually don't get them in until Saturday night. How's your business?"

"Slow. I think we scared away all the rustlers. Had some trouble with the Rocking Lazy M over fencing. McCarthy didn't fare too well on that one. He was a stubborn and mean old cuss."

"Yeah, I heard about that. He made a big mistake trying to come up against Walt Guthrie."

Jake let that one lie. Even though he and Johnny did all the work, Walt got the credit. Just as well since Walt had the reputation, and Jake was trying to decelerate his own rapid rise to fame. His name was more well known than he wanted. "Yer overhear any suspicious talk in the last few months?" he asked and took down half the shot of whiskey Alex had placed on the bar in front of him.

"As a matter of fact, there is a group of six cowboys from the Hashknife. They come in every Saturday night and play poker, visit Desi or Cherry. Got another new girl." He winked at Jake and made a small lecherous smile. "Just in time, too. Desi had to take time off and go to El Paso to bury her mother. Those Hashknife cowboys drink a lot of whiskey, too. But they always pay cash on the barrelhead. Anyway, one night a week or two ago, one of them was talking about bunching up some cows, and their leader shut him up fast and sharp. The others looked rather perturbed with him as well. It was obvious none of them wanted him talking. So, I add up one and one. They got more money than the usual cowpoke, and there is something they don't want other folk to know about. What does that equal to you?"

"Suspicion. Who's their leader?"

"Feller named Vern Conroy. Mean. Never smiles. None of them ever cross him. Not even if they think he's cheating at cards."

"Uh-huh. Think I met him last spring down at the Hashknife bunkhouse."

"You come back Saturday night, and you're likely to meet him again. Be right back." He slid down the bar and poured more beer and drinks for the men there. Jake thought about what he said. He remembered that when Wes loudly asked about any rustling by Hashknife crew, the bunkhouse went dead silent. It was a mean looking cowboy who started interrogating Jake. Probably this Conroy feller. Well, he aimed to find out and intended to stay over for the Saturday night investigation. In the meantime, it was Thursday, and he needed to fill his time while he waited for Saturday to roll around. Having completed his barkeep duties, Alex returned.

"Tell me about Cherry," Jake said.

"Well, you can ask her yourself. There she comes down the stairs."

Jake looked up to see a gorgeous young woman descending the stairs. She wore a cream-colored dress with lacy sleeves to her elbows. It had a low bodice that revealed the cleavage to her nice but not large bosom. There was a thin cream-colored belt pulled in snug at her waist, and the skirt was semi-form fitting to display her curvy figure. Her mass of brunette hair was piled on top of her head and pinned in place. Most distinctive, however, was her face with high cheekbones, soft brow, and clear, slightly olive-toned complexion from which her brilliant dark-gray eyes surveyed the room as if she were queen of the palace. Without doubt her full lips, natural in color, expressed in a word, haughtiness. Her look was defiant. And Jake was intrigued.

"Where's she hale from?"

"New Orleans. Think she might have some Creole in her."

"She high classed or vulgar?"

"What do you think, just looking at her?"

"Looks like she thinks we are beneath her. She's probably out of one a the better houses in New Orleans."

"You are very perceptive. That is where I think she is from, too. Won't answer any questions about why she is out here on the frontier in northwest Texas. And she is not saying anything about where she worked or what she was doing in New Orleans. Insists on a three-dollar minimum fee."

"Sounds about right I reckon. Runnin' from somethin' or someone. Seymour, Texas, ain't 'zactly the land a opportunity."

"Here she comes. I'll introduce you. You want Jake or Jonas?"

"Jonas V. Brighton."

She came up close to Jake but did not touch. "Let me introduce you two." They turned to face each other. "Cherry LeClaire meet Jonas V. Brighton," Alex said.

She held out her hand in the female fashion as a lady to a gentleman. "Nice to meet you," she said with just a twinge of a smile and critical eyes.

"My pleasure to meet you also," Jake said as he took her hand and lightly kissed the top in the French way.

"Oh. A gentleman. How nice but . . ." she trailed off as she leaned back a little and appraised Jake's garb. "Not attired as one."

"Ah," Jake smiled pleasantly. "Out West one wears most of the time what suits the occasion. Had I known I was to meet such a lovely lady as yourself, I assure you, I would have dressed appropriately for the occasion," Jake said with a slight dip of his head.

"Well, I thank you, sir, for the compliment. Perhaps you would take this occasion to buy a lady a drink?" And a slight smile of intrigue parted her lips.

"Of course. Alex, if you please."

Alex grinned and turned to retrieve the bottle of champagne from the cooler and pour a glass for Cherry. "There you are, sweetheart," he said as he set the glass on the bar. "And for the gentleman?" Alex said as he smiled professionally.

"The same."

And now it was time to watch a little squirming. As he set Jake's glass on the bar he said, "If the gentleman pleases, that will be two dollars." Jake did not flinch, but his left eye did tic once, and Alex saw it. He had to turn and look away to hide his involuntary grin.

"I understand you are from New Orleans," Jake said and then took a taste of the champagne. It took all he could muster not to pucker up his mouth at the strange tanginess of the bubbly liquid.

"Yes. And you?"

"Kansas City."

"Really. How interesting. What brings you out here?"

"I want to learn the ranching business."

"And are you?" A look of disdain came over her face.

"I would say so and also say that if folks are to stay in business here, they have to accept the cattle business and the cowboys who work it."

"Ah. How intriguing. A rather subtle jab. The gentleman has removed his gloves." She emptied her glass and took Jake's from him. "You've never had champagne before, have you?"

"No, I have not, but then I've never met

such an elegant lady."

"Even if she is a lady of ill repute, eh?" The smile grew larger.

"All right," Jake smiled in his pleasant way. "I guess the playacting is over, eh?"

"Yes. I would say so."

"Alex," Jake called. "Can you bring me a real drink. Thanks." When the drink was poured, he turned and moved a little closer to Cherry. "Let's start over. You can call me Jake."

"And you can call me Cherry LeClaire. See, you are the one who was playacting. I was true to myself the whole time."

Jake couldn't stop himself. He laughed and laughed. She played him smartly, and he liked that. He should have been embarrassed, but this was all of no consequence so why should he. The laughs kept coming, and Cherry was grinning along, too.

"So, what you are saying, hah, hah, hah, is that you are an elegant whore. Is that right?"

"Precisely. Now, would the gentleman care to escort the lady to her room?"

"With pleasure," he said, still chuckling. "And by the way, my name *is* Jonas V. Brighton."

Afterwards, they lay in bed, she smoking a dainty cigarillo and Jake his usual cigar. "You pulled a really good con on me."

"Well, and to be honest my real name is Clemence Le Claire. But that doesn't sound right for the business. So, I changed it to Cherry."

"You ever do any detective work?"

"Detective? That's a man's job."

"Not necessarily. There is a pretty good detective named Virginia Hudson working out of Kansas. She solved two murder cases."

"That's nice."

"You'd just as soon stick with whoring, huh?"

"For now, anyway. You know every whore thinks they will meet their Prince Charming and be carried off in a crystal carriage to the land of bliss." She chuckled and looked bemusedly at Jake.

"Yeah. That Desi is trying to get her hooks into me."

"Desi tries to get her hooks into any man she thinks might have some money."

"Yeah?"

"Yeah. You got money?" she said with a coy look as she sucked on the cigarillo.

"Maybe so and maybe not. You know that feller Vern Conroy?"

"He's a mean son of a bitch. I don't let him near me. He'd probably slit my throat if he didn't like the poke. Desi takes care of him. Hope he doesn't start bothering me now that she is gone for awhile."

"How about any of the other Hashknife boys. You know any of them?"

"There's this one kid comes by regularly. He's nice. Can't be more than nineteen."

"Well, look here. How'd you like to make some extra money?"

"Depends on what I have to do."

"Detective work."

"Huh?"

"You see I ride line for the Flying XC. You know what that means?"

"No."

"Line riders guard the cattle herd for the rancher. We ride out on the borders of the ranch and watch for strays and rustlers. We catch them and bring them in. You know what rustlers are, don't you?"

"Yeah. What's a stray?"

"Strays are cattle that wonder away from the herd and need to be brought back in. Now I have suspicions about that Hashknife outfit, and I need information. And I pay for it. If you were able to get that kid talking about things they have done or are planning to do and pass it on to me, I'd pay you. That's detective work."

"How much pay?"

"Well, that depends on the information

and what develops from it. Could be as little as five bucks or as much as fifty. What reward or other money I get for an arrest I would share with you."

"Uh-huh. Let me think about it."

"All right. I'll be pulling out on Sunday."

Saturday night Jake stepped through the doors of the Brazos about eight o'clock. The bar had a full line, two poker games were going, and many of the tables were occupied by people in various conversations. Pinky was working away on the ivories, and the piano music filled the room above all the cacophony of human voice. A haze of to-bacco smoke filled every square inch. Jake came behind a feller at the bar and waved to Alex, who came over a moment later with a glass of whiskey. Jake reached over and took the glass, sipped a little, and moseyed over to one poker game. He watched for awhile and then drifted to the Hashknife game. He stood across from the man he figured was Vern Conroy. He *was* the same feller as at the Hashknife bunkhouse. Jake was looking across the room when he heard Conroy say, "Hey, green peas. Yer want a play?" Jake looked down at him and pointed to his own chest. "Yeah, yer," he said most unpleasantly.

Jake pulled a chair over and squeezed in where room was made for him. The first hand went around, and he lost his ante. Next hand he called and lost. Same with the next. "Yer ain't doin' too good," Conroy said with a deadly stare at Jake. "Guess they don't teach yer very good up there at the Flying XC. Yer still workin' there?"

"Yep."

"Whatcha doin there? Washin' dishes?" He did not smile while the other cowboys chuckled.

"Ridin' line."

Conroy looked owly at Jake for a minute and said, "What'd yer say yer name is?"

"Never said. Not here and not at the bunkhouse last spring."

"Well, jackass, what is it?"

Jake stared hard at Conroy, and he stared back. Fifteen seconds and Jake said, "Jake Brighton."

"Rawhide Jake Brighton?"

"That's right."

"Wal, as I live and breathe. It's the famous killer. Rawhide Jake Brighton. Let me shake yer hand." He was not smiling, and his tone was not friendly.

He came around the table, and Jake stood up. Jake was not liking the situation. Quarters were too close. His gun hand was too far away from his pistol. The threat was real. And he treated it as such even as Conroy shook his hand and returned to his seat.

"All right. Now we kin play some poker with friends." He still did not smile, even once. They played a few more hands all of which Jake folded, and then he got some good cards. The bet was to Conroy. "I'll just bet three bucks," he said coyly.

He was called by two fellers and Jake. The rest folded. One of them had the deal. "How many?" he said to Jake.

"Two." Jake was holding three eights and drew a pair of fours to make a full house.

"Two," said Conroy and one other player took three and the other drew one.

"Five bucks," said Conroy.

One player called. The other folded. "Call and raise yer five bucks," Jake said.

The one player folded. That left Conroy and Jake. Conroy stared at Jake for a long minute. Jake stared back. "Call yer raise and raise yer 'nuther five bucks," Conroy said with a dare-you look in his eye and tone in his voice.

"Wal, yer roped me in this fer. Yer must have the cards. But I gotta see 'em. Call," Jake said as he tossed into the pot a five-dollar bill. He felt like he could have raised again, holding a full house like he was, but didn't want to take too big a pot and upset everybody.

"Yer damn right I got the cards. King high straight," Conroy said as he fanned the cards out on the table. He stared at Jake, still not smiling. Jake made no move, and Conroy started to rake in the pot.

"Sure, that's a good hand, but it don't beat a full house," Jake said as he laid his cards out on the table. He waited for the reaction. All he got was an evil eye as Conroy reversed his motion and pushed the pot toward Jake. "Nice draw," Conroy said. Jake acknowledged with a dip of his head and said, "Yer too." He did not want to gloat.

The game went on, and Jake played carefully always as second fiddle to Conroy when Conroy stayed in the game. Jake made enough in the one big pot he won along with a few little ones to still be ahead. He pulled his watch and saw that it was coming up on ten o'clock. "Wal, that's it fer me. I gotta be on the trail early tomorrow," Jake said. He traded coin for paper notes with one cowboy, picked up his money, and stuffed it in his pants pocket as he pushed back his chair and stood up.

Conroy pushed back, stood, and said, "Let's me and yer confab a minute over there." He motioned to an empty table in the corner behind them. Jake's antennae became fully arrayed. This was probably going to be the ice breaker moment. They pulled out chairs and sat down. Conroy got right to it. "I watched yer all night. Yer look to be a straight shooter so I gotta ask. How's ol' Walt treatin' yer?"

"Walt? He's fine." Jake let his gaze drop to the tabletop and spoke as if he were holding something back.

"Cowboyin' ain't agreein' with yer?"

Here it comes, the move to get inside. "Wal, it's a lotta stinkin' hard work, and it don't pay much."

"Mebe we kin hep yer with that. Ain't never gonna make any money in the cattle business unless yer own yer own herd."

"How do yer git yer own herd?"

"Wal, there's ways like bringin' in mavericks an' if yer kin get a bull and a couple a cows. Start small. And other ways, too." He shrugged. "But first yer gotta git a homestead to headquarter yer outfit and use the open range fer grazin'."

"Hear tell a lotta open range is gittin' fenced off."

"Yeah, that is a happenin'. But yer know, it bein' so dry and all, the Hashknife is lookin' for greener range. I thought yer, bein' a line rider an' all, might know a some open range we could run some critters onto."

"Which way yer wantin' to go?"

"North a here."

"Matter a fact I know a some open range a ways north a the Wichita. 'Bout twenty miles northwest a here. Good graze and browse and three springs that are still flowin'. Yer talk 'bout homesteadin'. I had my eye on this range for a while now."

"Any other outfit runnin' cattle in there?"

"Nah. Ever onced in a while I gotta chase some Flying XC strays outta there."

"Twenty miles, eh? Mind if I ride outta here tomorrow with yer, and yer kin show me the range if yer goin' thataway?" He did not smile, but his natural mean look did soften.

"Sure. I kin do that. I want to be off by sunup though, so I don't know 'bout yer, but I gotta git some shuteye."

"All right. Sure, I'll see yer at the stables just afore sunup then. I'll be saddled and ready to go."

"All right." Jake pushed back his chair, stood, and waited a few seconds for an offered hand if there was one. There wasn't.

In three hours, they arrived at the edge of the range Jake was talking about. He didn't want to answer a bunch of questions, so he trotted Jasper the whole way. What Jake knew and Conroy did not is that the range was owned by the Flying XC. Xavier Calhoun had a month earlier taken title to the land. Jake knew where it was because the surveyors, who made the plat for the deed, showed him. Fortunately, they had pulled up their stakes, so all that remained were the corner pins, which were covered with grass anyway.

He led Conroy to a knob hilltop so he could see out over the range. Jake pulled his stampede string tight as the wind threatened to blow off his hat. And he pointed into the wind to one of the springs. "See it just to the west of that bluff there?"

"Yeah, and I see the other two. Let's lope on down there and get a closer looksee."

They let the horses drink at each of the springs, and Conroy tested the water for all three. He also pulled some grass here and there and chewed it up, then spit it out. "I ain't no critter," he said. "But the grass still tastes sweet. Reckon this range'd do. Drive the herd up here after we cross the Brazos," he said as he gazed out to the southeast. "Where we crossed the Witchita is as good a place as any, lessin' yer know a better crossin'." Jake shook his head *no*. "An' yer say there ain't any other outfits runnin' stock in here?"

"That's right. Flying XC western boundary is three miles east. Calhoun likes to keep his herd on his property, an' Walt don't like strays, so I'm pretty much the onliest feller to ever git over here. An' like I said, that's just checkin' fer strays."

"Uh-huh." With a change of countenance Conroy said, "Wal, I'll have to check with Vandevert. Make sure it's okay with him. I'll keep yer up on it next time I see yer."

"All right. I gotta mosey on up north. Be seein' yer." Jake turned Jasper and spurred him into a lope. He went around a clump of mesquite and glanced back to see that Conroy had ridden off to the south. "Trap is set," Jake said out loud. He himself needed to check with Bill Vandevert in case Conroy was legit. Didn't think so but you never know. Problem was, how to do that without being seen by Conroy or one of his boys.

Jake waited there an hour then pointed Jasper southeast and headed for the Smith's post-making plant. As he neared the plant, he picked up the odor of burning mesquite and roasting meat. He was in time for noon dinner.

While consuming venison tenderloin,

beans, wild onions, and fresh baked bread along with plenty of hot coffee, Jake talked business with the Smiths. "So, what's yer production these days?" Jake asked.

Martin said, "We're kickin' out a hunnert posts a day. That's over two thousand a month takin' into account down time for maintenance, trips to town, and what have you. See that stack a posts yonder? It keeps gittin bigger. We need it to git smaller."

"Well, yer sellin' posts ain't yer?"

"Yeah."

"How many posts a day are yer sellin'?"

"Don't know. We don't sell 'em every day."

"Do yer know how many yer sell a month? Heck, I buy a thousand a month from yer."

"Yeah. You and the RG and the L Bar probably 'bout seventeen hunnert. More farmers are comin' in, too."

"So, what're yer moanin' 'bout. Yer production is keepin' up with yer sales and lettin' yer build an inventory for future sales. Good business sense I'd say. Speakin' a which, how much do I owe yer?"

Martin looked to Ed, who pulled a small ledger book from the back pocket of his bib overalls. He thumbed through the ledger and found the page he wanted. "Twenty-seven dollars," he said with a smile.

Jake took out his own ledger book,

checked an entry, and then wrote another entry with his pencil. Then he pulled a twenty and a ten from his pocket and gave the bills to Ed. "Keep the change," he said. "That equals sixty posts on me." Ed took the money with a squinched-up face. "I know you'd like gold better," said Jake, "but these here new bank notes are as good as gold. See, right here on the note it says, 'This Note Is Secured by Bonds of The United States Deposited with the U.S. Treasurer at Washington.' There ain't a bank in the whole country that won't give yer gold for this here note. It's jest easier to carry paper than sacks a gold everwhere I go."

"I still don't like it," Ed said.

"Don't worry, Ed. Yer know they always give us the gold at the bank in town."

Of course, Jake didn't tell them that he didn't trust banks and that is why he kept his money in the Flying XC safe.

"Wal, listen. It's been interestin', and I thank yer for the dinner, but now I gotta git back to Seymour. Can I take anything fer yer? Maybe a sack a gold to put on deposit? Hah, hah, hah."

Ed shook a fist at Jake as he trotted off to catch Jasper. Martin smiled.

Jake kept on a route to Seymour well to

the east to make sure he didn't run into Conroy by chance. When he came to the edge of town at mid-afternoon, he tied off Jasper to a rail around the corner from Main Street and took up a position from where he could watch the entrances to the Brazos, Aces Wild, and Quincy's Livery. Lucky he did. A half hour later Conroy's five men spilled out of the Aces Wild and crossed to Quincy's. Another twenty minutes and they were riding south out of town. Jake waited another quarter hour before he jumped in the saddle and rode east and then south. He got there in time to see Conroy's crew way across the Brazos. That satisfied him that they were gone, and he pointed Jasper back to town for Quincy's.

Quincy, with his hands in his pockets, sidled up to the stall gate where Jake was brushing Jasper and said, "Whatcha been up to, Rawhide?"

"Eh? Oh, howdy, Quincy. Just the usual. Ridin' the line."

"Uh-huh."

"Say, yer know Bill Vandevert. He ever come in here?"

"Nope."

"Wal, yer ever see him in town?"

"Yep."

Jake, out of Quincy's sight, rolled his eyes.

Why does he insist on playing these guessing games? He stood up and with brushes in both hands laid his arms over Jasper's back. "Would yer care to be more definitive?"

"By deefiniteeve yer mean say more?" Quincy said with a smiling smirk and gleam in his eyes.

"Exactly."

"No. I don't care to."

Jake rushed out of the stall to grab Quincy and shake the answers out of him. But Quincy was too quick. Like a monkey he was up the ladder to the hayloft, and just before Jake got to the ladder to climb up it, Quincy jerked it up and out of reach. "Hah, hah, hah," he cackled.

Jake seethed. "Yer gonna have to come down sometime, and when yer do, I am gonna beat the devil outta yer."

"Oh no," he squealed. "Please, massah. Please don't beat me. Hah, hah, hah!"

Well, it was just too humorous for Jake after all, and he started chuckling. "All right. Come on down and I won't beat yer."

"Say please."

Jake gritted his teeth and said, "Pleeease."

"That's better," Quincy said as he slid down the ladder.

Jake pulled off his hat and leaned against a post. "Now, Mister Brown, could yer please tell me when yer see Mister Vande-vert."

Quincy inched closer like a puppy tempting another puppy to chase her. "Wal . . ." he drug it out, and he was too close. Jake jumped him and wrapped him up in a bear hug. He squeezed, and Quincy screamed. "All right. All right." Jake released a little pressure. Quincy made one last attempt to escape by violently twisting his body and dropping to the floor. But Jake had him good and re-applied pressure. "All right. Take it easy. I 'as jest playin'."

"Yer too old to be playin'. Yer an adult. Not a kid. Now answer my question."

"He comes into town every Wednesday to the general store in a buckboard to pick up supplies. There. Are yer satisfied?"

Jake released his hold, and Quincy ran back up the ladder. "I lied. Hah, hah, hah."

Well, that was it. What's the use? Jake was beyond exasperation. He shook his head and then bent over to pick up his saddlebags and rifle. He pointed the rifle at Quincy who, like a scurrying rat, back crawled out of range. That brought a smile to Jake's face.

He walked directly to the general store only to see the closed sign. He forgot. It was Sunday. Wind was kicking up, so he buttoned his coat and turned up the collar, then tightened the stampede string of his hat. He turned around and walked against the wind up the pretty much deserted Main Street toward the hotel. Dust was flying, and the gusts roared. When he crossed McLain Street, a huge tumbleweed crashed into him before he saw it coming. No pain. Just a nuisance as he was sprayed with pieces of dried weed. He was still brushing it off when he came to the hotel entrance. He checked in and obtained the key to his usual room, went up the stairs, dropped his gear on the floor, propped his rifle against the wall near the bed, poured some water from the pitcher into the wash bowl on the dresser, and rinsed his face and hands. He wasn't in the mood for saloon action or Cherry so he thought he would have supper in the dining room and afterwards sit in the lobby reading newspapers and periodicals to catch up on the news while sipping a little whiskey and smoke a cigar. Then up to bed.

In the morning after breakfast, he stepped out of the hotel and nearly lost his hat in the buffeting and bellowing wind. He recovered quickly and walked to Quincy's through swirling dust and bits of debris. Hanging signs were swinging wildly in the wind and looked about to fly away. A flapping door could be heard banging against a wall somewhere. He hurried along and turned in to Quincy's barn without injury. Quincy didn't seem to be around, which was just as well because Jake was not in the mood for bantering. He fed and watered Jasper, saddled him and tied on his saddle-bags, and stuffed his rifle in its scabbard. He hung the bridle over the wall of the stall and waited for Jasper to finish his hay. That would probably be another fifteen to twenty minutes, so he decided to walk back to the general store. He dove into the wind and walked at a fast pace down the street with dust kicking up all around him. Even though he had a good hold on the door knob, the door slammed behind him as he stepped inside.

"Got some good wind out there today," said the bald man in white shirt with no collar, black garters around his upper arms, and a white apron tied about his waist. He was stocking a shelf of canned goods and had his back to Jake. He did not look to see who was there.

"Mornin' Bert," Jake said. "It's me, Jake Brighton."

"Oh, mornin', Jake. What can I get you?"

"Wal, don't need no supplies. I'm about to head outta town. But Quincy said Bill

Vandevert comes in every Wednesday for supplies. Is that right?"

"Yep. Just like clockwork. He'll show up about ten."

"All right. I need to see if he wants any more windmills. You got any more referrals for me?"

"Matter of fact there was a farmer named Schmidt in the other day asking about windmills. I think his place is west of town about ten miles and north of the river."

"Thanks. I'll look him up today since I ain't got nuthin' more important to do. Adios then."

"See you later."

His original intent was to ride out to the crew and deliver the payroll. But now his intent changed because money-in is always more important to develop than money-out. Both were needed of course in business, but there were priorities. Jake trotted Jasper for an hour fighting the wind and then slowed him to a walk. Soon he came upon a farmer in a field mowing hay with a two-horse team. He rode up to him, and the farmer reined in his team.

"Howdy," Jake said. "I'm lookin' for the Schmidt place. Would that be you?"

"Wal, that depends. Who are you, mister?"

"Name's Jake Brighton. Bert Stigler at the

store in town said he might be interested in a windmill."

"Wal then, guess I'd be Oscar Schmidt," he said with a smile and held out his hand. "Pleased to meet yer, Mister Brighton. Let me unhitch this team, and we can go into the house to sit down, and yer kin show me what yer got. Have some lemonade, too. Probably shouldn't be mowin' in this wind anyhow. Maybe it'll die down tomorrow."

He showed Jake into the house, and they sat at the kitchen table. Schmidt's wife brought lemonade while Jake spread out his Star Mill advertising literature. She was a well-endowed, obviously Germanic woman with thick blonde hair in a single braid down her back and striking blue eyes. He took note that she passed close to him, very close. He finished talking through the windmill, then started talking about drilling the well. "I know a fine driller by the name of Bill Waldron. Have yer heard of him? No. Wal, he is the best around these parts. Knows where to drill for the most flow, and he has one a those new rotary drills, steam powered, with his own four-legged derrick. Folds it up and hauls it on a wagon when he ain't drillin'."

"What's the price on all this?"

"Wal, I have an exclusive agreement with

the agent that has a license to represent Flint, Walling and Company — they make the Star Mill — that allows us to sell the Original Star Mill, ten-foot diameter, for eighty-five dollars. Bill'll drill the first fifty feet for ten bucks. Anythin' after that is twenty-five cents a foot down to sixty feet, then the price goes up to thirty cents a foot for every ten foot more down to eighty feet. So, for example, if you wanted to drill down to seventy foot, the cost would be ten bucks plus two dollars and fifty cents for the first extra ten foot and then three dollars for the next ten feet or a total cost of fifteen fifty. Sav — , er, understand? Eighty foot is all the pipe and casing he has. Usually around here though he hits a pretty good flow at fifty to sixty foot." Jake shifted in his chair and took a sip of lemonade. He sucked in his cheeks and pursed his lips. "Boy, that is lemony. Mind if I add a drop of sugar?"

Missus Schmidt said, "Not at all. Help yourself." She smiled pleasantly, and Jake thought he detected something as she stared into his eyes. Schmidt was going through the literature. Jake removed four lumps of sugar from the sugar bowl Missus Schmidt held out to him. "My, you must have quite a sweet tooth," she said huskily. "More?" she said and bent over to expose more cleavage. Jake glanced at Schmidt. He was still engrossed and seemed as if he didn't even hear them.

Jake gave her his best serious lover look deep into her eyes and said, "Yes, I do. Four is enough though." She grinned, and her bust revealed heavier breathing. But, alas, Schmidt spoke.

"How about shipping cost?" he said.

"Oh yeah. Sorry, forgot. That would be an additional three dollars. And we strongly suggest you build your own tower. We can provide plans for that."

"Fine. Can I keep this material?" Jake was in the middle of a big gulp of lemonade and nodded his head *yes*. "And how do I get in touch with yer?"

"I am in Seymour once a week." He glanced at Missus Schmidt. She smiled. "You can leave word with Bert Stigler, and I'll contact you."

"All right. Anything else?"

"No. That should do it. Just let me know when you are ready to order. There is, of course, a ten-dollar deposit."

"All right. Thank you," Schmidt said as he stepped out onto the porch and held the door for Jake. Jake looked back to the doorway to the bedroom, where she stood out of sight from her husband and removed

241

her blouse from her shoulder to reveal a lovely milk-white skin. She smiled seductively at Jake. He swallowed hard and hurried out the door. While he rode back to town hunkered down over the saddle with the wind blowing up his back, he thought about her. How easy would it be for him to stop by here when he was out on patrol and Mister Schmidt was working in the fields. How easy to have her. No. Not married women — ever. He shook his head as if to clear the cobwebs from his brain. But his mind naturally went to Mary Jane. And he sighed.

The next day, he carried the payroll to the crew. He was back in time for supper, and when he finished, he sat in a soft chair in the lobby with a brandy and a cigar. He lasted about an hour before his head started to nod and he went up to bed.

About nine thirty on Wednesday morning, he walked into Stigler's General Store. Bert was behind the counter by the cash register bent over some ledger books. "Mornin', Bert," Jake said cheerfully.

"Mornin', Jake. How'd it go at Schmidt's? Get an order?"

"Got it all made out right here." He

handed the paperwork to Bert. "All he has to do is come in and sign the order, leave the ten-dollar deposit, and then you can send it off, with a bill for your usual handling fee, of course."

"Of course. How was Missus Schmidt?" Bert asked with a lewd smile on his face.

"Whew! Old Oscar's got a tiger by the tail in that one. She always in heat like that?"

"She is every time she comes in here long as Oscar's not looking. But I wonder just how far she'd go."

"Yeah,wal, I ain't gonna find out. Far as I am concerned another man's wife is forbidden fruit. Nothing but trouble."

"I'm with you there."

"Seen Bill Vandevert yet today?"

"There he is pullin' up out front right now."

Vandevert came through the door and with heavy steps walked toward Jake and Bert at the counter. He was about Jake's height, maybe a little taller, looked wiry, with a square jaw, close trimmed brown goatee with a heavier mustache, no-nonsense expressive eyes, a ready-to-smile mouth, and hands that looked scarred and calloused. He was a few years younger than Jake. He was from Oregon and more educated probably because of his Kentuckian schoolteacher wife, Sadie, whom he'd met in Fort Griffin. Vandevert had some notoriety as a mail carrier from Camp Warner in Oregon to Fort Bidwell in northern California through hostile Modoc Indian country and as a bear killer — the story of which made the San Francisco newspapers. A fearless and steadfast man, he already had a reputation as a good, reliable range boss.

"Howdy, boys. Jake. Bert."

"Howdy, Bill," they both replied. "Got fresh coffee here. Want some?" Bert said.

"Believe I do."

"Here, I'll pour it. Think I'll have a mug, too," Jake said. He poured out two mugs, handed one to Vandevert, and said, "How those windmills working out?"

"Good. Most of 'em more than fifty gallon a minute. One thing we got in northwest Texas is plenty of wind."

"Glad to hear it. The Star is a good mill. Been around a while. Need any more?"

"Not yet." He smiled. "Of course, if we don't get any rain, may need a few more. Getin' more dry every day here and out at the Pecos range. Charlie's havin' a time of it."

"Charlie?" Jake inquired.

"Charlie Buster. He's the cow boss out there. Running thirty, forty thousand head."

"What about around here? Are you lookin' for more open range with grass and water to run in some critters?"

Vandevert's eyes widened, and he said, "Heck, no. Reckon we ain't goin' to see any rain for a long while. So, I'm slowly pullin' the herd in closer to those windmills you sold me. Got tanks I'm fillin' up. Got enough hay for the winter."

"You gonna ship this fall?"

"Think so. But Mister Simpson's been talkin' about trailin' herds up to his outfit in Montana. Don't think it's gonna happen anytime soon though."

"Simpson? Of the association?"

"Yeah. John Simpson. You heard of him."

"Yeah. He's our president and your manager, ain't he?"

"Yep. Major stockholder. Kinda famous around these parts. Him and Jim Couts started up the Hashknife. He's kinda famous, too. Bill Hughes and Simpson now."

"Yeah. I heard a him."

They talked a while longer about the weather, cattle prices, and what have you until Vandevert said, "Well I better get back to work." He drained his cup and said, "Been nice talking with you boys. Here's my order, Bert," he said as he handed Bert a piece of paper he pulled from his vest pocket. "While you're fillin' it, I'll go down to Lee's and pick up a couple of wagon tires."

So, there it was. Jake had his confirmation. Now all he had to do was wait until the crime was committed. Following Jim Loving's policy, he didn't want to inform Vandevert of what he suspected until he had the evidence — recovered rustled cattle and captured rustlers.

Two weeks later, on a late Monday afternoon, Jake stood at the bar talking to Alex while he enjoyed a beer. "Cooled off some," he said to Alex, who agreed and went down the bar to draw another beer. Cherry came down the stairs, and Jake motioned her over. "What do you want?" she said with a pout.

"Who put the burr under your saddle?" Jake said with a look of surprise.

"Haven't seen you in over two weeks. Think you can have your way with me whenever you please and then ride on out to who knows where and not come back until who knows when? Huh? Do you?" She took on her look of disdain and shot ocular daggers at him.

"Well — you are a — I mean — it's not like we're married or anything."

Then she smiled, and as always when she

246

did, it was a dazzling look she had in contrast to her typical haughtiness. "Just joshing you," she said as she threw a hip into Jake. "But I did miss you and . . . I have information."

Jake gathered in all she had to say and the next morning was on the trail before sunup headed north to Vernon. The wind blew his hat back, and his bandana blew from his neck like a pennant. Jasper's ears were back most of the time as he pushed against the headwind. It took them a half hour longer than normal to make the trip in an easy two days. He was thinking about making it in one day but because of the wind gave up the idea. When he arrived in Vernon, he found out that Wes was up at Doan's Crossing, so he headed right up there and waited for him at the hotel. He sat on the side porch out of the wind and watched the dust devils battling in the one road through Doan's settlement. The occasional wagon passing by destroyed the contest between the devils, and they had to regroup to continue the struggle. When he saw a particularly strong miniature cyclone charging down the road, he backed into the shelter of the hotel lobby and held the door against the force of the wind. It pelted the doors with stinging pebbles and dust particles so that it sounded as if they were being hailed upon. It lasted for just a few seconds and then moved on.

Jake stepped back outside only to see another big one coming on the other side of the road. Must have been twenty to thirty feet high and ten feet across. Right behind it a cowboy galloped his bay horse in chase of the dust devil. Quickly, Jake recognized the cowboy was Wes, who whooped and hollered and twirled his loop over his head. His hat flapped on his neck and shoulders on the stampede strings, and his mop of rusty hair flew in the wind. He stood in his stirrups and tossed the loop into the devil and pulled Noble to a sudden stop as if he had caught the devil. He shouted out a rebel yell that pierced the air above the rush of wind and laughed and laughed. Jake chuckled. Wild as the west Texas wind was his partner.

"Yer gonna brand him or what?" Jake called out. Wes turned his head to see and recognized Jake. He trotted Noble over to the porch as he coiled his rope.

"Howdy, pard. Brand who?"

"That devil yer just caught, hah, hah, hah."

Wes grinned and said, "Yer might just be surprised. Watcha yer doin' up here?"

"Wal, why don't yer put up ol' Noble and wash the dust off a yer. Then we can have a drink and I'll tell yer."

"All right. Be back in a few minutes." He sat his hat back on his head and tipped it at Jake, still grinning.

In the saloon, two wide planks on barrels standing on end served as the bar, and it already was too crowded with more cowboys coming in almost every minute. Jake edged in, filled a gap at the bar, and ordered a bottle with two glasses. But he wanted privacy. There was plenty of conversation and laughter noise to cover his talk to Wes if they were away from the throng. So, he and Wes moved over to sit at one of the tables in a corner. Jake poured the whiskey into the glasses, held up his glass, and said, "Here's how."

Wes raised his glass and responded, "Here's how." They clinked their glasses together. "Now what're yer hidin' under yer saddle blanket, pard?"

"Wal, how's yer rustler business goin'?"

Wes looked askance at Jake as he tossed down his whiskey. "Slower than molasses. Why?"

"Wal, yer remember when we were down at the Hashknife bunkhouse last spring and that mean lookin' cowboy was proddin' me?"

"Yeah."

"Turns out his name is Vern Conroy. He throws some weight around the crew of the Hashknife, and I think he's got himself a nice little rustlin' game goin' on."

"How's that?"

"Wal, Alex at the Brazos says he and five other cowboys from the Hashknife are in there every Saturday night playin' cards usually with more money than the average cowpuncher. So, I got into the game and befriended Conroy. He talked me into showin' him some open range up north of the Wichita. Says cuz a the comin' drought, the Hashknife is lookin' for more graze and water on open range. So, I take him on up there and show him that piece that Xavier Calhoun just bought. Yer know where the three good springs line up north to south? He likes it and says he has to talk to Bill Vandevert 'bout it. But I'm suspicious, so I talk to Bill myself without revealin' why and find out he is not lookin' for more range. In fact, he's pullin' the herd in closer to the windmill wells and tanks and hay storage he's got." Jake stared at Wes with a look of self satisfaction, pulled two cigars from his inside vest pocket, gave one to Wes, bit off the end, spat it out, scratched a match on the tabletop, held the flame to Wes's cigar, and then his own. He drank half the whiskey in his glass while Wes re-filled his glass. "What a yer think a that?" Jake said.

"Wal, Conroy's lyin' certain. But it ain't enough to arrest him."

"There's more. I also made a deal with Alex's new soiled dove, Cherry. One a Conroy's rustler crew likes her a whole lot. So, she gits information on Conroy's doin's for me, and I am payin' her a small part of our take when we run 'em in."

Wes raised his eyebrows once and let them fall. "Go on," he said.

"She tells me two nights ago that the kid says they're roundin' up cows and holdin' 'em south a the Brazos and gonna drive 'em north, so when they go he won't be able to come and see her for a while." Jake sat back in his chair with his cigar clamped in his teeth and folded his arms across his chest. He stared at Wes with a how-about-that look.

"When they leavin' on the drive?" Wes said through a cloud of cigar smoke he blew out.

"Cherry made the kid promise he would come and see her before they left. She'll let me know when that happens. What I think the weasel is doin' is cuttin' out small bunches of the critters they're bringin' in closer to the wells so as poor old Bill won't notice the loss until the roundup's finished. By that time, they'll be long gone with a herd they're makin' up south a the Brazos. They'll run 'em in on the Dodge City Trail behind all the other herds actin' just like they're authorized to do it. Won't be any tracks to follow. Then he'll swing 'em out to that range I showed him and hold 'em there to try and git some more weight on 'em."

"How many head d'ya think?"

"Wall, he's got five on his crew and him, so they can easy handle five, six hunnert."

"Maybe a thousand. Yeah, and we can't arrest 'em right now. Gotta wait until they git the critters off a the Hashknife range," Wes said with disgust.

"As soon as they come across the Brazos, they's open game, but we probably should let 'em git past town before we jump 'em in case the herd stampedes. Don't want it stampedin' through town." Jake poured himself another glass of whiskey. "You think we should git the sheriff involved?"

"Don't see how'd it hurt. We still git paid whether he's in on it or not. I just wonder about one a his deputies flappin' they's jaw."

"Yeah. We'd have to control that. Reckon you'd better come on down to Seymour and take up residence at Madison's."

"Reckon so. Yer ready for supper?"

"Yep."

Two weeks later the word came from Cherry. Conroy was starting the drive in two days. They had eight hundred head and were going all the way to Ogallala. Jake and Wes went to the sheriff's office and started by inquiring about his deputies' honesty and reliability.

"Wal, Ray, you know we are stock detectives and workin' in secret is a lotta our business," Wes said with a serious look on his face. "An' we got a sitchashun comin' up in yer county. Since we know about it ahead a time, it's probably good we let yer in on it. Yer kin ride with us or not. Don't make no never mind to us. But north a town we expect to arrest at least six rustlers with eight hundred head of rustled cattle. Now, I know yer kin keep quiet about it, but I don't know about yer deputies. So, what a yer say? Yer want a posse up with us?"

The sheriff spat a big glob of tobacco juice at the spittoon on the floor by his desk. It made a distinct ringing sound and spun the spittoon around a quarter turn. " 'Course I do. It's my job. It's my county. My deputies are good lawmen. I tell 'em this is secret, and they'll keep it secret." He stared fiercely at Wes and at Jake.

"All right. Glad to hear it, ain't we, Jake?"

"Yep. How many deputies yer have, Sheriff?"

"Three. So, one's gotta stay here in case the rest a us get kilt."

"All right. Reckon five lawmen oughta be able to bring in six rustlers, eh, Jake?"

"Yep. Here's the plan, Sheriff. Feller named Vern Conroy outta the Hashknife —"

"Know that mean varmint," the sheriff said in a low growl.

"All right, wal, he and his crew of five are rustlin' eight hundred head a Hashknife critters and bringin' 'em across the Brazos day after tomorrow. Let their tracks blend in with the other herds comin' acrost and fall in line with 'em. Actin' just like they's doin' what they's supposed to. Wal, since Wes is the known brand inspector 'round these parts, he's gonna station himself at the crossin' like he always does. Won't raise no suspicions. That weasel probably has his story all ready to go just in case he runs into Wes. Anyways, Wes'll inspect 'em as usual, and when he sees they's acrost the river, he'll come a runnin' for us. We set up the ambush right there just past where the trail turns north and gets rough. What a yer think?"

"I think y'all got a right smart plan there." He stroked his gray beard and said, "Y'all thinkin' 'bout slippin' up on 'em when they's in camp?"

"Yep. That's what we're thinkin'," Wes said. "We don't want to stampede the herd so we ain't gonna jump 'em while they's on the trail. Dependin' on what time they come acrost the river. We want 'em to be up in the rough country so's we can shadow 'em 'til they stop fer the night. That's 'bout fifteen mile from the Brazos so they can make it if they don't have to come too far before the river crossing."

"Uh-huh. Sounds like the best thing to do. When yer goin' to the river?"

"Soon as we're done here," Wes replied. "There ain't no moon so I reckon they won't try a night crossin'. Y'all can ride out in the mornin'. Better go separately so as not to cause any suspicions."

"We'll make a camp well off the trail and then go out to shadow 'em when we see 'em comin'," Jake said. "I'm headin' out today to locate the camp site. I'll see y'all when yer comin' and come down to meet yer."

"What're y'all thinkin' 'bout fer supplies?"

"Just saddlebags, no more'n three days.

Each man provides fer himself. Plenty of ammo," Jake said.

"All right then. I'll get my deputies ready, and we'll leave out in the mornin'."

At that moment Deputy Carson brought a cowboy out of the jail and released him saying, "All right, Buddy, yer had yer night to sleep it off in the hoosegow. Now git on back to the RG and git to work." He opened a desk drawer and took out a gun belt with a holstered pistol and handed it to the cowboy. "Here's yer rig. Now git," he said as he held the office door open.

"Who's that feller?" Jake said.

"Buddy Caldwell. He's a hand on the RG. Little too much whiskey last night," the sheriff said.

"Could he hear us talkin' there in the jail?" Jake nodded towards the door to the jail cells.

"Nah. Walls are too thick, and look how thick this door is. Could yer hear us, Carson?"

"No, sir. Didn't hear a word." The sheriff raked his look across Jake and Wes as if to say — *see?*

"All right. We'll be seein' y'all mañana," Wes said, and he and Jake walked out the door. At the entrance to the courthouse, Jake put a hand on Wes's arm to stop him from going any further. "What the —" Wes started to say.

"Let's just make sure that Buddy fellow ain't lurkin' around nowhere," Jake said as he searched from left to right for any sign of the cowboy. "I don't like loose ends, and that feller is a loose end. He saw us all together there in the sheriff's office. He might owe some favor or debt to Conroy even though he works on the RG. Could even be a Conroy spy reportin' on the RG so Conroy can raid old Bob."

"Sakes alive. Yer sure do have a eemajina-shun."

"Yer never know unless you know."

"Uh-huh. Wal, I don't see anyone, so I reckon I'll git saddled up and head out."

"All right. Good luck."

Jake waited a while longer and then went about town checking here and there for Caldwell. He checked at Stigler's General Store and the Brazos and the Aces Wild. He didn't see him anywhere, so he walked across to Quincy's and found him out in the corral fixing two broken rails. "Howdy, Quincy," Jake said most friendly-like.

"Howdy, yerself," Quincy said without looking up.

"What happened there?"

"Oh, that cussed drunkard Buddy Caldwell ran his horse into the fence last night and broke these top two rails."

"Buddy Caldwell of the Hashknife?" Jake deliberately misstated to see what Quincy knew. Otherwise, he could have been there wasting time playing games with Quincy.

"No, he's workin' on the RG. Plays cards all the time with the Hashknife boys though."

"Uh-huh. Wes still in the barn?"

"He pulled out a couple minutes ago."

"Thanks." Jake ran to the barn, slid his bridle over Jasper's nose, stuffed the bit in his mouth, smoothed out a saddle blanket on him, swung the saddle up, and cinched it tight all in less than sixty seconds. He started Jasper on a run out the doors, hung on to the saddle horn, made one hop, and vaulted into the saddle as he cleared the barn door. Quincy was watching the whole way and muttered, "Just made it."

Jake spurred Jasper into a gallop heading south out of town. In five minutes, he caught up with Wes, who was loping Noble along and had almost reached the river. Jake spurred and reined Jasper around in front of Noble to force him to stop. It took Wes by surprise, and he pulled his pistol, but when he saw it was Jake, he re-holstered the six-shooter.

"Yer loco?" Wes shouted. "I coulda kilt yer."

Jake reined around and brought Jasper up next to Noble. He said, "Quincy just told me that feller, Caldwell, plays cards all the time with the Hashknife crew."

Wes pushed his hat back on his head and said, "Whew. What a yer think?"

"I think we should assume that Conroy will know that somethin' was cookin' at the sheriff's office between us all. That means he's gonna be on the scout fer us, and we better stay alert."

"Uh-huh. Yer think I should camp out here tonight and tomorrow night case he's crazy enough to try a river crossin' in the dark?"

"Might be a good ideer just in case. I'll send the Stigler boy out to camp with yer so's yer can send him to alert Vandevert as soon as the rustled herd crosses the river."

"All right. Sounds good."

"See yer up the trail day after tomorrow."

Jake sat astride Jasper in the shade of a shelf of sandstone that jutted out from the cliff-side of a mesa formation that rose about two hundred feet from the rolling plain where the Western Trail passed through. The place where he chose to rest Jasper and his own saddle weary body was about three-quarters of the way up on the cliffside. Tucked into the shade as he was, it would be very difficult for anyone to see him with the naked eye, and he was well below the ridgeline so he was not silhouetted against the horizon. Although Jasper's black and white did not blend well with the terrain, he did blend in with the shadows. The color of Jake's shirt was long ago faded by sun and bleached by many months of washing. His britches were covered by his chaps of smooth brown leather, and his bandana was plain old beige paisley. He pulled off his hat and hung it on the saddle horn. Then with his bandana he mopped his face, head, and glistening chest exposed by the deep *V* of his partially unbuttoned shirt. Much earlier in the day he had undone all the buttons of his brown leather vest. Jake sat very straight and still. His hands were folded over the pommel of his saddle, right on top of the left in which he held the reins. He surveyed the terrain looking for a good camp site.

He found a high shelf with lots of mesquite cover on top and grass below and behind it. They could place a lookout on top, make a cold camp in the grass behind it, turn the horses out on hobbles, and water them at the Wichita a couple of miles to the north.

Then he rode up the trail a ways looking for a good ambush spot. He caught up with the tail end of a herd on the drive north. Fortunately, the wind was at his back as he followed the herd along until he found what he thought he remembered was there. It was like a canyon but not deep. Low mesas on either side of the trail provided high ground positions from which a man with a rifle would have good command of the ground below. He would put one man on each side, two men in front to stop the herd, and one in back to cut off any escape. Hopefully, there wouldn't be any gunplay. After all they were just cowboys and not killers. Or were they?

The next morning from the high shelf, Jake saw three riders coming. He put the glass on them and recognized the sheriff and his deputies. Behind them he saw a substantial herd coming. He cursed under his breath and hoped it would be through the canyon by the end of the day. Meanwhile, when he joined up with him, Jake explained his plan to the sheriff, who agreed completely. As luck would have it the herd was through the canyon and by sunset was bedded down beside the Wichita. Now all they had to do was wait for Wes to show.

At sunup, a chuck wagon and a small remuda arrived at the river's edge of the Brazos crossing. The point rider and the first of the little herd came up next. The rest were right behind them. Wes counted six cowboys. They drove the herd right on through the shallows and came out the other side. He trotted along beside as if he were inspecting brands and then rode Noble right up to the point rider. "Howdy," he said. "Yer the trail boss here?"

"Yep. JJ Robbins's my name. What's yers?"

"Wes Wilson."

"Oh, yeah. Heared a yer. Yer the brand inspector."

"That's right. I gotta enter yer name in the book. Let's see . . . these all Hashknife critters?" Wes wrote in his notebook.

"Yep."

"Where yer drivin' 'em?"

"Up to Ogallala. Boss says they got better prices there, and he's a testin' the water with this here little herd." Wes wrote again.

"How is old Mitch Harvey?"

"Who?"

"The cattle boss at the Hashknife? Ain't he?"

"No, sir. That'd be Bill Vandevert."

"Oh, yeah. What am I thinkin'? Oh well, say hi to Bill if yer see him 'fore I do. Good luck." That verified that at least the trail boss was a Hashknife hand so probably all the rest of them were, too. Wes turned Noble and trotted down the other side of the herd toward the rear looking at brands. As he rode by, he saw the Caldwell feller across the herd riding swing. He pretended he did not see him. What's worse though was that he looked carefully at the other four fellers, and none of them was Vern Conroy. He waited an hour before he put Noble in a trot back to town. At Quincy's he fed Noble and watered him. Once he was done, he rode at a trot out of town to the west for three miles and then turned northeast. In two hours, he came up on Jake's camp from behind. He slowed Noble to a walk, then stopped him. He pulled his spyglass from his saddlebag and surveyed the camp. Only Jake and the sheriff were there, so he went ahead and walked Noble on up to the camp.

"Where's the deputies?" Wes said as he stepped out of the saddle.

"Already have 'em in position on the mesas up thataway. One on each side. Here." He handed the spyglass to Wes. "You can see 'em from here. Look over the top a that red boulder yonder. See 'em?"

"Yep. But we got a sitchashun."

"What's that?"

"That Caldwell feller was ridin' swing with the herd when it crossed the Brazos, and Conroy was nowhere in sight."

Jake stood silent and stared blankly at Wes. Then he kicked a stone in the dirt and sent it flying.

"Gol dern it," the sheriff said and spat a stream of tobacco juice. "That means he's on to us. But he come on anyways. He thinks he's gonna get that herd through us."

"Wal, we'll see 'bout that," Wes said. And the boom of a rifle shot rolled down from the canyon. And then another. And then several. The men went to the ground on their stomachs, and Jake put the glass to his eye. What he saw exploded his temper. Standing on the red boulder in front of where Jake had the one shooter positioned was Conroy with a rifle on his hip pointed skyward in his right hand. His left arm was wrapped around a limp Deputy Carson, whom he let go to tumble like a rag doll off the boulder and over the cliff.

"That bastard," Jake said, and he shifted the glass to the other deputy whom he could see slumped back against some rocks. "That bastard," Jake snarled again. "He just threw Carson off the cliff, and Gates might be dead, too."

"Gimme that glass," Wes said as he jerked

it out of Jake's hand. "Son of a bitch. He's just sittin' there on that rock smokin' a cigarette. I'm gonna kill him," he roared.

"I gotta git to Gates," the sheriff said with a look of fearful determination.

"All right. But wait, fellers," Jake said in a dead serious, menacing tone. "He wants us to try and git to Gates, and he wants us to try and git to him. That's why he's tauntin' us. He knows what I know. He has the high ground and can pick us off one by one. So, we gotta be Injun-like and sneak up on him. He can't see us ride down off the back of this shelf. Sheriff, yer go ahead and ride down and go around and come up behind Gates. See if yer can git to him but don't expose yerself to Conroy. He seems to be a pretty good shot. If Gates's alive and holdin' on, it might be better to wait until me and Wes have taken care of Conroy."

The sheriff shook his head *yes* and spat.

"Wes, why don't yer ride down thataway and git up high and acrost from Conroy. Yer can keep him busy. Meanwhile I'll circle around to the north. After a ways, I'll turn south and try to git to him from behind. We can git him in a crossfire."

"Why yer the one to git up close? Too dangerous. You got boys to think 'bout. I ain't got nobody."

"Danger ain't never stopped us before."

"We never had time to think 'bout it before."

"Flip yer for it. Call it." Jake pulled a silver dollar from his pants and flipped it into the air.

"Heads." It landed tails.

"All right. Let's go. Wes, yer keep rounds a flyin' regular at that bastard. Yer got enough ammo?"

"Yep."

They mounted up and rode off. Jake got up toward the Wichita and hadn't heard any firing. So, he stopped and pulled out his spyglass to check on Conroy. He found the red boulder, but there was no Conroy to be seen. He shifted quickly over to Wes's position and saw him looking through his glass. But Jake could see that Wes was searching with the glass; he did not have visual contact on the enemy. Jake pulled the glass down and then nearly choked on his own saliva as a lump rose in his throat and his heart skipped a beat. There, riding at a gallop across the south end of the canyon, was Conroy. He was circling around to get in behind Wes and the sheriff, just like Jake was going to do to him. And neither Wes nor the sheriff knew where Conroy was.

Jake jammed the glass back in his saddlebag, spun Jasper around, and raced to head off Conroy. The big paint ran at full stride, jumping scrub clumps and small rock formations. A thick dust trail billowed out behind him. Jake stuck to the saddle and rode like a jockey in a stakes race. But it all was not fast enough, for he saw Conroy turn east and disappear behind an outcropping of boulders. Jake urged Jasper on faster, turned into the boulders, and reined in hard when he saw Conroy's horse grounded on a patch of dirt. Multiple gunshots were echoing in the little draw. He slid the Winchester from its scabbard and ran through the scrabble toward the sound of the gunshots. He arrived in time to see Conroy blasting away at Wes, who jumped over a boulder and slid down to the bottom. Conroy had run up to the top of the boulder and taken aim at Wes when Jake shouldered his rifle and yelled, "Conroy!" The outlaw spun and snapped a shot from his waist with his rifle, and at the same time Jake squeezed the trigger of his Winchester. A forty-four smashed right into the middle of Conroy's chest. He flew back and rolled down the boulder, landing a few yards away from Wes, never to move again.

"Wes?!" Jake called. "Yer all right?"

"Think I broke my arm."

It was then that Jake for the first time felt the pain in his right thigh and looking down saw his blood-soaked pant leg. He untied his bandana and tied it tight around the wound front and back. The bullet had gone in and come out cleanly. He scooted down the boulder and gently landed on the foot of his good leg right beside where Wes was sitting with his back against a boulder. "Let me see that arm," Jake said. "Yeah, it's broke sure. Yer want me to set it fer yer?"

"No, thanks. Think I'll let the doc do that. Whew. Glad yer came when yer did. Son of a bitch shot my rifle right outta my hand. See it over there? He's firing away at me and I jumped behind this rock but landed wrong, and my arm snapped. I couldn't git my pistol out with my left hand when he came to the top of the rock and was gonna plug me. Instead, yer plugged him, thank the Almighty. Guess we're even now." He feigned a sheepish countenance as he squinted up at Jake, then grinned.

Jake grinned and said, "Reckon so. Here, let me make a sling outta yer bandana." He fashioned the sling and gently supported the broken arm in it, then he helped Wes up by his good arm.

"Wal heck. Look at yer leg. Yer worse hurt than me," Wes exclaimed.

"Aw. Ain't nuthin'. Bullet went clean through."

"It's bleedin'."

"I got a bandage in my saddlebag I'll put on it."

Wes supported Jake on his good arm, and they hobbled over to where Jasper stood waiting. Jake rummaged through the saddlebag and pulled out a roll of gauze. Standing on one foot he said, "Here, hold this out like this," as he peeled off a strip of gauze. He pulled his knife and cut a length and then another one. He folded the two pieces into pads and said, "Hold these for a minute. Thanks." He dropped his gunbelt, his cartridge belt, untied his bandana from around his leg, shrugged his suspenders, and dropped his britches. He took one pad from Wes, put it on the entry wound, wrapped one wind of gauze around his leg, put the other pad on the exit wound and made several winds with the roll of gauze around both pads until the roll was exhausted. Then he slit the end into two strips and tied them tight. The pads colored a little red, but the flow did not spread, so the bleeding was staunched. "There. That should do it," he said. "Let's see what that sheriff is up to."

They gingerly mounted and rode over to

where the sheriff was with Gates. "Who goes there?" he called out.

"Yo. It's us, Wes and Jake," Wes called back. They saw a rifle barrel and a hat peek over a boulder, and then the sheriff popped up.

"I heard all the shootin'. What happened?" the sheriff said as he stepped out from his hiding place with his rifle at the ready. Jake recapped for him, and the sheriff said, "That varmint is the meanest snake I ever run into. Killed my one deputy and wounded my other. Wounded y'all, too. At least yer kilt him." Gates came out slowly. He had a bandage around his head. "He's all right. Bullet grazed the side of his head. Knocked him out cold. He's all right now though. Still kinda woozy, huh, Gates?" The deputy nodded his head. "All right y'all, yer wounded go on and git to the doctor in town. I'll pack in the bodies. We'll have to take care of that herd later. Y'all stay clear of 'em on yer way back to town. Don't want a spook 'em. Gates, if yer feel up to it, yer kin git up a posse so's when I git to town I can turn around and ride right back out with the posse. Won't be more'n a hour behind y'all." Gates nodded his head again.

"Don't think yer'll be needin' a posse, Sheriff. We sent a messenger to Bill Vandevert just as soon as that herd crossed the Brazos. Reckon Bill'll be along directly with a bunch a men," Wes said.

The three wounded riders headed southwest at a lope for a half hour, then slowed the horses to a walk. Trotting jarred them too much, so they loped and walked the horses. In another hour they saw the herd in the distance across the grassy plain and turned further west until it dropped from view. They continued to swing west for another few miles, then turned back to the south to head straight for town. Directly, they saw a bunch of riders approaching. Jake counted ten. When they met up Jake hollered, "Bill! They're headed right up the trail. 'Bout five mile. Sheriff is coming behind us with bodies. One is Conroy."

"Figures. Finally got himself killed. Yer see anyone else?"

"JJ Robbins says he's the trail boss, and Caldwell is with 'em. Six all together," Wes shouted.

Vandevert turned his head side to side and called out, "All right, boys. Let's get those beeves back." He and his crew spurred their horses, and in a cloud of dust, with whoops and yips, they galloped away to the northeast. Later Vandevert told what happened. It wasn't long and they caught up to the herd. The rustlers were so busy with the herd they did not see the cowboys coming until the drag riders and one of the swings were lassoed from their horses. The other swing took off at a run. When Robbins saw him go with cowboys chasing after him, he bolted, but his horse wasn't fast enough, and he ended up on the ground with a loop around him and a broken collarbone. The crew got the five rustlers trussed up and turned the herd around and moving to the south. Vandevert rode up beside Robbins and said, "What made you do it, JJ?"

"Needed the money. Yer know my missus died, and I ain't got nobody to watch after the three little shavers. My ma's doin' it now, but she ain't long for this earth." He wouldn't look at Bill.

"Ever rustled before?"

"Onced."

"Got away with it, huh?" Robbins nodded his head *yes.* "Thought you could get away with it again." Robbins nodded *yes.* "You should have come to me to see if there was something we could do. Now you're going to jail, and who's gonna care for your children?" Robbins hung his head and didn't answer. "Do you have any money?" He turned his head from side to side. "I can give you money for a wire. Do you have any relatives who could take in the children?" He nodded his head up and down. "All right then." Vandevert rode off.

He sent four men to take the prisoners to town for jailing, and he and the rest drove the herd back to the Hashknife. When they got to town with the rustlers, Wes was there at the jail waiting for them. Jake was over at the Madison with his leg up. The sheriff came in right behind them and left the horses with the bodies draped over them tied off to the rail outside. In no time a small crowd congregated. After housing the prisoners and hearing the story of the capture from one of the cowboys, the sheriff left and took the bodies to the undertaker. Along the way he had to tell of the events of the day as the little crowd followed beside and behind him. A few brave souls even jumped in front to ask questions. After depositing the bodies, he went to get the JP to view the corpses. Wes left and went over to the Madison, where he told Jake the story of what happened after Vandevert and his crew spurred away to catch up their herd. "Onliest one to git away was that Caldwell feller. Robbins said he had him out scoutin' ahead a the herd," Wes finished up.

"So, we get credit for six countin' Conroy or just one for Conroy since we didn't actually catch the others?" Jake asked.

"Way I look at it — and I think Jim would, too — if it wasn't for us, they might not've ever got caught. That's a lotta money we just saved the Hashknife. So, I'm sayin' eight hunnert head and six rustlers. That equals eight hunnert and thirty dollars. Our usual split — three hunnert fifty for yer and four hunnert and eighty fer me." Wes smiled sardonically and Jake glared at him. "Oh, all right, fifty-fifty," Wes said, and Jake grinned.

"I should get a bonus fer savin' yer life, again!"

"Wal now, I thought we was all square there," Wes said, and it was Jake's turn to grin sardonically.

The sheriff came in the door. "Inquest at ten tomorrow mornin', y'all. Yer know where. And while I am at it, I thank yer both for a fine job. Sorry yer got hurt." He sounded like he was building a lump in his throat, and then he turned quickly and went out the door.

The five rustlers stood in a line in front of Judge Anderson as he finished up their arraignment. "All right," he said. "Sheriff, please remove the prisoners to the jail. We'll wait for your return to begin the inquest." The sheriff and his deputy did as ordered.

Jake sat in the gallery with his leg up on a chair, and Wes was beside him with his splinted arm in a sling. The judge ignored them as he shuffled papers on his bench. The courtroom was otherwise silent. Presently, the sheriff returned.

"All right," Anderson said. "We open an inquest into the deaths of Miles Carson, Deputy Sheriff of Baylor County, Texas, and one Vern Conroy, alleged murderer and cattle rustler. Sheriff, please relate to the court the circumstances of these deaths as you know them."

The sheriff told what he knew with the caveat that he did not see either Carson or Conroy get shot.

"All right. Again, before the court are stock detectives Brighton and Wilson. Second time for Brighton in less than a year. First, the Charles Dalton killing and now this one. Gentlemen, do you agree with the sheriff's testimony as far as it goes? Yes. All right, please inform the court of your knowledge of the circumstances of the death of the two aforesaid individuals, Carson and Conroy." Both Jake and Wes related the circumstances as they occurred.

"Fine. Thank you both. Pursuant to the testimony of the witnesses the court finds that the death of Deputy Carson was murder by gunshot at the hands of Vern Conroy, and the death of Vern Conroy was homicide by gunshot at the hands of Jonas V. Brighton in defense of another. However, the court is concerned that here again it appears that detective Brighton may have exerted excessive force in subduing a suspect. After all, Detective Brighton, you were only shot in the leg. Could you have not afforded the same consideration to your victim during your actions? Perhaps only wounding him rather than killing him?"

Jake stood and leaned on his crutch. "Your Honor. As I understand it, your question goes to my intent. Would that be correct?"

"Yes."

"In other words, did I intend to kill Conroy or disable him so I could prevent him from killing my partner, Wes Wilson? Is that what the court would like to know?"

"Yes."

"Frankly, Judge, at the time I never thought of it one way or another. It all happened in a flash. My intent was to prevent the killing of my partner, and that is what I did. Don't forget I had but a short time before witnessed the murder of Deputy Carson at the hands of, as you call him, the victim, but who, as you yourself have just decided, was in fact a felon. That felon shot me in the leg because he spun and shot too fast. There is no doubt in my mind that he intended to kill detective Wilson and me and the sheriff and would have done so had I not shot him first. I took aim and fired so he could not fire again. There was not time to think about just winging him." Jake sat down.

"Very well. Thank you. However, for the record the court hereby admonishes you, Detective Brighton, to in the future, if you are confronted with a like situation, to consider the exercise of less deadly force. That is all. This inquest is closed."

As they hobbled out of the courthouse Jake said, "He didn't hear a word I said. He thinks we are rabid killers."

" 'Course he does. He's a Easterner. He's never been in a gunfight. And I ain't rabid. But if I am gonna shoot, I'm usually gonna shoot to kill," Wes said emphatically.

"Me too. It's too easy to git shot back if yer don't. Let's get a drink."

"Kinda early ain't it?"

"I need one to calm my anger. That judge ain't gonna be nuthin' but trouble. Second time he's taken me to task."

The following Wednesday morning with dust swirling around him, Bill Vandevert pulled his buckboard up to a stop at Madison's Boarding House and tied off his team to the hitch ring on the post outside. He pulled off his hat and bandana. The wind blew back his brown hair, and he mopped the sweat off his brow and his hatband. He looked through the dust haze to the sky. There was a little spit of rain last month. It wasn't much. Just enough to settle the dust. He turned his head slowly side to side with a look of disgust on his face. He mounted the steps and opened the door to see Jake and Wes sitting in chairs in the parlor reading newspapers, drinking coffee, and smoking cigars. Jake had his leg up on an ottoman, and Wes had the newspaper in his lap turning pages with his one good hand. They both looked up when Bill came through the door. Wes stood and Jake reached for his crutch. "No, no. Stay seated. Howdy, boys," Vandevert said with his hand held up, motioning them to sit back down.

"Howdy, Bill," Wes said. "What brings yer our way?" He pulled a chair around for Bill so as they could sit as one little group.

"Well, it occurred to me that I never thanked y'all for what you did. So, I thought I'd stop by and say thank you." Although younger than both Jake and Wes, he had the visage of a natural born leader about him.

His intelligent hazel eyes held their gaze without challenge or threat but with business-like firmness presenting as one who could not be pushed. "With your detective work y'all saved the Hashknife a lotta money, and it is much appreciated."

"Wal, it's our job, and we try to do our best. Glad to do it. Why don't yer set a spell and have some coffee and a cigar? Hashknife ain't gonna run away," Wes said with an affective smile.

"Believe I will. Thank you."

Wes arose and went to the sideboard in the dining room. One handed, he poured a cup of coffee and said, "Take anything with it?"

"No, just black. Thanks."

After they hashed over the events of the rustling for a few minutes, Jake said, "Well, I guess that feller Vern Conroy is gettin' kind of famous even as a dead man. Newspapers and folks are all talkin' 'bout how he slipped out eight hundred head right under your nose and killed a deputy sheriff while doin' it."

Vandevert took a drink of coffee, puffed a couple times on his cigar, and blew a cloud of blue smoke to the ceiling. For a moment he watched the smoke rise and then said, "You ever read any Shakespeare?"

"Who's that?" Wes said.

Jake smiled, slightly hidden under his mustache, and said, "He wrote plays way back when. The plays are in books now, and all the civilizee's read 'em. A lot of people think he was a very witty feller — even like a medicine man. But yer don't have to worry, Wes, cuz even though yer think I'm a civilizee, I don't read Shakespeare." Wes turned his head and blew a cloud of tobacco smoke, set his jaw, and did not turn his head back. Jake's smile grew.

"Well, I don't read him either, but my wife, Sadie, makes me sit after supper in the winter and listen to her read the books. Even still, there is one line I memorized. It's in a play about an ancient Roman emperor. One of them is making a speech and he says, 'The evil that men do lives after them; The good is oft interred with their bones.' What do you think of that? Ain't it the truth?"

Both Jake and Wes stared blankly at Bill. "I guess so," Jake said.

"It means that history almost always glosses over goodness when there is no heroism and almost always highlights infamy. Take for example that Vern Conroy. He'll be famous for a while because of the evil he did. But the ones who did the good, you boys, will probably be forgotten. You see what I mean?"

"Think so," Jake said as he and Wes nodded their heads.

"Or take that gunfight in Tombstone two years ago. The story made it into all the newspapers across the country all the way to New York City and out to San Francisco. And folks still talk about it, like we are now. Some folks side with the lawmen. Others say the outlaws were murdered by the lawmen. Now . . ." he paused and stared at them intently. "I think the whole affair was evil, and because of that, folks will be talkin' about it for a hundred years. They won't be talkin' about any good that came from it. And if they keep talkin' about the Conroy affair, which they will, eventually they'll get around to you, Jake. They'll talk about how you killed Conroy. But they won't talk about you savin' the lives of those cowboys who were fool enough to join up with Conroy or savin' eight hundred head a cattle. I ain't excludin' you, Wes. I'm just tryin' to show you what I am talkin' about. You see?"

"Yep," they both said in unison. "What yer sayin' is that as long as we're range detectives, only certain folks will appreciate what we do. But most folks will talk a long time 'bout us killin' outlaws," Wes said, and

Jake looked at him, a little astonished. "What'er yer gawking at? I kin figger things out yer know."

Jake grinned and poked him with his crutch. "I know. Yer the one who gave me the 'rawhide' moniker, and that's all people ever talk 'bout — who Rawhide Jake Brighton kilt. Yer said that would happen, and it has." Wes shrugged his shoulders.

Vandevert drained his cup, stood, and said, "Well, thanks for the coffee. I'll just keep this cigar and finish it on the ride back to the outfit. Good talking with y'all." He turned and went out the door.

"There goes a good man," Jake said.

"Edicated, too. But he ain't no civilizee. He's got grit," Wes said.

CHAPTER FIVE:
WEDDING BELLS
1884

Jake and Wes ate Christmas dinner at the Madison House. Jake was getting around without a crutch, and Wes had the splint off and was just about back to normal. They sat down to the table with Missus Madison and her son and young wife, and another stock detective Jim Loving sent over to fill in for Jake and Wes. The fencing crew was working close enough to Seymour that Boqin could come into town with Changlei and Niu to pick up supplies and payroll. Jake arranged for the bookkeeper at the Flying XC to wire the monthly remittance to him in Seymour. So, things were a little rough but still running along.

After dinner Wes said, "Wal, what a yer think? — We gonna be back in the saddle by spring?"

"Sure. But I don't think I'll be able to make it out 'til spring," Jake said with a sly smile.

"Uh-huh. Cold might be too hard on that leg," Wes replied and pushed his cheek out with his tongue. "So far it's been pretty dern cold, too. Wonder if there's gonna be any snow this winter?"

"Almanac says no. Gonna be a dry winter followed by drought. That's what's got everybody so jittery. Yer know two dry years in a row ain't good," Jake prognosticated.

"Uh-huh. Wal, saloons are closed. Want a play some rummy?"

"All right. But first, here's somethin' I got yer fer Christmas," Jake said, a little shaky in the voice. "Yer saved my life twice, and I know we're even but even still." He pulled a brand-new Winchester model 1873, 44-40 caliber rifle from behind the door to the dining room and offered it to Wes. "Since yer lost yers to the no-account Conroy and yer too cheap to buy yer own, I got yer a new one."

Wes looked back and forth from the rifle to Jake with an astounded look on his face. "Pard, I never —"

"Aw, go on. Take it."

"But I ain't got yer nuthin'." He looked down at the floor in a posture of shame, and when his gaze crossed Jake's boots he looked up with a cheery smile. "I just remembered, and this is the truth. I been lookin' at yer boots and thinkin' yer need a new pair, and I was gonna get 'em for yer. But I never got 'round to it. Tomorrow, though, we're goin' down to Stigler's, an' I'm buyin' yer a new pair a boots. That's my Christmas gift to yer. A little late is all." He grinned his old grin. "Now, gimme that rifle."

They pumped each other's hand and slapped each other's back. Then went to the parlor to pass the time away at a game of gin rummy.

Winter passed with no snow and no rain. Spring came with no rain. Jake was busier selling windmills than anything else. He was down at Seymour filling out orders and drilling contracts on a March early afternoon when Wes came riding in. They went over to the new Jenny's Café for dinner. Jenny had no whiskey, but she had beer, and they each ordered a beer along with their food. Wes took a drink from his mug and said, "Don't suppose yer heared the news from the Flyin' XC?"

"I was just there five days ago. What news?"

"Josh Walton got kicked by a mustang stallion. Like a fool he tried to rope the horse out in the corral so he could shoe it, but he ain't no cowboy." Over the rim of his mug Wes watched Jake's reaction.

"Was he kilt?"

"Dead as a doornail. Cracked his skull. Thought yer'd be a little more excited."

"What a yer mean?"

"Mary Jane Walton's a widow now." Wes smiled slightly, and so did Jake.

"They gonna have a funeral service?"

"Already did today. Can't leave 'em out too long this time a year. Git too ripe."

"Yer see Mary Jane afterwards?"

"Nope. I figger, give it 'bout a month before yer start sparkin' her."

"A month, huh? Yer sparkin' her?"

"Me?" Wes exclaimed as he leaned back in his chair and gave Jake an incredulous look. "Yer loco? I'm a long ways away from settlin' down with a wife and leetle shavers. No siree. Not me."

"Just wonderin'. Feller's gotta know who his competition is," Jake said as he jabbed his fork into fried chicken breast and picked up his knife. "Month, huh?"

Jake cleaned his plate with the last of a biscuit, drained his beer glass, wiped his mustache and mouth clean with the linen napkin, slid his chair back, and stood. "Where yer headin'?" Wes said.

"Down to the store. Got business to take

care of. See yer later."

"Howdy, Bert," Jake said as he walked through the doors of Stigler's General Store.

"Howdy, Jake. What can I get you?"

"Well, I need some fancy notepaper. The best you have."

"Got just the thing over here under the glass." He retrieved a boxed set of notepaper and matching envelopes. He opened the lid of the box as far as a red silk restraint ribbon on one side would allow. A matching ribbon ran diagonally across the notepaper in the box. "This is the very best money can buy. A full twenty-four sheets, silk, water-lined paper. Pure white, six by five inches. The very best grade."

"How much?"

"Fifty cents for the box."

"I'll take it. Can I borrow pen and ink from you?" Jake said as he dug a silver dollar out of his pants pocket and set it on the counter.

"Here's your change and a pen with a fine gold nib. It's an Excello. Sells for a dollar. Here's the ink. Dann's blue-black for ten cents."

Jake looked askance at Bert and said, "You are probably right. I should buy them instead of borrow as I think I said." Bert smiled and said nothing. "All right. Another dollar then. Here you go."

Bert placed the notepaper in one brown paper sack and the ink in another. "Would you like to carry this fine pen on your person?"

"All right. Thanks, Bert." Jake left and went to the parlor at the Madison. He sat down at the writing desk against one wall, took out a sheet of the notepaper and the ink, dipped his pen, and wrote:

Dearest Mary Jane,
I just learned of your tragic loss. Please accept my deepest sympathies. I hope to be up that way in a week or so and will stop by to be sure you are making out all right. If there is anything you need or I can do, please let me know at your earliest convenience. If need be, you can wire me here in Seymour.

May God bless you.
Very truly yours,
Jonas V. Brighton

He read it over a couple of times, thought about changing it, and decided it was fine. So, he addressed the envelope, stuffed it with the note, got up, and walked to the post office, where he posted the letter. "How long do you think?" he asked the postmaster.

"Well, we got hacks comin' every day now and goin' out to Wichita Falls. Used to be the Concord Stage would take the mail twice a week. So we's a lot faster now. They ride straight through. Changing riders and horses halfway. Takes 'em 'bout five hours. So, we say overnight to Wichita Falls. After that to the settlement, well, it's a little longer. Stage only runs onced a week to Vernon. Sooo — let's see. Today's Tuesday. Stage leaves on Thursday. Stops overnight at Harrold, so we can say it should be in the settlement probably Friday or Saturday."

Jake looked at the postmaster and sighed. "I guess you could've just said Saturday instead of giving me a postal lesson."

The postmaster squinched up his face and said, "However, we are human, and sometimes we lose a piece of mail." He stared at Jake with obvious suggestion written all over his face.

"Oh, no. Don't misunderstand me. It was interesting. I know you will take real good care of this letter." He smiled broadly in his most effective way.

The postmaster smiled back and said, "We'll do our best."

Jake tipped his hat and walked out the

door. Under his breath he said, "Dern well better take good care of the letter."

A week from Thursday he received a response from Mary Jane:

Dearest Jonas,
Thank you for your note. I do so appreciate it, and I do so anticipate your visit. I am doing as well as can be expected so am not in need of anything. Thank you for your offer. See you soon.

May God bless you.
Very truly yours,
Mary Jane.

Jake read the note and smiled. To himself he said, "Wes says a month, huh. I'm leaving tomorrow."

He stopped to check on the fencing crew. They were moving along nicely on the Flying XC southern border. He stopped at his usual halfway camp and the next day was in the bathtub at the Flying XC bunkhouse long before the crew came in at day's end. He bathed, shaved, put on clean underwear, and dug his black suit out of his valise. It was badly wrinkled, but as luck would have it, Chan was ironing his own clothes and pressed Jake's suit as best he could. It still had some wrinkles but would have to do.

He mounted up and was gone before anyone except Chan knew he was there. Along the way to the settlement, he stopped to pick a bouquet of bluebonnets.

At the store in the settlement, he persuaded one of the store-owner's boys to run a note over to Mary Jane announcing his arrival at her place in the next half hour. It would have been impolite just to show up on her doorstep without giving her an opportunity to clean up herself. When the boy returned Jake asked him what she said. "She screamed and slammed the door in my face." Jake smiled delightedly and gave the boy two copper pennies.

Thinking he better give her a little extra time, he waited forty minutes and then walked over to the Calhoun house with his bouquet.

She was amazing. In the short time she had available, she made herself gorgeous. The fragrance of lavender about her was intoxicating. She wore her thick and shiny auburn hair swept up to the top of her head, with frizzled bangs over her forehead. Adorning her slim figure was a dark-plum colored day dress of silk taffeta with plunging neckline. Her deep-blue eyes gleamed against her fair complexion as over her high cheekbones they focused on Jake and virtually danced with good cheer. Her nose was petite over her full lips set in a little mischievous smile. Her chin was strong and had just enough prominence to give her an exotic appearance with hints of underlying riotous intent. Jake felt weak kneed and somewhat silly. He beamed his admiration as he held the flowers in both hands against his chest. Just a few minutes ago he was full of male confidence on the hunt for a mate. Now he could barely stand, and, strangely, his voice seemed to have disappeared.

"Why, Mister Brighton, what a surprise. I've been a widow barely two weeks, and you come courting. My goodness. I presume the flowers are for me. Come in." Her smile and the twinkle in her eyes were the most playful he had ever seen in any woman of any repute — ill or otherwise. He stepped across the threshold and held the door back so it would not slam. Once inside, he froze. "Come in, come in. The Calhouns have gone to their mansion in Denton. We are alone. I trust you'll behave yourself." Was it his imagination, or did the twinkle in her eye jump out at him? "Good gracious. What's the matter with you? Cat got your tongue?" Certainly, now her smile was that of a mischievous little imp. "Why, I do believe you are smitten. Have I smitten you,

Mister Brighton?"

"Uh . . . I feel funny. You are, uh, the most beautiful woman I have ever seen."

She melted, and they rushed each other, falling into a mad embrace of swirling emotion, kissing, and fondling. Mary Jane let herself go limp, and Jake eased her down on the sofa. He positioned himself and devoured her in luscious kisses as she did him. In between kisses they gasped for air as they panted hot breath upon each other. Mary Jane's face became dewy, and Jake could feel the perspiration pop out on his forehead. He was about to make his move when she suddenly screamed, "No!" She pushed him back and sat up, straightening her dress and re-pinning her hair. She stood and stepped to the middle of the room, where she stopped and placed her hands on her hips.

"This is not right. Of course, I am no virgin, but I am no whore neither. You'll do right by me, Mister Brighton, before there is any hanky-panky between us. As you can tell I am easily swayed, so I expect you to be an honorable man."

"Will you marry me then?"

"Why . . . we hardly know each other but . . . yes, I will." She flew into his arms, and they fell back onto the sofa, her on top of him.

"Hold on. Hold on. I am doing the honorable thing. We must wait 'til we are hitched," Jake said as he lifted her off him and to his side. "Mary Jane. I love you and want to do right by you."

"Oh, Jake. I love you, too," she said as she laid her head on his shoulder. And they stayed in that embrace on the sofa for some long and tender moments. Then she said, "Would you like some tea? I have water on the stove."

They were sitting in the parlor next to each other with their teacups and tea service on the coffee table in front of them when the doorbell rang. Jake straightened his vest, and Mary Jane rose to answer the door. "Oh, hello, Missus Higgins. Come in, please."

The older matron wearing her hat and brown visiting dress came in carrying a basket of food all wrapped up in a red and white checkered towel. "I brought you some vittles so's you don't have to cook or go out if you don't want to," she said with a smile, which gradually faded as she turned her head to see Jake standing in the parlor. "Are you receiving visitors?"

"Yes. This is our, or now, my dear friend,

Jonas Brighton. He rode all the way from Seymour to look in on me to make sure I am fine and take care of any chores that might need doing. It's hard to think of things without Josh. I am sorry." Mary Jane dropped her head to her chest and dabbed her eye with her hanky.

"Nice to meet you, Mister Brighton. Well, if I can be of any help . . ."

"Would you like a cup of tea?"

"Don't mind if I do." Missus Higgins placed herself in a chair across from the sofa. "Thank you," she said as Mary Jane handed her a cup full of steaming tea on a saucer. She blew off the steam and took a sip from the cup. She lowered the cup and saucer to her lap and said, "Well, my goodness, do you think the Lord will send some rain our way?"

"If only we could divine the Lord's will," Jake smiled. "For the weather and in love and life." He continued to smile at Missus Higgins, who was obviously becoming uncomfortable under Jake's steady gaze. But she wouldn't budge. Finally, Jake tired of the small talk and said, "I had better take my leave, Mary Jane. Have some business at the Flying XC. I will finish those chores tomorrow. Good day, Missus Higgins."

"I'll see you to the door," Mary Jane said.

At the door Jake whispered, "I'll be back after dark" and blew her a kiss.

An hour after dark Jake stabled Jasper in the barn behind the Calhoun house. He looked around furtively and then sprinted for the back door to the house. Mary Jane was there and waiting. She opened the door for him, he slipped inside, she shut the door quickly and was in his arms. They kissed long with passion. Then Mary Jane stepped back.

"You see there are many Missus Higgins types around, and if my honor is to remain unsullied, we have to be very careful."

"Why don't we just go to Wichita Falls tomorrow and see Judge Howard?"

"That wouldn't be proper. Not enough time has elapsed since Josh's death."

"Aw, who cares?"

"Oh, my Jonas. I do."

"Oh. Uh-huh."

"Besides, we need to get to know about each other. Let's sit down here at the table. Want some coffee?"

"Got any whiskey?"

"Josh never drank. I can borrow some of Mister Calhoun's if you promise to pay it back."

"Let's see what it is. Make sure it is available out here."

Jake poured himself three fingers of Overholt into one of two glasses she set on the table. Then started pouring in the other glass and said, "Say when." When there were about two fingers of whisky in the glass, she said, "When." He pulled a cigar from his vest, held it up, and asked, "All right?" She nodded *yes.* He smiled and lit up.

"I know all I need to know. From the first moment I saw you, I fell in love, but you were forbidden fruit. So, I went about my business and tried to put you out of my mind."

"And I was attracted to you. As the months went by you were always on my mind. Josh was steadfast and a good provider, but he wasn't the fun-loving type. And was not the best in bed. At first, he was after me all the time. But after the children were born, he seldom made advances. We had six children. Three are still living and all out on their own now. So, it was about three years into the marriage when my love for him began to fade, and ever since I've just been doing my duty."

"So, you *were* flirting with me the first time we met."

"Yes, I'm afraid I was. But I felt like I was trapped in an empty marriage, and I suppose my eye just naturally wandered. All I could assume is that my future was going to be a cook and housekeeper married to a blacksmith for the rest of my days. You were the first in a long time to come around who tickled my fancy. Not much to choose from out here."

"Well, why did you marry him?"

"Security, I suppose. I was sixteen, and my father was pushing me to marry. We're from Kansas City, Missourah. He was a clerk for the city and didn't make much salary. All he could do to support a family of ten counting himself. Getting me and my sisters married meant one less mouth for him to feed, and he could save the difference. I always admired Josh. He was different back then. He was an apprentice smithy when we met. I always tried to encourage him to open his own shop, but he was always too afraid of the risk. Not like you." She smiled affectionately. "You have a regular job and a business on the side."

"Two." He made a small grin. "Two businesses on the side. I sell windmills and drilling services, too."

She arched her eyebrows and said, "See. I knew there was something special about you. Anyway, Josh went to work for Mister Calhoun in seventy-two. We came out here with Xavier in seventy-eight. I have a son in

Fort Worth. William. He sells real estate. Another in Austin who is in the first class of the University of Texas. Thomas. Wants to be a lawyer. Xavier got him in. Paying his tuition on the promise that Thomas will work for the Calhouns when he is a lawyer. And our little Alice. She is in Decatur married to a successful shop owner. Millinery. No grandchildren. So that's the short of it. Just been passing time the last few years. What about you?"

Jake went through a summary of his life's story, and when he finished Mary Jane said, "I don't know if I like that stock detective work. Sounds really dangerous to me."

"It has its risks. But the pay and bonuses are good. And you said risk taking makes a man special." Again, he gave her a small affectionate grin.

Over the next couple of months Jake worked his schedule around so he could spend as much time as possible with Mary Jane. They got to know each other a lot better, and their love grew from the mere physical to mutual admiration, respect, and dedication. Jake was discovering that, even though Mary Jane was a little oversexed, she was an honest, moral woman who controlled her urges. He started feeling a little guilty. So, late in April he rode the fifty miles to Henrietta, stopping overnight at about halfway in Wichita Falls. The next day he trotted Jasper up to the hitching post in front of St. Mary's Church. It was a wooden building with a low steeple over the front doors. Jake looked up at the steeple, took a deep breath, and walked around to the side to find the door to the parish office. He asked the secretary about an available priest to hear his confession.

"Confessions are on Saturday mornings," she said.

"Yes, ma'am. I wonder if an exception might be made. I rode fifty miles, and I am carrying a heavy load of guilt." He tried to look as pitiful as he could.

She seemed to look more sympathetic and said, "Well, you are in luck. Father is in his office. I'll check to see if he can see you."

Jake sat in a pew, and the priest placed a chair in front of him. Then he blessed the proceeding saying in a soothing voice, "In the name of the Father, the Son, and the Holy Spirit. What ails you, my son?"

Jake stared at the floor and said, "Well, Father, I have two boys living with my sister-in-law in Independence, Kansas. I provide for them with money to help my sister-in-law and her new husband. My wife and little girl were killed in a cyclone in seventy-six. I been unmarried ever since. And . . . I been . . . well, dallying with ladies of ill repute." He glanced up to see if there was any reaction. None. "I am to marry real soon, and that's part a the reason I'm here. Also, I am a stock detective working for the Stock-Raisers' Association of North-West Texas. I chase rustlers. I had to kill some who were gonna kill me."

"How many?"

"Six. And one feller that was gonna kill a friend of mine. And another me and another feller shot together. That'd be eight." Jake fell silent. "Maybe more," he said sheepishly.

After a long minute the priest said, "Anything else?"

"No, sir. That's about it."

"Are you sorry for these sins?" That caught Jake by surprise. He forgot about that part. It had been a long, long time since he went to confession, and he hadn't thought about it. Sorry? Not really. The interval became awkward.

"Fornication is a sin against the body that God created. Killing is a violation of the Sixth Commandment. Both are offenses against God. You should be sorry for offending your Heavenly Father."

"Yes. When you put it like that, I am sorry for offending God for fornication and killing. I am sorry I had to kill those men. But I ain't sorry for them. They tried to kill me, and they were all bad men."

"Perhaps another occupation would be in order, my son. For your penance, pray three Our Fathers and five Hail Marys and pray and meditate upon the possibilities for a new direction to take for your life in your new marriage. Now, please make your prayer of contrition." He handed Jake a prayer card to recite from. When he was finished, the priest went through the rite of absolution, and it was over. They stood, and Jake shook the priest's hand and tried to give him ten dollars. "Will you take this, Father?" he said as he pressed the note into the priest's hand.

"Please, just give it to the secretary for the parish." He smiled kindly at Jake as they walked back to the office.

On May 16, 1884, a Friday, Mary Jane and Jake stood before Judge Howard in Wichita Falls and were officially hitched. The Catholic folks they knew had urged them to be married in the church. Some of the folks on the ranch and around the settlement thought they got married in a fever. When the subjects came up, they just gazed adoringly at each other and smiled. Walt and Millie Guthrie seemed to know something of how the lovebirds felt and had a little reception for them on Sunday. They had cake and punch, which seemed to taste stronger as the day went on, humorous speeches were made, and the two singing cowboys of the Flying XC crew worked up a special little performance for the newlyweds. It all was very nice, and Mary Jane was again a happy woman.

Chapter Six:
A Friend Is a Friend

A week after the wedding, Jake was settled in at Mary Jane's room in the Calhoun house and figured he better get back to work. His leg was healed up, and he didn't have any hitch in his giddy-up, so he felt fit and thought that if he didn't get back out on the range, he would soon get fat from Mary Jane's delicious cooking.

The spring roundup was finished and the cattle shipped out of Wichita Falls to Fort Worth on the new Fort Worth and Denver Railroad. Except for what Calhoun and Walt Guthrie figured the ranch could sustain in the drought, almost the whole herd was shipped. So, Jake decided to head way west into the open range grassland and search south to the north for any strays that got missed in the roundup or any stock snaked away by rustlers. Walt had to let a lot of cowboys go because the smaller herd reduced the need for cowboy labor. Calhoun was generous and paid each cowboy they had to let go a month's wages as severance pay. Many of the cowboys headed west all the way to California, and some went north looking for work. But a few hung around, and they were the desperate ones who, in their minds, would be forced to steal a beef to sell for money to survive on. They were the ones Jake would be on the lookout for. He planned to work his way north to Doan's Crossing and help Wes out with the inspections at the Red River for a few days. After that, he intended to hurry back to the settlement and his Mary Jane. He'd be gone for a week.

On the second day out, he came up against the rough mesquite covered hills around the confluence of the Middle Fork and North Fork of the Wichita River, where he saw of all things a bison bull, three cows, and two calves. They were grazing the grass along the base of the hills, and Jake watched them through his spyglass for a good ten minutes and then moved off to give them a wide berth as he continued west. He came to the top of a ridge and down the other side to another span of grass with another hill of mesquite to the west of it. The North Wichita made a bend into and then out of the big meadow that he bisected from east to west to see if he would cut any trail and pick up some sign. He did.

He reined in Jasper and stepped out of the saddle, got down on one knee, and examined the hoofprints. They were fresh. Not more than three days old. And mixed in with the livestock prints was the sign of three shod horses. Jake followed the trail of trampled grass heading north and determined there were probably about a dozen cows and three horses. After about a mile he came across the sign of a fast-moving horse that appeared to have run into the bunch from the east. Then the trail was all a mess as it looked like the cows scattered and there was a skirmish.

That set off alarms, and he snapped his head up from studying the ground, to survey the surrounding area to check for ambushers or other varmints. When he did, he saw a trail of trampled grass heading off to the west into the hills. He pulled his rifle from the scabbard, rested it across his lap, and touched his spurs to Jasper's sides. They moved off to the west generally paralleling the trail of trampled grass. He kept his head on a swivel and looked sharply about him, alert for any sign of movement or color or standout shapes. Halfway along, he saw something in the mesquite he couldn't quite make out, but it didn't look natural. He took out his spyglass and sighted in. A slight shock went through him as he saw a man, naked from the waist up, tied to a big mesquite bush in a standing position. He pulled down the glass and slowly, carefully looked around him again for any sign of anything. The only thing moving was a flock of buzzards flying in circles over the spot where the man was trussed up. Holding Jasper to a slow walk, he approached.

About fifty yards out, he stopped and again looked through his spyglass. It looked like the man was unconscious, as there was no movement from him. Two buzzards were perched on a branch off to the side of the man. Jake looked behind him for the hundredth time and to his sides and then peered into the mesquite. The sun was still high so he could see pretty good into the bushes. There was no horse around anywhere he could see. He went ahead and walked Jasper up to the man, and the perched buzzards flew off. From the saddle, he saw that the feller was sunburned bright red, and his face was blistered and swollen. He looked to be alive, but his breathing was shallow, and he was surely unconscious.

"Hey, mister. You awake?" Jake questioned. No response. "Hey!" Jake said loudly. Still no response. He stepped out of the saddle and looked closely at the feller. He looked familiar, but his face was such a mess he couldn't really recognize him. Jake looked about the man for any kind of weapon, pistol, or knife. Nothing. So, he got his canteen and poured a trickle of water over the man's head of grayish hair that was mottled with blood clots. That revived him, and he stuck out his swollen tongue to catch the water slipping over his nose. When he opened his eyes, Jake recognized him. "Sticker Joe!" he exclaimed in a shocked voice.

"Water," Sticker groaned.

Gently, Jake held the canteen to Sticker's lips, which cracked and bled as soon as he touched them. Sticker went after the canteen like a calf to the tit. He choked and coughed, and water sprayed out of his mouth. "Careful now. Not too much at once," Jake said. "Let's git yer outta the sun."

Jake looked around for a hat or shirt, but there was nothing, so he took off his hat, set it gently on Sticker's head, and pulled the stampede string tight. Then he wrapped his bandana around his own head like a scarf and reached around with his knife to cut Sticker loose. He was prepared to catch a falling man, but Sticker Joe just slipped a little and groaned heavily. Then Jake saw why. He was impaled on the mesquite thorns. "Oh Jesus, Mary, and Joseph! They got yer stuck on to the mesquite stickers." Jake felt a little nausea creep up. He fought it down and said, "Gonna have to pull yer off one at a time real easy-like."

"Here. This is the way to do it." Spurlock groaned. In halting speech, he said, "Take my hands and pull me off all at once. Straight off. Don't want any thorns breaking off and leavin' some a the sticker in me."

"Yer sure?"

"Yep. Trust me. My handle ain't Sticker fer nuthin. This is how I got it. Now here. Pull me. Pull hard, straight, and fast." He held out his hands.

Jake reached out and took Sticker's two wrists, squeezed, and pulled him toward his chest. The victim never screamed or yelled or cursed. He just groaned, passed out, and fell into Jake's arms. Jake looked down toward the river and spied a small grove of plateau oak trees along a drainage creek at the river. He laid Spurlock down and said, "Gotta git yer down to that shade. Then I kin doctor yer up." He went to his saddlebag, pulled out a clean shirt, and wrapped it around Spurlock. Then he poured a little more water on Sticker's head, and he came to. "Okay, Sticker, we gotta ride double down to that oak grove, so I'll help yer into the saddle. Yer sit in front a me. Here we go." Jake lifted him up and into the saddle and then vaulted himself up.

They made it to the grove without incident. Jake laid Sticker out on his tarp, then went about setting up a camp. He got a fire going and found a good-sized rock with a bowl hollowed in it and took it up to the camp. Then he started carrying water from the river in his tin stew pot and filled the hollow in the rock. He boiled up water, let it cool somewhat, and gently washed Sticker's head, neck, and upper body, front and back, while Sticker continued to drink water from the canteen.

Once he finished washing and cooling Sticker, Jake said, "What do I need to do 'bout them sticker holes?"

Sticker was coming around more and more and answered, "Wal, first we need to see if there be any that need cut out." He unwrapped the shirt off him and rolled over on his stomach, which caused him to hiss at the sting from his sunburned skin on the tarp. Jake looked his back over, slow and deliberate.

"I see ten holes, and two of 'em look like

there's some sticker in 'em."

"Okay. Cut 'em out."

Jake performed the minor surgery and took gauze pads from his first-aid kit to press on the wounds. Sticker said, "Yer got any soap?"

"Yep. Got a bar in my saddlebag."

"Any sugar?"

"Yup."

"Okay. Cut shavings off the soap and mix it in with the sugar to make a paste."

Jake set a tin plate on the rock and shaved off his bar of soap. Then he crushed his sugar cubes and made a paste like Sticker said.

"Okay, now make a poultice of dry moss mixed in the paste and put it on each hole with mud on top. Git the pison out."

Jake got the poultices all on Sticker's back, then said, "Got some bacon and hardtack. Yer want ta et?"

"Tomorrow." And he fell asleep.

In the morning, Jake had coffee going when Sticker woke up. He rolled over and sat up. "Smells good," he said. "I'll have some and some a that bacon if yer be fixin' it."

"Comin' right up. Yer lookin' a dern sight better. Swellin's down. Still red and blistered though."

"Uh-huh. 'Magine them poultices have felled off."

"Yep. When yer sat up. Here yer go." Jake handed him a tin cup of coffee.

"Wal, guess those dern fools ain't got rid of ol' Sticker Joe after all."

"What happened?"

"Wal, yer ever meet that raunchy cowboy on the spread named Sideways Bill?"

Jake turned his head side to side.

"Wal, I been keepin' a eye on him a long time. This was his second year. I knowed he was a thief. Just could never get the goods on him. Wal, he was one a the cowboys let go. He and two others he pardnered up with. None of 'em took it easy. 'Fact they was hoppin' mad. Might yer have some ter-baccy?"

"Cigar."

"No chaw? Okay I guess that'll do." He took a minute to light up and then continued. "So, when they rode off to the west I trailed 'em. Make sure they wasn't takin' no Flyin' XC stock with 'em. Sure enuff. I caught 'em. Only thing is, they corraled me and threw me afore I could git my shootin' iron pulled. They's thought it was real funny to crucify me, is what they's said, on a sticker bush. Hrrumph." He took a long drag off the cigar and paused a minute.

"Cuz my handle is Sticker Joe, yer see? Said I didn't look so tough stuck to that sticker bush, and they's laughed it up real big. But what they's don't know is I got a guardian angel thas been protectin' me all my life. From the day them Comanch kilt my fambly to this very time when she sent yer to save me." He smiled impishly and said, "Yeah, my angel is a girl. Yer got one?"

"I dunno. Guess so."

"Wal, I'd look into it if I were yer, Mister Rawhide Jake Brighton. Oh yeah. I 'member yer, and like Walt Guthrie I guess I'm beholdin' to yer. Much obliged." He held out his hand for a shake.

Jake was a little taken aback and choked up a tad. The great Sticker Joe Spurlock was beholden to him. "The honor is mine," Jake said and smiled admirably at Joe as he shook hands.

"Yeah, and I don't even mind if yer let it go to yer head." He smiled and chuckled. Jake smiled back at his new friend.

"Wal, then how'd yer git the Sticker Joe handle anyhow? I heared from Johnny Raymer that yer hogtied some ragin' bull and pulled a sticker outta him, and he was yer pet ever after."

"Yeah, I heared that one afore. I think I'm a little giddy. Ain't normally this much a talker. Must be the sun. Don't yer tell no one," he said with a scowl at Jake. Then he gulped some coffee and puffed his cigar. "Truth is, it was a bull, but he ain't no pet. Long years ago, we was movin' the bulls, and one got into a bunch a mesquite and wouldn't come out. So, I got off my horse and ran up and looped that bull. Wal, he tried to git me and charged outta that mesquite, but I got away, and he ran back into the bushes. But I still had my rope and a loop around him. So, I got back up on my horse, dallied my rope, and started to drag him out. He was stronger and pulled me and my horse into the bush. That son of a bitch gored my horse real bad. He's screamin', and that devil is roarin'. We're crashing around in the brush. My horse went down, and the devil came after us. I jumped free and shot that devil three times right between the eyes. Me and my horse got all stickered up. My horse died. I liked that horse a lot. I climbed outta the brush all full a stickers. Wal, they's called me Sticker Joe behind my back at first, and then I didn't care. So, it's stuck with me ever since. And yer are one a the few fellers who know the truth. Keep it thataway."

"Yer can count on it." Jake started frying up the bacon and chunking the hardtack.

"More coffee?" he said. Sticker nodded his head, and Jake filled his cup. "That rustlers' trail looks like it is headin' north."

"Yeah. I know where they's goin'. They's gonna make camp 'bout five miles outta Vernon on the Pease and drop that bunch a critters there. Then they's gonna go into town and blow that severance pay they's got on whiskey, women, and cards. They'll come on back to they's camp all drunk, and that's when I git 'em." He stared across the river into the distance and puffed his cigar. Took a gulp of coffee and said in a kind of mystical way, "They took my horse, my weapons, my hat, even the shirt off my back. More'n that, they took my pride. They's prob'ly up in Vernon right now bragging all over how they crucified Sticker Joe Spurlock. Wal, I aim to git my horse and all my gear back, kill 'em, and ride into Vernon trailin' they's corpses so everone can see that ol' Sticker Joe is really as tough as they thought." He looked over at Jake with a *so-there* look. Jake tipped his hat.

"Don't blame yer one bit," Jake said as he spooned out bacon chunks onto a tin plate. "Reckon we head out tomorrow mornin'. Take it slow and easy ridin' double. Water at the Pease."

"Yup."

In the morning Sticker Joe had his strength back, took Jake's hand, and swung up behind him in the saddle. Jake touched his spurs to Jasper's sides, and the big paint started off with a double load — easy for him.

Just like Spurlock had predicted, in the afternoon, as they approached the Pease, they saw smoke curling up about two miles distant, and it wasn't long before they came across a few head of cattle with the Flying XC brand on them. Slowly they came closer to the camp, and when they were about thirty yards out, they dismounted, and Jake pulled his Winchester out of the scabbard. Sticker Joe said quiet-like, "Mind if I borrow yer pistol?"

"My pleasure," Jake said. "It's a double-action forty-four. All yer gotta do is pull the trigger."

"Uh-huh. Guess I knowed that."

Jake smiled and said, "Gettin' tougher, huh. Here — take the holster and pistol belt in case yer gotta reload. I got this here other cartridge belt." Jake threw Jasper's reins up around his neck and tied them together at the ends so they hung loosely and wouldn't impede Jasper's grazing while he was loose on the grass. Then they slowly crept toward the camp, crouching to camouflage themselves as much as possible. Slowly, slowly, closer they came. So far so good. There was no alarm sounded. But Jake felt a nudge on his back and immediately knew what it was. Jasper had followed them and wanted his candy. So, Jake dug out two pieces and handed them to Jasper, who munched happily. He looked over at Sticker, who was staring severely at Jake.

When they were ten yards out, they got down on their bellies and crawled in the rest of the way to come upon the camp. There was no movement, and the only sound was a crescendo of deep-throated snoring.

Jake looked at Sticker and he at Jake like they couldn't believe their luck. "Let's snake they's weapons away from 'em and then wake 'em up," Jake whispered.

"No. I want 'em to try and put up a fight. That way I won't be accused a murder. You go over to that side. I'll go this way. Don't shoot unless yer need to save my life . . . agin'." He smiled ever so slightly.

They stood and separated. When they were inside the camp perimeter Jake picked up a distinct odor of whiskey in the air. They were probably sleeping off the night before. Then Sticker Joe bellowed, "Wal, lookee here. It's the Sideways Bill gang, and who's here facin' 'em?"

The three cowboys sat up and rubbed their eyes. Then surprise showed on their faces and almost at the same time they went for their six-shooters. Sticker shot the fastest one first and Sideways Bill second. The third cowboy had a bead on Sticker, and his pistol was cocked. Jake shot him in the shoulder of his shooting hand. He dropped to his knees and tried to reach for his pistol on the ground with his left hand. Sticker walked over and shot him in the heart. That killed him. Then Sticker turned back to Sideways Bill, who was lying on his back holding his gut with both hands that were covered in blood. "Wal, lookee here. Sideways Bill's been shot by the man he crucified. Ol' Sticker Joe Spurlock must be resurrected." Sideways Bill scrunched up his face in a vile hateful look and started to say something when Sticker cut him off with a shot to the heart. That killed him.

Sticker handed Jake his hat and picked up his own hat off Sideways Bill's saddle and set it deliberately, but tenderly, on his own head. Then he unbuckled his gun belt that Bill had on, shoved him over with his boot, pulled his belt and holster off the body, and snatched up his pistol off the ground. "Shirt's ruint," he said and went right off out into the grass to find his horse. Jake caught Jasper and started out to catch the rustlers' horses.

They trotted into town trailing the three horses with their cargo of corpses behind them. A small throng of people was around them when they tied off at the sheriff's office. Sticker stepped up onto the boardwalk and turned around to face the crowd. There was a collective audible gasp as the people looked upon Sticker's hideous blistered face. Even so, he called out, "Wal, I guess that no-account cattle rustler was bragging around how he crucified ol' Sticker Joe Spurlock. Guess yer can see I ain't dead. I been resurrected with the help of my pardner Rawhide Jake Brighton and kilt the vermin that tried to kill me. There they are." He pointed to the corpses on the horses at the rail. "They's dead. I ain't. That's it. End of story." He turned away and went into the sheriff's office followed by the sheriff and Jake.

The story for long after went around how Rawhide Jake Brighton rescued the impaled Sticker Joe Spurlock and how they got vengeance by killing the three would-be killers. Of course, after a few tellings, the story got more and more wild. But the two tough hombres were in any case friends forever.

Jake went on up to Doan's Crossing, and Sticker Joe trailed the small bunch of cattle back to the Flying XC. At Doan's, Jake and Wes were at the bar, and Wes said, "Wal, yer been here for two drinks already. Yer gonna tell me 'bout it or what?"

"Tell yer 'bout what?"

Wes rolled his eyes and said, "Yer and Sticker Joe, a course."

"The word already up here?" Jake looked incredulous.

Wes nodded his head and said, "News travels fast."

"All right. Yer buy me a Overholt, and I'll tell yer all about it."

"Why yer hornswoggling, two-bit tinhorn." Wes feigned insult and looked at Jake like one greatly offended. "All right. Tell me."

Jake grinned and began the story. When he finished he said, "That's it. End of story."

"Did yer get a receipt for the rustlers and cattle?"

Jake took on a sheepish look and said, "Plumb fergot."

"Wal, no matter. Yer can pick it up from

the sheriff on yer way back. Anyhow, yer a hero. Even more a legend now. Yer fame'll go far and wide. Here's how." He held up his glass, and Jake clinked his against it, saying, "Here's how." With the mutual admiration of good friends in their eyes, they smiled at each other and tossed down their drinks.

CHAPTER SEVEN:
THE LAST STRAW
1884–1885

Riding in the grass on the high plateau just south of the Brazos, Jake trotted Jasper heading east. The range was used mostly by Bob Goree's RG outfit. Jake's intent was to nose around the grassland generally following the river, cross back over at the Seymour crossing, and bunk at the hotel for the night. The grass was dry and brown with little if any nutrition for any critter wanting to graze. For that very reason, he was packing extra oats for Jasper, and Jake could tell he was liking it because he was more lively than usual. The year before rain was scarce. This year so far it was nonexistent. All the old-timers were calling it a drought for sure.

He came up to an area known as the breaks because a series of gulches lined up west to east and ran in a north-south direction along a big bend in the river. Down below the upper plateau of grassland, probably two hundred feet, was the river. The soil of the plateau there had been carried away to the bottomland of the river by rainstorms when there were storms. The gullies left behind were wide enough to run a few critters through. With the river right below, there was plenty of water for cattle but no grass. The little mesas and sharp walls of the ravines were pretty much covered with mesquite. Where the red dirt was exposed, it was bone dry. Well into autumn as it was, Jake had his coat on but unbuttoned. And in the crisp morning air he smelled the odor of burning mesquite carried on the stiff breeze blowing from east to west. He searched the breaks for smoke but could see none. Someone had a fire going nearby, and he intended to investigate.

Every time he went from the grass into a gap of the breaks the scent diminished and, in some cases, disappeared. So, he stayed in the grass until the odor was gone, and then he backtracked to pick it up again. He decided it was coming from a particularly wide ravine. Slowly, cautiously, quietly he walked Jasper into the gulch. No sooner was he out of the grass than he picked up the sign of a recent passing of livestock. Another three or four hundred yards and the little gorge opened to a low-lying field of sparse mesquite and grass. There were about twenty cows with calves in the field. The mesquite fire was off to the east side underneath a jagged ledge of one of the little mesas about a hundred yards distant from where Jake sat on Jasper. There was a feller squatted down by the fire with his back to Jake.

Jake pulled his Winchester from the scabbard and held it across his lap while he eased Jasper toward the camp. About twenty yards out he hollered, "Hello the camp."

The feller stood, turned around, and hollered back, "Hello yerself."

He was a cowboy in chaps and wore a sidearm. Looked like he was in his late twenties. He stood probably about an inch under six foot tall, had a strong looking build and black hair on head and face. There was a rifle leaned up against a log a little way away from the fire. Jake kept coming slowly, and at about five yards he reined in Jasper and said, "Was riding by and smelled yer fire. Thought maybe yer might have a cup a coffee." He thought he saw a running iron in the fire but couldn't be sure.

"Wal sure. Matter a fact, I got a fresh pot. Come on down off that hoss and set a spell." He smiled friendly-like.

Jake re-sheathed his rifle, kicked his leg over Jasper's neck, and slid out of the saddle so he could keep his eyes on the feller. "Thank ye. Kinda cool today."

"Sure is. I been here by the fire all mornin'. Gittin' ready to move those critters back on out to the grass. Lettin' it warm up a bit first," he said, still smiling.

"What outfit yer workin' fer?"

"RG."

"Uh-huh. Runnin' iron a standard tool at the RG?"

Lightning fast, he drew, and Jake was looking down the business end of a large bore Colt before he could even twitch a finger toward his pistol. He stood stark still. The friendly smile on the feller's face was gone, replaced by the look of a very dangerous hombre. And he had the drop on Jake with his .45 pointed at Jake's gut. The hammer on the six-gun was back, so the pistol was ready to fire. Jake's body muscles involuntarily tightened, but he felt no fear and showed none. Instead, he scowled in anger at his assailant. He was angry with the feller and with himself for falling victim to this gunman. But what to do?

"Yer a pretty fast draw," Jake said, glaring at the feller, who returned his glare without flinching. And he had the look of evil about him.

"Damn fast," the rustler said in a low growl.

"Yer a gunman then?"

"Some say so. I don't give it no never mind."

"From around these parts?"

"Maybe I am and maybe I ain't." He held the Colt steady, still pointed at Jake's gut. He gave no sign of nervousness or impatience. He held his ground like he had done this before.

"How come yer ain't a lawman instead of a rustler? With that fast draw, yer'd be pretty effective."

"Ain't none a yer business, but jest so as yer know, I hate law dogs. Yer a law dog?"

"No. I ride line for the Flyin' XC. That's what I am a doin' out here."

"Wal then, yer give me no choice. Yer just like a law dog. I gotta kill yer or yer'll kill me. Won't yer?"

"Prob'ly. Ever kill a man before? It ain't easy. Stays with —"

"Yer ain't the first and yer ain't the last. So quit the jawin'."

"Wal, if yer gonna kill me, why don't yer pull the trigger. Yer all cocked and ready to fire."

"Drop yer pistol belts first."

"Yer ain't even gonna give me a chance, huh?"

"That's right. Now with your left hand yer unbuckle those belts, or I'll drop yer where yer stand."

Jake knew the feller was going to kill him sure one way or the other. There had to be some way out of this situation. He couldn't draw on him. He was covered outright. And even if he broke left or right to draw and fire, he was sure he would be shot first. This feller seemed to be too handy with a pistol and would react quickly with a sure aim.

"Last time. Drop them belts or yer die right here."

"And if I do?"

"We gonna take a little walk down to the river."

"So, I die by the river."

The feller shrugged his shoulders and said, "Yer seem like a brave feller. Not afraid to die are yer?"

"They ain't no man can buy his own ransom or pay a price to the Almighty for his life. A man ain't got no know-how to ransom his soul. He can't buy a immortal soul. Every man comes to the grave. So, I ain't afraid to die. Are you?"

He didn't answer, and Jake said no more. Maybe a walk to the river would be to his advantage. Buy some time. What he needed was movement and distraction. Even though he would be without his .44 he had his little thirty-two pocket pistol in his vest. He unbuckled his gun and ammo belts and let them drop at his feet.

"All right. Let's go, preacher man. That-away. And keep yer hands up where I can see 'em." He motioned with his head and kept a very close watch on Jake.

"Why we goin' to the river?" Jake called back over his shoulder.

"Cuz I ain't got the time or the gitty-up to bury yer. I could leave yer lying, but that don't set well with me. So, I'll let the current take yer downstream, and somebody'll pull yer out and plant yer."

"Mighty good a yer," Jake said in full-fledged sarcasm.

Jake walked slowly, keeping a keen eye out for any opportunity to cause a distraction. And then he saw it. A few feet ahead, the wide path they traversed took a steep incline down. The surface was loose dirt and stones exposed by rain wash, almost like shale. It looked like it ran for at least ten feet. Jake stepped on to it and had to lower his hands out to his side to keep his balance, as with each step he slid a little. He had to step carefully and watch where he stepped to prevent his boots from skidding out from underneath him. The feller behind him had to be in the same predicament. Jake listened with full attention to what was happening behind him.

When he heard the feller slide in the gravel, he snatched his thirty-two from his vest, spun around, took sure aim, and shot the feller right in the middle of his forehead. A look of surprise came across the rustler's face, and that was his expression while he convulsed, choked, and died in sixty seconds. The feller dropped his pistol, and it fired when it hit the ground. The bullet splayed gravel around Jake's feet without any further damage.

Jake said out loud as he stared down at the lifeless face of the rustler, "Yer were right. I weren't the last one you kilt. Yer were." He pocketed his pistol and knelt beside the body to go through the feller's pockets. There was a bone-handle jackknife, about twenty dollars in notes and ten dollars in gold pieces, and of all things a folded-up wanted poster. Jake unfolded the bill and looked at it in surprise because there was a likeness of the wanted man that matched the man he had just killed. His name was John Dove, and he was wanted for murder and cattle rustling in Palo Pinto

County. Five-hundred-dollar reward dead or alive. "Aw shoot," Jake swore. "Now I gotta cart yer body into town to claim the reward." He picked up the outlaw's pistol and looked around for Jasper.

He whistled up Jasper and looped a rope around Dove's ankles and drug him back up to the camp area. Jake bent over and pulled the running iron out of the fire and tossed it in the dirt. Then he swung into the saddle and set out to catch the feller's horse. He brought the horse to the camp and first went through the saddlebags. Nothing there of any note, so he re-looped the rope around the man's chest under his arms and flung the other end up and around a mesquite limb. He tied the rope to Jasper's saddle horn. Then he walked Jasper ahead a little, raised up Dove's body to where he wanted it, and dropped Jasper's reins to the ground. He walked Dove's horse around under the body and whistled Jasper back to slacken the rope. As easy as could be he let the body down on Dove's horse. He got it turned around, draped over the saddle, and securely cinched down the hands and feet. The cargo was ready. Jake glanced up at the sun and estimated he could make it to Seymour well before sundown but not if he had to push the bunch of RG cow and calf pairs into town, too. So, he decided to leave them there, planning to tell Goree where to find them. He spat on the running iron. There was no sizzle, so he tested for heat with his bare hand. The iron was warm but not hot, and he slid it along with Dove's pistol into his own saddlebag, mounted, and rode off, trailing Dove's horse behind him.

The shadows were leaning east when Jake tied off Jasper on the hitching rail in front of the brand new, stone courthouse. He stepped into the sheriff's office, and as luck would have it the sheriff was sitting at his desk. Looked like he was doing some paperwork.

"Howdy, Sheriff. I got another one fer yer," Jake said.

"Howdy, Rawhide. What'er yer got this time?"

"Wal, I think it is John Dove. Wanted dead or alive outta Palo Pinto County."

"Mmmm. Let me see." The sheriff stepped over to the wall that held a bulletin board to which the posters were tacked up in groups of eight or so. He rifled through them and came to the one on John Dove. "Yep. Here it is. Five hundred dollars reward dead or alive. Murder and cattle rustling. Let's go take a looksee." He grabbed his hat, and they walked out to the hitching rail.

One of the deputies came out and joined them. The sheriff walked around to the side of Dove's horse, lifted John Dove's dead head by the hair, and held the wanted poster next to his face. "Yep. That's him all right. How'd yer know it was him?"

"He had this poster in his pocket." Jake handed it over to the sheriff, who unfolded it and with a glance said, "Wal, ain't that a stroke a luck. Might as well a had his own callin' card. I'll just keep this fer the inquest," he said as he refolded the poster. "Looks like purty fancy shootin'. One shot, eh? Let's go back inside, and yer kin tell me all 'bout it. Gates, will yer take the body down to the undertaker and the hoss over to Quincy for impound," he said to the deputy.

"Here. I took these off him after I shot him," Jake said as he pulled out the running iron and pistol from his saddlebag and handed them to the sheriff. "Evidence," he said with a serious nod of his head.

"Yep," the sheriff responded.

Jake went through the whole story in detail for the sheriff, and when he finished the sheriff said, "All right. Looks like yer got a clean shootin' here. I'll wire the sheriff in Palo Pinto and arrange for the reward money. Meantime, stay in town. JP Inquest at ten tomorrow mornin'."

"I'll be at the hotel," Jake said as he sat his hat on his head, went out, and walked Jasper down to the livery.

"Wal, yer keep comin' back like a bad penny," Quincy said to Jake with a smirk as Jake stuck his head in Quincy's office door.

"I guess this bad penny is bringin' yer plenty a business what with my own stable fees and those of the county for impounds. What a yer got to say to that, yer old scorpion?"

"Wal, at least yer a bright shiny bad penny," Quincy said with a grin as they shook hands. "Who'd yer git this time?"

Jake led Jasper to a stall, pulled off the saddle and tack, and was carrying them to the tack room when Quincy said loudly, "Wal? Yer deef or what?"

"Wanted feller outta Palo Pinto County. Name's John Dove," Jake called back over his shoulder.

"I heared a him. Texas Ranger told me all 'bout him a while back. On his trail but had to break off for somethin' else. He didn't say what, but he said Dove was wanted for a murder in Fort Smith, and he ran to Mineral Wells. Workin' in one a the spas. Killed a feller there over some woman. He escaped to the Bottoms right next to Fort Griffin . . . yer heared 'bout that place, right?"

"No. Can't say I have," Jake said as he slipped a bag of oats over Jasper's muzzle and began brushing him.

"What? Lawman like yer don't know about Babylon on the Brazos?"

"Ain't no lawman. I'm a line rider for the Flyin' XC."

"Uh-huh. Even still yer shoulda heared a it." He stared at Jake for a minute with a quizzical look about him and then apparently gave it up. "Hell-town place if ever there was one. Not as bad as Tascosa but as bad as Dodge City or Deadwood. Maybe worse. Lotta hardcases used to roost there. John Wesley Hardin for one. Yer heared a him for sure." Jake nodded his head *yes.* "Wal, anyway, the other hardcase we is discussin', John Dove, he gits the idee to steal cattle from a ranch he knows 'bout in east Palo Pinto County and drive 'em to Fort Griffin to sell to what was left a the army and to the outlaws and riff-raff in the Bottoms. Only he gits caught red handed, but he kills a deputy and breaks outta jail, and I guess makes it here, huh?"

"Reckon so," Jake said as he forked hay into Jasper's trough. Then he put a bucket of water on the stand outside the stall door, slipped the oat bag off, and shut the door to hold Jasper in for the night. "Wal, reckon I'll git a shave and a bath down at the barber. Nice talkin' to yer, Quincy." He picked up his rifle and saddlebags and walked out the door, leaving Quincy with his mouth hanging open. The stableman made a dismissive wave at Jake's back and retreated to his office.

On the way back from the barber shop Jake stopped in at the Brazos for a drink before supper. "Howdy, Alex," he said to the owner/bartender who came down the bar with a bottle of whiskey and a glass.

"Hello, Jake. Heard you brought in another body. Wanted man dead or alive, eh?"

"Reckon so."

"Judge Anderson ain't gonna like that."

"What a yer mean?"

"Oh, he's been on a terror lately. A month back Deputy Gates shot a wanted horse thief. Didn't kill him but Anderson almost threw him in jail for assault. And he almost got shot himself as the thief got a bullet off before Gates fired. So, if I were you, I'd get Carter Collier to stand by and defend you if need be."

"Ah, it's only an inquest. I don't need to pay for no lawyer," Jake said, and a little

335

agitated, he tossed down his drink. "And the feller said he was gonna kill me. Besides, he was wanted dead or alive. Give me anuther."

"Just letting you know what's going on around here," Alex said as he poured Jake's whiskey.

"I appreciate it, Alex. You've always been a big help to me." Jake smiled as he drank down half the glass of whiskey. Then unmistakably, the fragrance of Desi's perfume tickled his nose, and the soft feel of her breast against his arm and her warm breath on his neck and her arm around his back and her firm mound of Venus pressed against his thigh had an immediate effect on him. Still without turning to face her he downed his drink and remained facing the bar, as he did not want her to see his arousal. So, he turned his head, smiled at her, and said, "Howdy, Desi." Then he glanced back at Alex, who had a small grin on his face and made a gesture with the bottle to inquire if Jake wanted another drink, to which Jake with a slight turn of his head politely refused.

"Oh, my handsome Jake. I miss you so much," Desi cooed.

Jake looked firmly into Desi's eyes and said, "Wal, Desi, I gotta break the news to yer one way or anuther, so I'll just come out and say it. I'm married now, and I can't be foolin' 'round no more." She went limp as if to faint, and Jake caught her before she fell to the floor only to have her sneak her hand to his crotch and grin alluringly at the feel of his hardness.

"I see. You still love Desi." She circled her red lips with her tongue and lusted him with her luscious eyes. Her trick managed to accomplish not what she apparently wanted as Jake regained control of himself and gently pushed her away.

"No more," he said in a low tone of warning. Desi stepped in, slapped him hard across the face, spun a one-eighty, sashayed away from him, stopped, lifted her skirts and stuck out her bare butt at him, then went upstairs. Alex chuckled, as did a few of the patrons who were close by. "Think she got the message?" Jake said to Alex.

"I think you did, too."

"Yeah. That smarts," Jake said as he rubbed his red cheek.

Justice of the Peace Anderson came into his courtroom, and everyone stood. Of course, the only ones there were Jake, the sheriff, and Deputy Gates.

"Good morning," the judge said as he

337

took his seat behind his table. Jake and the sheriff responded and took their seats.

"Well, Mister Brighton, I see here you are before me again with another corpse. Becoming rather habitual, wouldn't you say?" Jake kept quiet.

The judge continued. "This morning I examined the corpus delecti of a male, approximately thirty years of age, apparently known as John Dove. Shot once through the forehead with a smaller caliber weapon, no exit wound, and I can confidently say that is the cause of death to wit: homicide by a cranial gunshot. I am less confident regarding the circumstance and manner of death as related to me by Sheriff Thompson. Before me is one Jonas V. Brighton aka Rawhide Jake Brighton, who is the self-avowed shooter in this case. Mister Brighton, kindly tell the court in your own words what happened in this shooting incident."

Jake stood and related the whole story in detail, and the judge listened seemingly with interest. "And so yesterday afternoon I turned the body over to Sheriff Thompson," Jake finished. He stood waiting for reply from the judge, who reclined the back of his chair, swiveled to the right, and stared at the ceiling as if he were contemplating all that Jake said. Then he swiveled back to face the room and let the chair back come forward.

"Please, take your seat, Mister Brighton. As I said, I am less confident in your story as to the manner of death."

"Your Honor, he was wanted dead or alive for murdering at least three people. One of them was a deputy. I don't see how *his* manner of death is relevant."

"That is exactly my concern. You knew he was wanted dead or alive, and so you took the easy way and executed him. The bullet hole looks more like an assassin's shot than one inflicted in a gunfight. And if that is the case, then you, too, are culpable for murder."

"Your Honor, I did not know he was wanted dead or alive at the time I shot him to save my own life."

"Then how did you know he was wanted dead or alive for murdering at least three people, one a deputy, is what I believe you said?"

Jake had to think back. How did he know that? He got a little queasy as he could sense an imaginary noose tightening around his neck. But fortunately, just before he broke out in a sweat, he remembered it was Quincy who told him about the three murders. "Your Honor, when I was stabling my horse yesterday, Quincy told me that a while back a Texas Ranger came into town on John Dove's trail and told Quincy about the man. Said the Ranger had to break off his investigation to attend to some other matter and left town."

The judge turned to the sheriff. "Any Texas Rangers been in town in the last six months or a year?"

"Not that I recall, Your Honor."

"And a Texas Ranger in town would make a courtesy call on you, wouldn't he?"

"Reckon so."

"Please have one of your deputies fetch Quincy to immediately appear here before me. We'll recess until he arrives."

Jake walked outside on to the porch of the courthouse building. He lit a cigar and looked out over in the direction of the river. He was looking but not seeing. He took a few puffs of the cigar and then said, "This son of a bitch wants to hang me." And that made him mad. *Who did he think he was anyway?*

Five minutes and Quincy came up trotting a little black mare. He rode bareback. "What's —" he started to say when Jake motioned him to be quiet and go into the judge's little courtroom.

"Mister Quincy Brown is before me. That

is your correct name, isn't it?"

"Wal, yeah, Judge. Yer know that."

"It is for the record, Mister Brown."

For the record? There was no recorder there. What kind of game was the judge playing?

"Now, Mister Brown, Mister Brighton states that yesterday afternoon you told him that a Texas Ranger told you that the deceased, Mister John Dove, was wanted dead or alive by Palo Pinto County for murder and cattle rustling and was wanted in Fort Smith, Arkansas, for murder. Is that correct?"

"By deeceesed yer mean the dead feller?"

"Yes."

"Sure as rain, which a course we ain't had now for more'n a year, that's what the ranger told me."

"The ranger did not call on the sheriff. Do you know why that is?"

"No, sir. Alls I know is that he stabled his horse and went down to the telegraph office. 'Bout a half hour later he come back. Saddled his horse and rode outta town."

"All right. That will be all. Thank you, Mister Brown. You may go."

"Thank ye, Paul. I brung that little black mare just in case yer want a take anuther looksee at her."

341

"I said, you may depart." Judge Paul Anderson raised his voice and glared at Quincy, who scooted toot sweet out of the courtroom.

"Well, the independent testimony appears to corroborate certain aspects of your story, but I still suspect an execution rather than self defense. Further, according to your own testimony you did not identify yourself as a so-called stock detective of the Stock-Raisers Association."

"Your Honor," Jake said with exasperation in his voice. "I was working undercover, and now again you have exposed my cover."

"Well, now, isn't that just too bad, Mister Rawhide Jake Brighton." The skin on the judge's face tightened, and he bared his clenched teeth as he took on a severe glower aimed directly at Jake. "You so-called detectives roam around the range killing whomever you damn well please and expect the courts to pat you on the back and tell you what a good job you are doing. Well, that doesn't happen in my jurisdiction. Truth and the law rule here."

"I wonder what Deputy Gates has to say to that," Jake snarled.

The sheriff snapped his head around to look at Jake as if he had just said the most incredulous thing. The judge stiffened even more and looked like he was about to explode. Then he relaxed and folded his hands in front of him on the desk. "The decision of the inquisitor in this judicial inquiry into the death of one named John Dove is that the said deceased died from a gunshot wound to the head inflicted by Jonas V. Brighton under suspicious circumstances and the case is therefore referred to District Court for trial —"

"Some inquisitor you are. You can't even allow the preponderance of evidence in a case that is clearly a justified homicide. You are a disgrace to your office." Jake blurted out his angry interruption of the judge's declaration and pointed a very stiff and direct index finger at the judge.

A faint smile showed under the judge's mustache as he said, "Jonas V. Brighton, you are under arrest for suspicion of murder. Sheriff, take him into custody."

Jake threw up his hands in exasperation and called out, "What a kangaroo court."

"Bail is set at ten thousand dollars."

"All right. That is pure hogwash," Jake yelled. The judge stood and waved Jake away as if he were a king and Jake was a knave. The sheriff and Deputy Gates each took a hold of Jake's arms and hustled him out of the courtroom.

■ ■ ■ ■

Two weeks later Wes rode up to the back porch of Xavier Calhoun's house, dismounted, and dropped Nobel's reins to the ground to hold him there, which he was apparently happy to do since he immediately started cropping the grass of the lawn. "Stay here, boy," Wes said as he draped his arm around Nobel's neck and gently patted him while looking around for any sign of Jasper. Just a few seconds more and he was startled by the screen door slamming against the porch wall.

"Wes, oh, Wes!" Mary Jane cried. "Have you seen Jake? He's been gone two weeks now. Never this long before. I am worried to death." She held her skirt up and flew down the porch steps and then suddenly stopped and fell to her knees. "Oh, no. Please, God. No. You have bad news. Tell me. Please don't let it be."

"Now, now. Let's not get all lathered up fer nuthin'. I'm sure he's fine." He reached out his hand to her to help her up. "Here. Come on up here now." And he held her while she wept.

She dabbed at her tears with her hanky. "I've just been so worried. But if something did happen to him, you would have heard, wouldn't you?"

"Oh, sure. Right away I woulda heard." Her weeping fell off, and Wes said softly, "Feel better now?"

Mary Jane nodded her head and lifted it to smile modestly at Wes.

"I came to talk some business with him. But yer say he ain't been home for over two weeks?"

"Yes." She nodded her head and let out a pitiful sigh.

"Wal, he probably got on a trail last minute and has to stay with it. Fencing crew is workin' to the west. I stopped there on the way here. Boqin said Jake hasn't been there since the last payday. I'll head on down to Seymour. See if I can find anything out. I'll wire yer as soon as I know anything or even when I git there to let yer know one way or ta' other."

"Thanks, Wes. You're a good friend." She smiled weakly at Wes.

Wes trotted Nobel into Seymour and turned into Quincy's lot. He stepped out of the saddle, stretched, and rubbed his back. He had held Nobel to a good pace all the way and rode straight through as the crow flies instead of following the longer trail that was developing more and more between

Seymour and the Flying XC settlement. He walked Nobel into the barn and settled him in an empty stall, then unsaddled the big feller and pulled off his tack. He set a pail of water on a milk stool outside the stall door and latched the door closed. Nobel turned around in the stall, hung his head over the door, stuck his muzzle in the pail, and sucked water a long time, nearly emptying the pail. "Sorry about that, boy. But we was in a hurry. I'll feed ya in a couple a hours," Wes said as he stroked Nobel's shoulders.

"Wal, another bad penny shows up," Quincy said as he came walking up behind Wes.

"Howdy, Quincy."

"Yep. The other bad penny last showed up a couple weeks ago. He ain't left yet and prob'ly won't for a good long spell."

"What a yer talkin' 'bout?"

"I'm a talkin' 'bout yer pardner got hisself thrown in jail."

"He's in jail?"

"Yep," Quincy said with a grin.

Wes took two steps toward Quincy, and Quincy took two steps back. "Out with it. What happened?" Wes shouted.

"All right, all right. Calm down. Ain't no need to shout. Yer know I treat y'all pretty good here in this livery. Yer don't have to go and do like yer done." Wes took another step toward him, and Quincy took another back, but Wes was becoming more ferocious looking by the second.

"Wal, all right. I guess Jake done kilt some wanted feller named John Dove. Brought the body in for the inquest, and Judge Anderson didn't like the way Jake done the killin', so he arrested him and threw him in jail to stand trial fer murder. That's it."

Wes pulled his hat off and slapped his thigh with it. "That high and mighty son of a bitch. Wal, he crossed the line this time." He stomped out of the barn and marched down the street to the stone courthouse where the sheriff's office and jail were located.

"Wal, there goes one mad bull, snortin' all the way," Quincy said to no one. Puffs of dust kicked up with every heavy step Wes took and made a little dust trail that lingered in the still air behind him. He ran up the courthouse steps into the front hall, turned, and stomped over to the sheriff's office, where he threw open the door. It crashed against the wall, and the sheriff jumped up from behind his desk.

"Now, jest calm down, Wes. I been 'spectin' yer. But I cain't do nuthin' 'til yer cool off. Gates, get in here." He yelled the last.

"Jest want to talk to Jake. Nuthin' else — long as I don't see that scarecrow judge."

Gates hurried in through the side door that led to the jail. "What's wro — ? Oh. Howdy, Wes," he said.

"Wes wants to see Jake. Go ahead and take him in. Leave yer shootin' iron and toad sticker here, Wes," the sheriff said in a voice that trembled just a little.

When Wes walked in, Jake was standing at the iron bars with his hands folded behind his back. He stuck his right hand through the bars and said, "Glad to see you, pard." They shook hands. "Took yer long enough to git here." Jake grinned.

"Yeah. So, what the heck happened?"

Jake told him the whole story and then finished with, "So that fool judge arrests me and charges me with murder. Worse than that he set bail at ten thousand dollars. Of course, I ain't got that kinda money. So, I'm stuck here, and he's up there in his brand-new courtroom cacklin' away."

"Yer hired a lawyer?"

"Nah. Can't bring myself to pay a lawyer when I ain't in the wrong. Gotta do somethin' purty quick though. We owe the Smiths for posts, and the crew payday is in two weeks."

"I kin handle all that. Yer got the money?"

"Yeah. Sheriff's got it. Yer'll need 'bout three hundred to pay the Smiths and make the payroll. I'll tell the sheriff to give it to yer."

"Meanwhile, Mary Jane is worried sick. I told her I would send a wire soon as I knew anythin'."

"Yeah, I suspected as much. Poor thing. I thank yer fer that, pard."

"And, too, I'm a gonna git a wire off to Jim. He'll be here in no time, and we'll git yer loose." Wes grinned and winked at Jake.

Three days later, Jim Loving sat in a leather easy chair sipping whiskey and smoking a fine cigar. Next to him in a matching chair sat the honorable Charles P. Falenash, District Judge of Baylor County, direct descendant of one of Stephen Austin's Old Three Hundred Families, a Texian through and through who fought in the Mexican War of 1846 and was currently influential around the legislature. He and Jim were long-time friends. They were in the judge's chambers, where they had been reminiscing for about a half hour when the judge said, "So, did you come in on the stage or ride over? Strike that. I think I know the answer. You haven't ever ridden in a stagecoach, have you?"

"Once. And only once. Can't stand 'em. Been in the saddle all my life. Guess I ain't gonna change now."

"Well, let's get to the reason for your visit."

"Yes, let's," Jim said and puffed his cigar. "You familiar with Judge Paul Anderson's background?"

"No. Can't say as I am other than he was appointed by the Supreme Court to fill the vacancy for a justice of the peace when the county was organized nearly five years ago now. Shoulda been an election by now. Hell, I was elected only two years ago. So, what about him?"

"Well, he ain't never been elected because he is controversial, and that is putting it mildly. I think he is a radical maverick. He ain't even Texan. Hails from Arkansas. Came to Texas ten years ago and ran for JP of Blanco County. He was defeated, but he was hanging around Austin and got himself appointed JP down in Kimble County when it organized eight years ago. Two years later there was an election, and he was defeated. Folks did not like him at all. So, he went to his friends in the Supreme Court bureaucracy and got appointed here in Baylor County. He must be pulling some other strings to hold off an election."

"How do you come to know all this about him?"

Jim sipped his whiskey, then said, "A few years back I had occasion to look up his background when he tried to railroad one of my detectives. Seems to have a grudge against stock detectives. And now he's got his hooks into another one a my boys. Which means he's agitatin' the association."

"Jonas Brighton."

"Yup."

"When you wired me, I figured it was something like that so I reviewed the case with the DA and . . . well, I don't know, Jim. There is only his testimony. No other witnesses, and that bullet hole is mighty suspicious. Maybe a jury of his peers does need to decide guilt or innocence."

"I talked with Jake and heard his story in detail. I believe every word. If you go to trial, it will be an agitation to all the members of the association, and they will pay for his defense. Plus, those big cattlemen will probably take it as a personal affront since they set up the stock detective corps. We will call Xavier Calhoun, Robert Goree, Walt Guthrie, Wes Wilson, me, and the likes of all of us who will testify as character witnesses. All highly respected and influential individuals. Plus, this John Dove feller I understand was wanted dead or alive by Palo Pinto County. Hell, Charlie, the Texas Rangers were on the culprit's trail. Personally, I don't see the problem here."

"Anderson thinks Brighton executed Dove."

"Because he was shot in the forehead? You hear tell Jake's story on how that happened?" Jim sipped a little whiskey and stared keenly at Falenash. *Was Charles listening or not?*

"And I ain't making a threat, but when the jury returns a not-guilty verdict, the association might sue the county for malicious prosecution and Judge Paul Anderson personally for false arrest. Now, we don't have to go through all that bad blood if you will just dismiss the case as it should be and officially inquire of the county election board as to why there has not been an election for justice of the peace. Then the whole thing'll blow over, and the association'll be happy." He smiled at Charles.

"Well, you make a good argument. You should have been a lawyer. Let me sleep on it. Meantime, how about some supper? Betty'll be really glad to see you."

"Sure. Sounds good. If I recollect rightly, she is a mighty good cook."

■ ■ ■ ■

Ten o'clock in the morning, the sheriff came in and unlocked Jake's cell door. "Let's go Jake. Yer a free man. Case's been dismissed."

" 'Bout time," Jake grumbled as he snatched his coat off the bunk. "Somebody finally come to their senses, eh?"

"Yeah, Judge Falenash. He ain't got no ax to grind, and he's ten times smarter than Anderson. But yer didn't hear me say that. Jim Loving's waitin' fer yer in my office." The sheriff gave Jake a knowing, collaborative smile.

"Thanks, Jim," Jake said as he came across the sheriff's office and shook hands with Jim, who gave Jake a slap on the back and draped an arm over his shoulder.

"All in a day's work for the Stock-Raisers' Association of North-West Texas. Now you gotta get back out on the range and kill some more bad men, hah, hah, hah." They all laughed.

Mary Jane saw him coming, as she had been waiting by the window ever since she received Jake's wire two days ago. She was flying down the back porch steps when he jumped from the saddle. She fell into his

353

arms, and he squeezed her tight. For a few minutes they stayed like that, swaying a little in the breeze. Then Mary Jane said, "It's cool out here. Let's go inside. I got hot water. I'll boil it and make some coffee."

Jake kissed her affectionately, leaned back, and said, "Let me get Jasper settled, and I'll be right in." He was back in fifteen minutes and stepped up to the porch, where he pulled off his boots and spurs and left them there.

They sat at the kitchen table, which was covered with red and white checked oilcloth. Mary Jane poured the coffee and sat down across the corner of the table from Jake. She took his free hand in hers and said, "I was worried sick for a week before I got Wes's wire from Seymour. And then I worried more about what was going to happen to you in court. Jake, I know you made no promises when we married, and I knew all about what you were doing, but I never thought the worry would be like this. I don't want to ever do it again." She stared deep into his eyes with pleading in her own eyes. "We've been married only six months, and this happened. And before we were married you and Wes were both almost killed, I don't know how many times I ain't heard about. I just don't like it," she said with a little anger in her voice.

"Well, funny you should bring this up because I am sick and tired of dealin' with that rogue judge Anderson. Seems like one way or another whether I am guilty or not I end up in jail. But, you know, it started when I was a kid at Andersonville. Then four years in the Kansas State Pen. Then Missourah and now here in Texas. Everywhere I go I get thrown in jail, and I am downright tired of it. And this time just for doin' my job." He shook his head from side to side and took a drink of coffee from his cup. "So, I am thinkin' about quittin' Texas."

Mary Jane eyed him curiously and said, "What do you have in mind?"

"Got plenty a money from the fencin' business, sales commissions, and rewards and stuff. Thinkin' about takin' the winter off. Keep the fencin' crew workin' and in the spring ride down and talk to Bill Vandevert. I hear the Hashknife is workin' on a big deal to sell the Pecos herd to investors from New York City. It's called the Aztec Land and Cattle Company. Supposedly, they are buyin' up a bunch of grassland in Arizona and will ship the herd there. That'd be over thirty thousand head saved from the drought. Of course, they gotta keep the Hashknife brand. So, there'll be Hashknife in Texas and in Arizona. Bill Vandevert is supposed to be goin' to Arizona. Maybe I'll see if we can tag along." He looked across the top of his cup with gleaming eyes that betrayed the smile he wore. "What a yer think of that?"

"What would you be doin' for Bill Vandevert?"

"Same thing as now. Stock detective."

"Uh-huh." Mary Jane dropped her eyes to stare absently at the tabletop. Jake did not miss it.

"But you never know. Down the road in Arizona something more better might come along," he said cheerily.

Mary Jane beamed with glistening eyes, about to spill over with a flush of tears. "I love you," she said huskily.

"Let's see how much," Jake said seductively as he took her hand, and they hurried to the bedroom.

A month later, Wes was over for supper. After the meal was finished, Mary Jane was pouring coffee, and Jake waited until she sat back down before he said, "Wal, pard, we been ridin' this range for two years now. But" — he hesitated — "looks like we might be comin' up to the end a the trail."

Wes looked suspiciously at first Jake and

then Mary Jane. "What a yer mean?"

"Wal, we're thinkin' 'bout movin' to Arizona."

"Arizona!? Are yer crazy? Or now yer wanna be a Indian fighter?" Wes slapped the flat of his hand down on the tabletop.

"No. Ain't gonna be no Indian fighter."

"Wal, them 'pache is still raisin' hell out there yer know?"

"Not where we're thinkin' 'bout headin'. And they got Geronimo on the reservation now."

"All right. So's what's this all 'bout?"

"Wal, seems like whatever I do in detective work, I end up gettin' thrown in jail one way or ta other. Started in Manhattan when that feller was gonna shoot me, and me and another feller shot him and kilt him. Didn't get jailed then but they were trying hard to charge me. Then in Missourah, they arrested me and made me a jailhouse snitch to try and get evidence on Frank James. I told yer all this. The last straw is that jackass judge Anderson jailin' me for killin' John Dove, who was wanted dead or alive. I'm gettin' sick of it, and I got Mary Jane to think of now, too. So, I'm thinkin' real serious 'bout a change in scenery and even quittin' the posse. And the Hashknife might be our ticket to ride. 'Sides, Mary Jane don't like me riskin' my life out there on the range all the time."

"Hashknife? What a yer mean?"

"Wal, yer heard that the Continental partners are workin' on a big deal to sell the Pecos herd to an outfit called the Aztec Land and Cattle Company. That's 'bout thirty thousand head now. Feller named Henry Warren is the manager for Aztec. He's part of Continental, too. Never met him. You?"

Wes shook his head *no.*

"Hear tell, if the deal is sealed, Warren is gonna round up the whole herd, break 'em up into smaller herds, and trail 'em up the Pecos and Rio Grande and then west to Arizona. Later on, he'll trail the herds to Isleta, near Albuquerque. Then ship 'em by train to a place called Holbrook up in Navajo country. Ain't no Apaches up there."

"All thirty thousand a them? Probably got a big herd a horses, too."

"Couple thousand I hear tell is in the deal. The Aztec company has a big spread up there. Continental, Buster's outfit, is hit real hard by the drought, and they's sellin' the herd to Henry Warren and the Aztec company to get what they can before they ever die off, I guess."

"Who do yer hear tell all this from? I ain't

never heared none of it."

"Vandevert."

"Bill Vandevert told yer all this?"

"Yep."

"That a fact?" Wes whistled. "What's he gonna do?"

"Said he's goin' on out there probably next year."

"You talk to Vandervert 'bout goin' with 'em yet?"

"Yep. But we ain't waitin' 'round 'til next year."

"How come Arizona?"

"Wal, just different scenery, I guess."

"What 'bout the fencin' company we got?"

"Wal, if yer don't take no offense I would give my share to Boqin. He can manage his Chinese laborers and the business, and yer can rake in the pesos. How's that sound?"

"Wal, that part sounds all right, but I ain't likin' yer quittin' the range." He stared at them both with sad eyes and then dropped his gaze to the floor. "Got any whiskey?" he said in a low and quiet voice.

Mary Jane pulled a bottle down from a cupboard and three glasses from another. She set the glasses and bottle on the table. Jake poured.

"We been through a lot together, pard. Saved each other's lives almost more times

359

than I can 'member," Wes said as he shot a quick glance at Mary Jane. She was staring directly at him.

"I didn't have anything to do with this, Wes. Jake came to this decision all on his own. And I ain't been naggin' him at all."

"That's right. She ain't said nothin' or acted out or nothin'. I know she don't like me out on the range chasin' rustlers. But, like she herself said, she knew my line a work when we got married, and she ain't ever tried to steer me in some other direction. 'Course, we'd both be lyin' if we didn't admit she's happy about us movin' and me maybe quittin'." He shot a quick glance at Mary Jane. "Anuther thing that bothers me a little is Jim. He's done a lot for me includin' springin' me outta jail. Feel like I owe him and am desertin' him. What a yer think?"

Wes nodded his head and smiled pleasantly at Mary Jane. "Aw, I think yer done plenty lot for ol' Jim and the association. Him springin' yer outta jail was as much fer him and the association as it was fer yer. And now that yer are hitched to Mary Jane, wal, I don't know. Yer know what his rule is. But, what the heck. Here's how," he called out as he held up his glass. Jake and Mary Jane answered back, "Here's how," and they

all clinked glasses and downed their whis-
kies. "Wonder if that Rawhide handle I gave
yer will follow yer on out to Arizona."

ONE MORE TIME

Book Three continues the narrative of the life and times of Jake and Mary Jane as they say adiós to Texas and take up residence in Springerville, Apache County, in the Arizona Territory. Jake is appointed Springerville District Constable and opens a blacksmith shop and a saloon in the Round Valley town. He does some detective work that goes a long way to help rid the county of the "desperados" who were like a plague on the land. He takes out Ike Clanton of Tombstone infamy, one of the worst, and others. Although law enforcement in general appreciates Jake's work, many in the civilian population are less enthusiastic about his shoot-first-ask-questions-later modus operandi. But it earns him an appointment as a special deputy United States marshal working in Arizona until he and Mary Jane head off into the sunset on their way to California. There they are finally blessed with a little one, Jake is injured in a riding accident, he plays a major role in capturing California's most notorious outlaw of the day, and he gathers the evidence for the arrest of train robbers in Los Angeles County. They retire to Orange County, where Mary Jane passes, and Jake remarries. Subsequently his health fails, and he leaves this earth at the age of eighty-one.

ABOUT THE AUTHOR

Back in the day, as they say, there were plenty of old West stories on TV to flood a boy's imagination. Those fanciful memories stayed with **JD Arnold** all through his Vietnam era military service, helicopter piloting, deputy sheriff, and death investigator time, with a last change of gears to a more sedate CPA career. Finally, now that he's quit his day job, his imagination came to fruition with the previous Book One and this Book Two of the trilogy on Jonas V. Brighton. Book Three is due out in 2023. Also in the works are three more novels: *Lone Star Folk* and *Lone Star Pride,* and a family saga set north of the Mogollon Rim in Arizona.

Jeff, Diane, and Sofie, their canine love, live by the polo fields in Indio. Their children and grandchildren reside in the next county over to the west. He wishes peace for everyone, always.